D0011040

"The believabl[...] Harper is enhanced by the addition of highly dimensional supporting characters, and a minor mystery subplot increases the tension by a notch. This is a fine addition to a strong series."—*Publishers Weekly* on *Lone Rider*

"Captivating sensuality."—*Publishers Weekly* on *Wind River Wrangler*, a Publishers Marketplace Buzz Books 2016 selection

"Moving and real . . . impossible to put down."—*Publishers Weekly* on *Wind River Rancher* (starred review)

"Cowboy who is also a former Special Forces operator? Check. Woman on the run from her past? Check. This contemporary Western wraps together suspense and romance in a rugged Wyoming package."—Amazon.com's Omnivoracious, "9 Romances I Can't Wait to Read," on *Wind River Wrangler*

"Set against the stunning beauty of Wyoming's Grand Tetons, *Wind River Wrangler* is Lindsay McKenna at her finest! A *tour de force* of heart-stopping drama, gut-wrenching emotion, and the searing joy of two wounded souls learning to love again."—International bestselling author Merline Lovelace

"McKenna does a beautiful job of illustrating difficult topics through the development of well-formed, sympathetic characters."—*Publishers Weekly* on *Wolf Haven* (starred review)

WIND RIVER PROTECTOR

LINDSAY McKENNA

ZEBRA BOOKS
KENSINGTON PUBLISHING CORP.
www.kensingtonbooks.com

To all my readers who love romance and happy endings!

Chapter One

"Well, hell!"

Captain Andrea Whitcomb hissed out the epithet. She was in trouble. Her harness bit deeply into her shoulders as she hauled back on the stick of her A-10 Warthog, having swooped within fifty feet of a hill peppered with Taliban guns firing back at her. The Gatling gun beneath the nose of the aircraft made her entire body shake from the fire power she'd just delivered against the enemy.

It was dusk, the lurid red color of the sunset dying behind the Afghanistan mountains to the west. Her A-10 had a helluva lot of armor, especially around the seat of the cockpit where she sat, but bullets had done damage to both engines on her stalwart close air support jet. Her gloves were sweaty with adrenaline as she felt the gravity pinning her back against the seat. She silently pleaded with the ailing combat jet to climb and get the hell out of bullet range of her attackers.

Jerking a glance to her left, looking through NVGs, night vision goggles, she saw the Black Hawk helicopter was trying to make an escape out of that deadly valley.

It had just dropped a SEAL team near the wall of the canyon when it came under fire. She had been called in from another mission to protect the Army helo. It was always dangerous dropping or picking up black ops, and it was done after dark, if possible.

This time? She was in trouble. And so was the Black Hawk. The Taliban weren't stupid. They had the helo caught in a bracket, heavy fire aimed at its rotor assembly area. Their enemy knew if they could destroy that one mechanical mechanism, the helo was grounded and everyone on it would eventually be killed—by them.

Sucking in a breath of oxygen through her mask, eyes narrowed, Andy saw the warning black smoke issuing from the helo's two turbo engines. *Not good. Not good at all.* There was a mountain range to the north end of this box-canyon-type valley and the helo was hobbling along, clawing for air and trying to get away from the bullets of the Taliban, too.

Her gaze snapped to the engine indicator, the dials telling her she was in equally bad shape as that limping-along Army helo. From muscle memory, she went into ejection-seat mode. First, mayday calls to Bagram. Her combat jet would have to be destroyed, provided she could safely eject out of the crippled craft. Nothing could be left of it to be picked through and then sold to China or Russia, who would want avionics, for starters, from the jet. There were so many top-secret black boxes on this jet, they had to be destroyed, instead of hoping a fire or explosion would do the job. She set the detonation assembly.

Her gloved hand flew over the cockpit array, prepping the jet for the series of internalized explosions that would be initiated upon crashing to the ground. Hopefully, with her ejected, the parachute opening and being far enough away from where the A-10 augured in, she'd survive this.

A landing area was critical. She had a GPS radio on her flight suit and that would continually broadcast her whereabouts. That way, she could be picked up by either the Air Force or some other rescue operator helo that might be nearby. Sweat stood out on her upper lip, her mind moving at the speed of a computer.

The Warthog's engines, that specific whistling sound that was protected by the helmet she wore, couldn't be heard. But she could feel it lag and then a burst of surging power, and then her indicators would drop once more. She was losing power and altitude little by little. Barely at six thousand feet, heading north into those mountains, she could no longer see the Black Hawk because it was below her somewhere, barely creeping along at about fifteen hundred feet or so. Was it carrying a three- or four-man crew on board? Andy didn't know. She completed her eject list and searched the rugged mountains looming up ahead of her. The ravines were covered with hardscrabble trees that clung to their rocky surface. The tallest peaks were at ten thousand feet. For the next minute, she homed in on where she wanted to eject, what the terrain looked like and if she could survive it once she jettisoned out of the cockpit.

The first engine flamed out. The craft listed for a moment before she used the rudders beneath her flight boots, and the stick, to keep the Warthog flying level, flying toward her objective in the darkening sky. *One down.* An A-10 could handle losing an engine and make it back to base provided it wasn't shot up and coughing, like the second one was doing right now.

For a moment, the faces of her adopted mother and father, Steve and Maud, flashed before her eyes. She had been put on the step of a fire station and a firefighter had found her one cool May morning. She had been abandoned. Andy never found out who her mother was, but as luck would have it, she had been adopted months later and greatly loved by her new parents, who lived in Wind River, Wyoming.

She didn't want to die! Not like this. Andy had spent years in the Air Force, and every rotation back into Afghanistan provided close air support to men and women on the ground. She loved her life, her mission. But now things were coming to an end. And she wasn't sure if she'd survive.

For a moment, her attention was torn to eleven o'clock, to the left of where she flew. There was a small explosion, and she knew it had to be the Black Hawk hitting the rocky mountainside below and to the port side of her jet. It was the same area where she was going to eject into. Praying that the crew and two pilots made it out safely, her gaze flickered between the engine dial and where the small fire was below her. Then she focused on her own plight.

And then there was a huge explosion, a rolling red, yellow and orange fireball bursting out into the ebony darkness, lighting up a huge area around the helo. No one could survive that second explosion. Her heart ached for the crew.

The second engine sputtered and died. It flamed out, and she shut off the fuel line to it.

Automatically, her muscles puckered. Grabbing the lever, the cockpit Plexiglas separated with a loud bang around her.

Wind slammed and pummeled her masked and helmeted face. She was glad she had the NVGs in place over her eyes. Gritting her teeth, she initiated the ejection. In seconds, there was an explosion beneath her seat. Andy bit back a cry as her tightened nylon harness bit hard into her shoulders. Thrust into the cold darkness, the seat blew away from the now plumeting A-10.

Enclosed in darkness, Andy kept her elbows tightly pinned against her body. She kept her hands and arms stiff, holding them in place as the seat continued skyward. Just as the seat separated from her, she tumbled, hearing her chute begin to open somewhere above her.

Would it open completely? Her mind rattled between dying and wanting desperately to live. She was twenty-six years old, her whole life before her. If she made it out of this crash? She would leave the Air Force and find something in aviation. She loved to fly; she did not want to give it up, but she had to find something safer. The future wasn't an issue; surviving this situation was.

She swung like a pendulum through the night, wind gusts pummeling her. She could see she was going to land somewhere along the edge of a ravine. There were scrub trees everywhere. There was no way she was going to avoid tangling with one of them.

Just then, the A-10 plunged down onto the mountainside to the right of her. It was a thousand feet higher in elevation from where she was presently drifting downward. Automatically, she opened her mouth to balance the pressure inside and outside her lungs. The pressure waves from the crash were like fists slamming into her. Yellow and orange fire erupted into several fireballs, telling her the string of explosions were the ones designed to destroy all the avionics. The whole area lit up in a surreal, shadowy reddish glow for a few seconds. It blinded her; she'd stupidly looked at the explosion and it blew her vision in the NVGs. She swung several more times in the sky, several smaller explosions occurring at the crash site.

The ground came up fast. Getting some of her night vision back, she saw the trees looming beneath her dangling boots. She kept her knees soft and slightly bent. In seconds, she slammed into a tree, branches and limbs snapping and breaking off beneath her. Leaves, twigs blew up around her. Andy's legs were pummeled as her ascent slowed dramatically, her body crashing through the tree, bruises blooming all over her legs and arms.

She hit the ground, rocks biting into her one-piece flight uniform, letting out an "oooffff . . ." The straps of the chute gave her a soft landing. And then they untangled from the branches and the chute collapsed nearby.

Heart pounding, fear tunneling through her, Andy had no idea if there were Taliban nearby. They did not have night vision equipment and were known to camp at dark. Was she safe? Not safe? Was there a group in this ravine? She didn't know.

Disoriented from the landing, she pulled off her helmet, setting it nearby. She unstrapped her pistol, keeping it easy to reach after sliding a round into the chamber, the safety off. Now, after all those yearly training sessions for just such a situation, Andy knew what to do. She made sure her GPS radio was on and broadcasting an invisible location beacon signal to anyone who might be hunting to pick her up.

The explosion she'd seen earlier showed she was about half a mile farther up on the ravine than the spot where the Black Hawk had crashed. Had anyone survived? She looked around, trying not to sob for air, adrenaline making her gasp. With trembling hands, she unsnapped the chute from her harness, dropping it to the ground.

Through her NVGs she couldn't see far because of the thickets in the ravine itself.

First things first. She started to get up as two more minor but powerful explosions went off above her. Andy stood on shaky knees as she scrambled up the hill, slipping, falling on the field of rocks. Luckily, her Nomex gloves were on, protecting her hands from being sliced and cut, but her knees didn't fare as well. Getting to the chute, she gathered it up between her arms. Taking it down to the tree she'd crashed through, she pushed it toward the trunk, getting down on her hands and knees, digging a hole to hide it from prying enemy eyes.

She wasn't going to need the helmet either, so she dug another hole with effort, her knuckles bruised from all the smaller rocks she hit. It was nearly impossible to dig deep enough because there was more rock than soil. Andy wondered how these trees survived on this windswept ridge. Lucky it was August and not the snow season. She wondered how anything survived in this godforsaken place known as the Sandbox.

Pulling up the cuff of her flight-suit sleeve, she saw it was 2100, nine p.m. Standing, she looked around. Above and below her, there were two fires: the Black Hawk burning below, and above, her beloved A-10.

She looked up into the cloudless sky, the stars so close she thought she could reach out and touch them. It was a moonless night. Keying her hearing, she took off the rubber band and repositioned her shoulder-length chestnut hair into a ponytail. Where was the enemy? She didn't know. Never had she felt so naked and vulnerable as now. And scared. It was as real as it would ever get for Andy. The adrenaline was still pounding through her veins, and her hands were shaky as she touched the butt of her pistol, which lay across her chest on top of the Kevlar vest she wore.

The wind was powerful and came blasting through the area in unexpected gusts, sometimes pushing her a step sideways or backward. She was glad her flight suit was a desert-tan color so it wouldn't stick out like a sore thumb night or day. Not that the Taliban traveled at night. They rarely did.

For the first time since joining the Air Force, Andy

wished she wasn't in the military. She knew the dangers of A-10 jet jockeys being hit by enemy fire. It had happened to her many times before, usually bullets down the fuselage. Tonight? The enemy had gotten lucky and she was the unlucky one. Would an Air Force helo pick her up? How soon? She knew she had to try to call in and pulled the radio from her pocket.

Her night vision goggles had been affixed to her helmet, but she'd taken them off and hung them around her neck. She didn't want to bother with them at the moment. Time was of the essence. However, without moonlight she couldn't see her hand in front of her face. It was that black. Fingers trembling, she brought the radio up to her eyes, barely seeing the outline of it. Frowning, she couldn't find the green light on it that indicated it was working.

No . . .

Taking off her flight glove, she stuffed it in a leg pocket. Running her fingers across the top of the device, she cut her fingertip. Her heart sank in earnest. The top part of her radio was broken. That was why there was no green light. She must have struck it with the limbs of the tree as she parachuted to safety.

Looking around, fear snaking through her, Andy knew without her GPS radio working to signal where she was located, there would be no help coming except from the A-10 seconds before it augured in. Lifting her chin, she saw the flames of her crashed jet rapidly dwindling, more like a candle in the ebony night instead of the bonfire before. Her only hope was to remain near the wreckage. Someone, somewhere, would have to have fixed the last location of the GPS. They would send a helicopter crew out to the area and rescue her. She had to remain here. If it was cluttered with Taliban nearby? Her rescuers would not pick her up.

A shiver went through her. It was ass-freezing-cold on top of the ravine. She wrapped her arms around herself after pulling on the glove once again. It was bitterly cold. And until daylight came, Andy had no idea how far away her jet was, or how to get close to it to be seen by a rescue crew. And Taliban could be anywhere. If the jet was out on a bare spot on the slope, she would be seen by some sharp-eyed enemy for sure.

Heart sinking, she remained near the tree, unsure what to do. Her radio wasn't working, so no one would be able to find her. All she had on her flight vest were a few protein bars in her thigh pockets. And no water. This didn't look good.

"Hey!"

Whirling around, Andy stumbled and nearly fell. Her heart banged in her chest, her throat closed as the deep male voice came out of the night.

"I'm friendly, don't shoot!"

Her hand was already around the grip of the pistol as she righted herself, eyes huge as a dark shape—at least six feet tall—emerged from the inkiness of the ravine. "Who are you?" she demanded.

"Lieutenant Dev Mitchell. Are you the pilot from that A-10?"

Gulping, relieved, her eyes narrowed as the man came toward her. She could barely see the outline of his flight suit. "Y-yes. You're from the Black Hawk that crashed earlier?"

He halted. "I am. The only survivor. Who are you?"

"Captain Andrea Whitcomb, US Air Force. I was flying that A-10 until I got hit in both engines."

He gripped her arm. "Are you injured? Can you walk?"

She felt the strength of his fingers around her upper arm. Under ordinary circumstances, she'd have jerked away. But these weren't ordinary circumstances at all. "I'm okay . . . just bruises. Shook up for sure."

"Did you hide your chute?"

"Under this tree here. My GPS radio is damaged. No one can find where I'm at."

"I found you."

She saw his teeth white against the deep shadows of his craggy features. "How?"

He pointed to a set of NVG goggles around his neck. "These. Where's your helmet? Are the NVGs good on them?"

"Yes," she said. "I took them off my helmet before burying it. They are here, around my neck."

He released her. "We gotta get the hell outta here. The Taliban will come in at dawn, looking for us, searching for black boxes on both aircraft. We can't hang around here."

"B-but," she stammered, fear rising in her, "don't you have a GPS radio?"

"I do and it works, but we can't stay around these wrecks. Even a SAR, Search-and-Rescue, crew can't land in the middle of the Taliban closing in on where those birds are located. We have to leave. I'm in touch with them. SAR will track and follow my GPS coordinates until it's safe to come in and pick us up. This is very heavy enemy territory. We gotta leave. Now."

She turned, then moved to beneath the boughs of the tree, trying to stay out of the wind. So much of her fear had abated because the other pilot was there. And he sounded like he knew what he was talking about. "You seem to know what to do."

Again, that cocky grin. "Yeah. Not my first rodeo, Captain. You good enough to travel? The farther away we get from here at night, the better off we'll be. It's August; the sun's gonna come up early. We need to find a cave or someplace to hide when dawn comes. Right now we're in

Taliban central. We need to head west," and he pointed across the ravine. "There's a firebase about forty miles as the crow flies in that direction. We have to climb up and over the mountain range to reach it."

"Forty miles?" she managed, her voice raspy. "We're walking to it?"

"Yeah. It's that or stay here and get hunted down by Taliban, who will sure as hell behead us, and we'll show up on videos across the internet. I don't think you want that."

"Hell no!" She heard him give a low chuckle.

"You saved our ass after we unloaded that SEAL group. They got away and blended into the wall of the canyon and made their escape. Thanks."

"What about your other crew?"

She heard his voice lower, a lot of hidden emotion behind it. "Dead. We crashed. I was the only one who got out."

"Oh, God . . . I'm sorry, so sorry."

"Ready?" he rasped. "We're going to go down into this ravine and climb up the other side. We have about five hours of night to hide us, and then we'll have targets on our backs."

"Roger that." Andy settled the NVGs into place over her eyes. The wind shifted, and she could smell his flight suit, the strong odor of smoke and grease contained in it. "Are you okay? Did you get hurt?"

"Some first degree burns on the back of my neck and top of my ears is all. I'm okay. I have some water bottles in my leg pockets. Are you thirsty?" He pulled on his NVGs and then gripped her gloved hand with his.

"No, but I'm sure I will be. I have no water on me."

He grunted. "You'll have it whenever you want. Come on."

Andy could barely see Mitchell's face. It was his soft voice, with almost, she swore, an Irish lilt to it, that helped her steady her own fear. She wished she could see his face.

Was he married? Have a wife and kids at home? Most likely. What must they be feeling right now? She knew without a doubt that her own parents would be receiving a call from the Pentagon that she was MIA, missing in action. Andy's heart filled with anguish; she knew it would tear them up, and her three adopted siblings.

His hand was strong and guiding without hurting her fingers. He led her down the steep, rocky slope, and they were quickly devoured from anyone's sight beneath the scrub trees that stubbornly lived in the unstable ravine. There was no time to talk and no time to look around. She could see his broad set of shoulders against the nap of the trees sometimes. He was four inches taller than her, his stride ground-eating. Picking up on his urgency, very soon she was out of breath, rasping and forcing herself to keep up with him. They were at a high elevation and her body wasn't used to it. All she could see around them was darkness and the outlines of trees. The NVGs made everything a grainy green, and she kept her gaze down so she wouldn't stumble or trip over the rocks, some of them the size of cantaloupes and watermelons. It was a hard, rugged landscape, no question about that.

Dev Mitchell cursed silently as the Air Force pilot who had saved his life struggled to keep up. They had spent three hours on the run, getting as far away from the crash sites as they could. She was a trooper, had grit and never complained or asked him to slow down. The price of physical weakness would be capture, something he wanted to avoid at any cost. Once they breasted the first ridge, he stopped and told her to sit down and rest under a group of pine trees. Handing her a bottle of water, he stepped out to get the best radio signal he could find and called Bagram.

No stranger to the routine of being found by a SAR crew, Dev gave their GPS location. The answer he got in return chilled his blood. He had stepped away from Captain Whitcomb to make the call. She was green to what it meant to crash and then survive in this hellish country. Oh, he knew she had gone through all kinds of training, but this was the real thing, which was very different. Pulling out his notebook, he quickly wrote down some coordinates, shoving the pen back into his shirt pocket. Signing off, he quickly moved back to the pilot. Through his NVGs, he could see she had an oval face, a clean-looking nose and a nicely shaped mouth. Maybe in her mid-twenties at most. He was twenty-six himself. Liking her self-reliance, her pluck and determination, he knelt down in front of her, pushing up his NVGs.

"I contacted Bagram," he said in a low tone, his face inches from her, not wanting his voice to carry in case Taliban were nearby. "They've given me coordinates for a place for us to hole up. It's about a mile down the other side of this ridge."

"Hole up?"

He heard the fatigue in her voice. The alarm. His mouth thinned for a moment. "I was informed we're right in the middle of Taliban central. Where those birds crashed? We were a mile away from a large group of one hundred soldiers. Bagram has our location. They want us to go to a tunnel complex just down a mile on this ridge and hide out there. They can't bring in a Search-and-Rescue, SAR, to fly us out until the Taliban leave this area so it's safe enough to pick us up."

Groaning, she said, "How long?"

"As long as it takes. No one knows. We'll be safer resting in a cave or a tunnel complex during daylight hours."

"Yeah, but the Taliban use them, too. Did they tell you that?"

He grinned. "Yes. This isn't going to be easy, Captain Whitcomb."

"My name's Andy."

"Call me Dev. Nice to meet you. Are you hydrated? Are you ready to hoof it?"

She nodded. "Let's go." She handed him half a bottle of water. "You need to drink, too."

Taking it, he stood up and backed out of the grove, drinking the water she'd saved for him. There was a lot to like about this feisty female pilot. She was a team player; she thought of others and not just herself. As she joined him, he stuck the emptied plastic bottle into one of the thigh pockets of his flight suit. He didn't want to leave evidence behind. The Taliban would spot an American water bottle like a hawk spotting his next meal. It would tell them they were on the right path to finding them and he wanted to avoid that at all costs.

"How you holding up?"

"Sore and tired. You?"

"Same. If we get lucky, we'll find a place to hole up and then we can sleep."

She snorted. "Someone has to stay awake and play guard dog."

"I'll take first watch," he assured her, smiling. He pulled down his NVGs, seeing that pretty mouth of hers twist into a wry grin. She was a good partner to have. "Let's go."

The first time she actually saw Dev Mitchell was when he located a series of tunnels and found a cave that had a water source in it, plus light coming in from the top of it through a craggy, broken opening. It was the gray of dawn when he led her into it, after going in first, pistol drawn, to ensure no Taliban had taken up overnight residence in it. The place was empty.

The first thing he did after getting her in the cave was to walk outside, call Bagram, and give them their GPS. When he returned, she saw the exhaustion in his face. He had red hair and the greenest eyes she'd ever seen. His beard darkened his oval face and strong jawline. There was nothing weak-looking about Dev Mitchell. The darkness beneath his eyes, however, told Andy he was suffering over the loss of his crew. As he took off his gloves, she saw they, too, had been burned, his hands reddened with first degree burns, as well as his wrist area, where his Nomex fire-retardant flight suit had ridden up to expose his flesh. Her heart was heavy for him.

"Bagram has a Reaper drone at ten thousand feet flying over our area. It has a camera and it knows our GPS. The operator is watching for any Taliban wandering into our area and they'll call us if that happens."

"How long until they can rescue us?"

Shrugging, he put his NVGs on a rocky ledge near where the water seeped into a small nearby pool. "Unknown. This place is crawling with Taliban because it's close to the Pakistan border." His mouth flexed. "They think in a day or two."

"I found two protein bars in my pocket," she offered.

He gave her a one-cornered quirk of his mouth. "I have four. We'll share."

"Well, I wanted to lose a few pounds anyway."

"I like your spirit, Andy."

She warmed when his voice dropped to a deep, almost velvety sound. "Black humor comes with being in the military." She pointed to his reddened wrists. "Those look like more than first degree burns."

He sat down, leaning against the wall, tipping back his head and closing his eyes as he stretched out his long legs. "The wind blew the Black Hawk into the slope. We crashed on the right side, the pilot's side." Grimacing, his voice soft, he rasped, "I couldn't save him. And our crew chief died on impact. Fire was everywhere. I cut his harness and tried to drag him out, but the fire drove me back." He opened his eyes and touched one of his blistered ears. "I couldn't do it. I was choking on the smoke, couldn't see, and I finally fell back and out the sprung door. I crawled away and made it to safety before the main explosion occurred." He rubbed his face wearily. "It was a bitch of a mission. If you hadn't been on station to suppress the Taliban fire, the SEALs wouldn't have gotten into the brush and escaped."

"I couldn't pull it off," she offered quietly, giving him a sympathetic look. "Whoever those guys were on the ground? They had armor-piercing rounds. Usually they don't. But this group did."

"Yeah, believe me, when those rounds came tearing into our Hawk, we knew we were in trouble." He gave her a grateful look. "You tried to save us. I saw how low you flew, taking their gunfire away from aiming at us. You put yourself in the line of fire so we could get away."

She sighed and nodded. "It wasn't good enough. I'm sorry. So? You had only one crew chief on board? Usually there are two."

"There were supposed to be," Dev admitted. And he lifted his chin, holding her gaze. "I guess the only good news is our other crew chief stayed behind because his wife was having a baby and they had her on a video feed."

"Thank God," Andy whispered unsteadily. "At least he didn't die. And you didn't either, so that's the second piece of good news out of all of this, Dev." She wanted to use his name, and it rolled easily off her tongue. Almost like a prayer. "You saved me, too. I didn't know where the hell I was, my radio was broken and I knew how much trouble I was in."

"Three pieces of good news out of this," he agreed tiredly. "Look, you need to eat a bit, drink water," and he handed her a bottle, "and then go to sleep. I've got purification tablets to put into our bottles to keep the water in this pool from giving us some parasite. Plus, we'll refill the bottles tonight before we leave. Water is everything."

"Wake me in two hours? I'll take over the watch."

"No, I'll let you sleep four hours."

"Can you stay awake that long?" she asked, opening up her protein bar. She ate half and gave Dev the other half.

"Fear will keep me awake," he answered wryly.

She laughed softly, not wanting the sound to carry. "You're tough, Mitchell. Really tough." Her heart expanded when he gave her a little-boy smile, his face lighting up. Most of all, she liked the freckles across his nose and cheeks. Surely of Irish descent? Maybe they'd get time later to talk.

"I think it's called a will to live instead of die," he responded drily, quickly eating the other half of the protein bar. He pulled out the third bottle and drank half of it, then offered her the rest. Andy took it and thanked him.

"Even though we're Army and Air Force, we're getting along pretty good together," she teased, finishing off that water.

Dev dropped tablets into the three empty bottles and held them under the small stream coming out of the wall of the cave. "Yeah, we are." And his eyes sparkled as he gave her an intense look. "I'm just sorry I didn't meet you under better circumstances."

Chapter Two

Four years later
June 3

"Andy, look out! Drone! Three o'clock!"

There was no time to react. A drone smashed into the side of her Black Hawk Los Angeles Police Department helicopter. It hit with such force, it shattered the drone, the plastic pieces raining down across the cockpit window. Instantly, the helo sagged, the power in one engine suddenly quitting on her.

Andy didn't even have time to curse.

Bob Covington, her copilot, shot his gloved hand on the throttles located above their seats in the overhead, instantly shutting off the fuel line to the lost engine above them.

They were at three thousand feet, heading for home over the sprawling California city near dusk. Her feet danced on the rudders, her hands tight around the cyclic and collective as the bird sagged downward. They could fly with one engine, but she had no idea if the drone that struck them had sent shrapnel into one engine or both.

"Where to land?" she demanded, working to keep the Black Hawk steady. They were slowly losing altitude.

Luckily, they weren't over the skyscrapers in central LA, but in a suburb.

"Open baseball field at six o'clock, Andy. About a mile away."

"Roger that." She banked the helo gently, not wanting to stress the only engine any more than she had to. In the helmet she wore, the visor down to protect her eyes, she heard Bob putting out a Mayday with their helo terminal in the city. He rattled off the GPS and told them a drone had struck very close to the rotor assembly on top of their bird.

Would they make it down okay?

Shades of the past came racing back to her as she watched her altimeter continue to unwind. The crash of her A-10 in the mountains of Afghanistan hit her full force. After getting rescued, she'd left the Air Force, wanting something safer. She'd learned to fly a helicopter and was immediately hired by the LA Police Department. She loved the varied routine of a law enforcement officer.

"We're set for a hard landing, if need be," Bob said, his voice tight.

"Roger that. I see the landing area," she replied. It was an empty green baseball field, used by the nearby high school, she would bet. Fortunately, it was Sunday and dusk, with no game and no people around. The vibration she normally felt as comforting made her anxious, and she stuffed the feeling deep within her. They were moving lower and lower. She watched for the electric lines and any other flight issues as she guided the limping Hawk toward the field.

They were twenty feet from landing when the second engine suddenly quit.

Too late!

"Brace!" Andy yelled out. They were too low to pull up the nose and catch air to soften the landing.

This was going to be a nasty, hard landing.

The helo slammed into the field, nose first. The Plexiglas exploded inward, showering both of them. She was jerked hard, her neck snapping back against the seat. The bird had augured in, the nose buried in two feet of plowed-up dirt. She'd yanked her feet off the pedals just in time. The nose had buckled and part of it caved in an inch from where she'd pulled up her flight boots. If her feet had been on the rudders, she'd be trapped, or they might have been cut off.

God! That was close!

"Exit!" Andy ordered in a croak, yanking at her harness, smelling the fumes of the fuel entering their cabin.

"Roger!" Covington answered. He instantly shut off the fuel line above him, then wrenched the harness off his body.

The door on the right was jammed because of the nose auguring in slightly to her side. Turning in the seat, she jammed her flight boots against it.

The door popped open.

Instantly, Andy bailed out.

Covington was already out, running around the nose to come and get her away from the bird. The smell of fuel was heavy in the air. Despite him shutting off the fuel, the hard landing could have broken the line, and it was dripping somewhere above them. There was a chance of fire.

Andy fell to her knees into a headlong dive. She scrambled upward and Bob grabbed her arm, hauling her forward. If this bird blew, if the fuel bladder had been punctured by the landing, they could be toast.

Andy ran hard, keeping up with Bob, who had wrapped his hand around her arm as they raced away from the helo.

Finally, when they arrived at the bleacher boxes, they turned quickly, gasping for air, breathing hard. Andy used her shoulder radio to call in the emergency landing, gave the police dispatcher their location and said to call the fire department to the scene.

Bob shook his head, taking off his helmet and setting it on a wooden bleacher, running his hands through his thinning gray and black hair.

"That was close," he said in a shaky voice. "You okay, Andy?"

"Yeah, just shook up. You?" and she sized up Bob, who was in his early fifties. Even in the dusk, he looked pale. Andy was sure she looked the same way.

"Bruises, nothing else. A damned drone! I hope they find the kid or adult who flew it into us."

Andy studied the helo in the coming darkness. The blades had stopped turning and it looked like a wounded bird, half the nose buried beneath the sod. "I'm sure they'll expend every effort to find the person who did this."

Rubbing his jaw, he looked up, hearing fire sirens coming their way. "There are gonna be more like this in the future. It sucks."

Andy nodded, adrenaline racing through her and making her hyperalert. They could have died. That engine could have stopped at fifty feet and she'd have no way to do anything to save them. They'd have dropped out of the sky like a rock. That she was sure of because ten feet versus fifty made all the difference in the world. The fuel bladder could have exploded on impact, for starters.

She remembered Lieutenant Dev Mitchell's Black Hawk helo, which had been hit with enemy gunfire and exploded. He'd been the only survivor. Shaking her head, she tried to purge the memory from her mind. That was four years ago, but this crash brought back that night to her starkly. And the five days they were on the run, avoiding the Taliban who were hunting them.

It had been a harrowing experience, and once they got

picked up and taken back to Bagram, all Andy wanted to do was leave the military. Life was too precious. She might have wanted a career in the military, but that crash and subsequent life-and-death dodging of the enemy every day made her walk away from it. Besides, her adopted parents were relieved, and so was she. Staring at the broken helo out on the grassy area, her heart still pounding beneath her vest, she removed her gloves. The sirens of the approaching fire engines filled the air. A few people had pulled over on the four-lane street, getting out, looking through the wire cyclone fence at the broken helo.

Andy felt shaky, knowing it was the letdown of adrenaline. Maybe this was a sign. Just like her A-10 taking fire and her having to bail out. Pulling off her helmet, she tucked it beneath her left arm, watching the three fire engines approach from the other side of the diamond. Controlled chaos. Andy was sure NTSB investigators had already been notified.

"We're going to have a lot of paperwork to fill out," Bob said grimly, shaking his head. "All because of a stupid drone and an irresponsible owner."

Nodding, Andy pulled out her personal cell phone, turning it on. "I'm going to call my parents. I'm sure they'll hear about this sooner or later, and I don't want them to find out on the TV or internet."

"Yeah," he said, tugging his cell phone out of his pocket, "I gotta call Jodi."

"She always has a police scanner on," Andy said. "Try to beat her to the call."

"Yes," he agreed, putting the phone to his ear and then walking a few feet away from her.

Andy took the moment to connect with Maud and Steve Whitcomb.

"Hello."

It was Maud, her mother. "Hey, Mom, Andy here," she

said, trying to sound upbeat. "I was just in a helo accident and I'm fine," she stressed. "And so is Bob, my copilot. A drone flew into the helo and I . . . uh . . . it was a hard landing, but we aren't hurt." She knew her mother would not take this news well.

"No! Andy, are you really okay?"

"Yeah," she said wryly, "just hurt feelings that I didn't see that damned drone first." She heard her mother's ragged sigh. "Really, we're both fine. We walked away from it. That's all that counts." She wanted to soothe her mom, not inflame the situation.

"This is twice, Andy!" She muttered something away from the phone and then said, "After the first crash, you know your dad and I wanted you to get into something safer."

"I know, I know," she muttered. "I did, Mom."

"You didn't do this on purpose," Maud said, her voice low with stress, reeling from the shock of the call.

"You're right about that," Andy said, forcing a chuckle she felt she needed to boost her mother's mood, "this is two. Third one I could . . . well, you know."

"Things come in threes, Andy. Is there any way we can get you to come home for a week when this incident is all over? I'm sure there will be a lot of questions by investigators, papers or reports to hand in."

"All of that," Andy assured her. "Look, let me call you back? I see our watch commander. He just drove up. The firefighters are here as well. I'll talk to you later. Make sure Dad knows I'm fine. Okay?"

"Yes, I will. Can we Skype when you get home? I know you probably have a million things to take care of first."

"I promise," she whispered, suddenly wanting to cry. That shook Andy. She wasn't normally like this. But she was four years older and she wasn't the ballsy young woman who had joined the military to make a difference, to fight for her country.

"I'll call Sky, Gabe and Luke. I'm sure they'll hear about this crash sooner, not later," Maud said.

"Thanks, Mom, I appreciate that. I'll get hold of you tonight when things calm down. I love you and Dad. Just know that." She heard a small intake of Maud's breath and swore she could feel the roiling emotions in her tone, the shock and reeling from the news she'd crashed—again. And walked away from it—again.

"We love you so much, honey. We'll wait for your call."

The shakiness subsided as the minutes wore on. By the time night had come, she and Bob were picked up and taken back to their precinct. It was there that Andy spent the next three hours. By the time she drove home to her apartment, she felt gutted. Her brothers and sister had each called her, wanting to be reassured she was okay. Andy was the oldest of the four who were all adopted by Maud and Steve. Her mother couldn't have children—a genetic affliction—and they had opened their hearts to the two boys and two girls. Never had she felt so loved as with her ranching parents in Wyoming. Gabe, Luke and Sky were truly her family, too. There was nothing but love shared between all of them.

Weariness crashed over her, and when she got in her apartment, she took off the flight suit and boots and went for a long shower, as hot as she could stand it. When she emerged later, it felt as if her feet were made of concrete. Wanting to do nothing but sleep, she forced herself to pick up her cell phone and call her parents.

Steve, her father, answered.

"Hi, Dad, it's me."

"You sound tired, Punkin."

Warming to the endearment, she sat down on her bed, pushing the slippers off her feet. "I'm whipped, Dad. I wanted to call to let you know I'm okay. Got all the reams of paperwork filled out, I'm home, had a hot shower and now I'm going to bed."

"Sounds good. Can you call us tomorrow morning sometime? I know your mother has something to tell you."

Groaning, Andy said, "I hope it's not bad news."

Steve laughed a little. "No, it's not, Punkin. I promise. Hit the sack. We'll talk by Skype tomorrow."

She nodded. "Thanks for understanding, Dad. Tell Mom I love her, too."

"I will. We'll talk soon. Love you."

She turned off the cell and placed it on her bed stand because she was off duty the next three days. Tomorrow afternoon she had to see a flight surgeon for a thorough checkup. All part of the NTSB investigation. Andy was looking forward to these days off. She crawled into her queen-size bed, snuggled in and promptly spiraled into a deep sleep.

Her dream began almost as soon as she slept, one she'd had before. There was Dev Mitchell's Irish good looks, red strands mixed with his sable-colored hair, those intense green eyes, the color almost magical because the shade seemed to change depending upon the light or lack of it. Sometimes, in bright sunlight as they sat inside the cave or another place of hiding during the day, the color reminded her of fresh, young green leaves sprouting after a hard winter, spring just around the corner. At dusk, his eyes took on a more olive quality. And when he'd tease her, which was often as a way to keep her spirits up when they were running for their lives, Andy swore they were a gorgeous emerald green. She'd always thought he was somewhat magical but had never given it voice. It had been her secret, and it was one of the few positives in their unexpected meeting.

Dev Mitchell had protected her. She outranked him, though they were near the same age and had been in the military almost the same amount of time. More than once, he had shielded her in those dangerous moments, and Andy was grateful. She wasn't the athlete he was either. She rode a combat jet in the sky. He'd said that if he wasn't flying or jogging at the air base where he was stationed, he worked out at a gym. She was not a gym or jogging person. There were too many times to count when she'd slowed him down and her physical weakness had put them in dire jeopardy. Through it all, he never once blamed her. He only doubled down and used creative ways to hide them from the ever-present Taliban.

The dream shifted, and she was standing with him in an interrogation office, just finishing up their interview with agents after they were returned to their base. They had left the building together, and Andy knew this stalwart pilot was going to walk out of her life. She didn't want that to happen. Dev and his squadron were based at Jalalabad—J-bad—and she was here at Bagram. Already he'd been informed that after the interview, he was to be picked up by Humvee, taken to the helo terminal and flown back to J-bad.

Just as she was going to say something, the Humvee pulled up. Dev had turned to her, his face darkly shadowed because there were few lights on the base come nightfall. During their run for freedom, Andy had admitted to him that if she got out of this alive, she was going to hand in her papers and leave the military.

"Wait, Dev," she said.

He smiled tiredly down at her. "They need me now, Andy. I have to go."

"I just want to say thank you," she said a little breathlessly, clinging to his gaze, those thick lashes of his framing his dark green eyes as he studied her at the curbside.

He handed her a business card from his pocket. "This is

where I'm at presently. I get moved around a lot, but you should be able to contact me here if you want."

She took the card. "Yes, I want to do that, Dev. I don't want to lose touch with you . . ."

He reached out with his long, spare hand and gently pushed some errant strands of her hair away from her temple. "You're leaving the Air Force. A new chapter in your life. I truly wish you well, Andy. We made a good team out there."

And he turned and disappeared into the Humvee.

Andy stood there on the curb, watching the Humvee take off down the street. She wanted to throw up her hands and stop it. Her chest ached. Tears smarted in her eyes. There was something in his eyes, a kind of sadness, as he reached out to her. So much she wanted to say, and yet she was such a coward, her throat with a lump in it, the words stuck.

But he'd given her his squadron's card and she gripped it, afraid she'd lose it. But they both knew circumstances weren't right for them. Andy didn't even know whether Dev was married with a passel of kids. They'd never spoken in personal terms during those five days, in part because they were being hunted and talking could get them found by the sharp ears of their enemy. She didn't know about Dev, but she was scared out of her wits. The specter of being beheaded, her parents seeing the video on the internet, haunted her.

Andy moaned and briefly awoke. For a moment, she forgot where she was, still tied to that dream that came at least four times a year. She'd never heard from Dev again after the rescue party brought them to Bagram's hospital. Later, when she wasn't able to locate Dev, she departed the military in Bagram and finished signing the exit papers at Travis Air Force Base, near San Francisco. From there,

Andy had decided she didn't want to leave flying, though she didn't want to become an airline pilot, Helicopters had always drawn her, and she wasn't ready to leave her risk-taking days behind her either.

Sighing, she turned over, pulling the sheet across her shoulders, burrowing her face into the pillow. Dev's face reappeared, and it comforted her. It always had. Especially out in the wilds of Afghanistan, where she felt like the hunted. Had he been married? Did he have children? Where was he now? She dropped back into a dreamless sleep as she asked that last question, and it remained unanswered, as always.

Andy's heart burst when she saw her parents appear on the Apple computer screen, sitting together at their office desk. She had slept in late, getting up at nine a.m., unheard of in her world. It served to tell her how much the hard landing had taken out of her last night. After grabbing a quick breakfast, she'd sat down and Skyped them. Her mother, Maud, was as beautiful as ever, her silver and black hair short and shining, and she was wearing a red tee, her favorite color, and faded jeans with a brown leather belt. Her father, Steve, was in a blue chambray shirt, sleeves rolled up to his elbows, in jeans as well. She absorbed the love for her shining in their eyes.

"You look tired," Maud said gently, pointing to under her own eyes.

"I had a restless night's sleep, Mom."

"Walking away from a crash would do that to anyone," Steve said, giving her a warm look meant to make her feel better.

"I was dreaming of that guy who saved my butt four years ago in that crash in Afghanistan," she admitted.

"You still dream of him?" Maud asked.

Quirking her lips, Andy said, "Yes. Silly, isn't it?"

"No," Maud said. "He saved your life. I wouldn't forget him either."

"That's true," she murmured, looking at Dev in a new light. "I just wish I could have had more time with him. He was a nice person."

"Some things aren't meant to be, Punkin."

She nodded, holding her father's thoughtful gaze. "Ever the philosopher in our family," she teased.

"I think every family needs a risk-taker," Maud said, smiling, "and a philosopher. One steps on the accelerator, the other steps on the brake."

"Hmmm," Andy murmured, "that's true of us, for sure. Dev Mitchell acted like the accelerator in our unexpected coming together and I was the brake. But to be fair to him, he knew how to survive that crash and I didn't. I was always dragging my feet."

"You said one time," Steve said, "that you just weren't physically able to keep up with him, that he had to rest more often because of you. That's not putting on the brakes, Punkin. Just because you weren't in as great shape as he was didn't mean you didn't bring intelligence and insight to your situation. We know you did."

"That was true," she agreed. Sighing, she opened her hands. "I feel like I've just closed the next chapter of my life. I felt that way after the crash of my A-10."

"Seems like it," Maud said. "You know that for the last three years we've been fully involved in getting the state of Wyoming and the federal government to build a regional airport in Wind River."

Nodding, she said, "Yes, a very exciting project. God knows, the Wind River Valley needs something like this to pull them out of poverty and give the people a place to get good jobs. I can't think of an area that needs it more."

"Which is why your dad and I have been working so hard to make it happen. I have some news for you, Andy. And I think you might be interested."

"Oh? What?" She lifted her cup of coffee and took a sip.

"Well," Maud began, excitement in her tone, "we've had two possibilities hanging fire. One was that we're trying to get federal approval for a helicopter for our local hospital. The other was getting a helicopter for law enforcement in Lincoln County. Sarah Carter, the sheriff, just called me yesterday to tell me that the feds had finally approved the money to go ahead and purchase a Black Hawk helicopter, along with employing four pilots and copilots, plus a two-person ground crew that would include crew chiefs. It's a huge win for us. Sarah is over the moon." Maud leaned forward, her eyes sparkling. "Andy, they've hired a director and he has put out a want-ad for pilots and copilots. Is this something you might want to be involved in? I know Wind River Valley isn't LA, but it would allow you to do what you love most, which is fly."

"You'd be back home with us," Steve said. "That's something we always wished would happen with our children. We know you have your own lives to lead, but with this regional airport getting ready to open in July of this year, there are finally some serious opportunities for you and maybe Sky, Luke and Gabe, too."

"Seriously?" Andy sat up. "Wow, that's really good news. So? They're hiring?"

"Yes," Maud said, hopefulness in her tone. "They're taking résumés right now. I talked to Pete Turner, who has just been hired as director of operations for the sheriff's department, and he said he's already hired one pilot, who will be assistant director. They're now looking to fill three other slots. Might you be interested?"

"This is so funny." Andy laughed and shook her head. "I woke up this morning asking myself what the hell I was doing with my life. I was wishing I was home with you, in the valley."

Maud made a small sound of surprise. "Then why don't you come home, Andy? We don't have many drone operators in this area. And you know our criminal issues sure aren't anywhere near what LA has."

"It would be quieter," Steve assured her. "Pete was saying that the biggest issue in the valley is drug running. Sarah said crime was actually down to a new low in Lincoln County. You might be bored on some days, but at least you'd be safe."

"And close to us. We'd love to have you back with us, Andy."

Andy saw her mother's eyes glisten with tears. "I miss both of you so much," she quavered. "That sounds like it's a fit for me. I woke up knowing I no longer wanted to work here in the city. It's just too big, too much pollution, and I guess I'm growing up or getting older. I want some peace and quiet. I miss the clean air of Wyoming, the winters and everything in between."

"Well," Maud said, "you know Sky flies a sky crane helicopter water tanker for the US Forest Service?"

"Yes."

"They're putting in a huge wildfire operational facility here, along with the ten-thousand-foot runway. They're almost done with the aerial facility at the airport. They're going to be hiring people to run it."

"Wow," Andy said, "I didn't realize that. Will they have a firefighting crew stationed at the airport?"

"That's what's planned," Steve said.

Sitting back, Andy whispered, "This is stunning news . . . Have you told Sky about this?"

"We were waiting for the final decision and it just came through," Maud said. "There are still some minor road-blocks that have to be ironed out. As soon as they are, I'll let her know."

"Wouldn't that be great if Sky could come home, too? I know she misses the valley. Every time we talk she sounds homesick."

"I know," Maud said. "And your dad has already talked with Luke. He's a Hotshot firefighter stationed in Boise, Idaho, but he'd like to get into the action here, join the crew they're assembling right now at the airport."

"That's wonderful," Andy whispered. "Three of us might be coming home." She pressed her hand to her heart. "I can't tell you how good this makes me feel."

"Or us," Steve said gently. "We miss our kids."

"What about Gabe? He's working for the DEA over in San Diego. Is there a job opening for him, too?" she asked.

"No," Steve said. "Not that we know of."

"Well, maybe that will change," Andy said. "I love our valley. We have so many friends we grew up with still there."

"Come on home," Maud said, smiling. "Wind River is growing. As a matter of fact, I think I told you that a whole new condo unit was built on the outside of town?"

"Yes. Are there any condos open for lease?"

"As a matter of fact," Maud said, "there are. Maybe one for you, but you're welcome to have your old bedroom back here at the ranch."

Laughing, Andy said, "I'll take you up on it, but I think a condo in the long run, if I get a job, sounds great. And I'd only be twenty minutes from the front gate of the ranch. I'm sure we'd be together a lot more often, and I love the idea of moving home." She saw her parents' face go soft and knew in that instant that going home, her home, was the most important decision she'd made lately. Her throat tightened, her voice off-key. "I've really missed you two, the ranch and the valley. I've been looking at my life like chapters in a book I'm writing and living. My first chapter was being abandoned, my mother leaving me on the steps of the fire department. And then you stepped in, adopted and loved me." She felt tears leaking out of her eyes. Wiping them away, she managed, "My second chapter was graduating from college. My third chapter was military service, my love of flying. My fourth chapter was leaving it, learning to fly a helicopter and working with the LAPD."

"And now? Your fifth chapter is coming home," Maud whispered, wiping her eyes. "Full circle."

"I've always missed you and home. It's never far from my mind. You gave me and three other adopted kids a real chance to have a family who loved all of us. We all owe you two so much." And never were her words more genuine than in that moment. Sky, Gabe, Luke and she had been abandoned and then rescued by Maud and Steve. All of them were very young with no memory of their biological mothers. She had been the first child they'd brought to their ranch, and then six months later, they adopted Sky. Two years later, Gabe and Luke came into their household.

Steve gave her a wobbly smile. He put his arm around Maud, giving her a fond look and then gazed at her. "Come on home, Punkin. This is where your heart is, no matter where in the world you travel or work. We'll always be here. The ranch will be here."

"Sounds awfully good to me," she whispered, choking up. "I don't know what the next chapter will bring, but at least I'll be home, and that means everything to me."

Chapter Three

June 11
Monday

"Andy?" Dev Mitchell blinked twice to make sure he was seeing correctly. He was standing in line at Kassie's Café to grab breakfast when he saw her walk into the busy and popular Wind River restaurant. She carried a briefcase in her left hand. It was cloudy outside and, at six a.m., below freezing in the valley. Dressed in a long, black nylon jacket that fell to her hips, she wore a bright red muffler around her neck, black leather gloves on her hands and a pair of sensible jeans and work boots. On her head was a bright red knit cap, her once-short chestnut hair now shoulder length and longer than when he'd known her four years earlier. Best of all, as he met her widening gray eyes, which were framed with thick lashes, he saw that she recognized him, too. He grinned lopsidedly, shocked, and stepped out of line, walking back to where she stood.

"It's really you?" Andy asked, breathless, disbelief in her tone as she gazed up at him. "Dev Mitchell?"

He laughed, feeling a little giddy along with the pleasant shock rolling through him. He held out his hand to her.

"Yeah, it's me. Of all the places in the world, Andy, we meet here."

She shook his hand. "It's so good to see you again! What are you doing in Wind River?" and she released his warm, firm hand.

"I was just hired a week ago to become the assistant flight operations manager for the Lincoln County Sheriff's Office. Everyone told me Kassie's was the place to go for breakfast and I was trying it out. How about you? If I remember right," his smile deepened, "you said you lived in western Wyoming."

"I was born here in Wind River," she said, meeting his smile with one of her own. "Gosh, this is incredible! I'd lost touch with you when you left in that Humvee for Bagram's helo facility for that flight back to your squadron. There was so much I wanted to say, to thank you for."

"I know," he said, his smile dissolving, apology in his voice. "I was needed back at my black ops airbase ASAP; that's why I had to leave. When I returned, I was put back on the flight roster. We were short of pilots and I was flying every other day for three weeks until we got some new pilots transferred in to ease our schedule."

"Oh," she said, gesturing for him to come and stand in line with her. "I tried to find you, but you literally disappeared."

"Not on purpose," he admitted. He gave her a warm look. "It's nice to see you again, though. When I finally got back to Bagram about a month later, I visited the squadron you flew with, and they said you'd handed in your papers and left the Air Force shortly after returning from the crash." He shrugged. "Not that I could blame you. We had a rough five days playing cat and mouse with the Taliban."

"It broke me," she admitted, her smile gone, now more serious. "My mom and dad were always worried for me because I flew a combat jet in close quarters. After the crash and them not hearing from me because we were on the run, it broke them, too. I just didn't want to put them or myself into a situation like we got caught in again."

"I understand," he murmured, sympathetic. They inched forward in the line. At six a.m., the café was filled to capacity. It was the place where everyone went, his boss, Pete Turner, had told him. He was glad he'd come this morning. "Are you still flying?" he asked her.

"Yes. When I left the Air Force, I went to a civilian helicopter training school and got a license to fly Black Hawks."

His eyes sparkled. "Ah . . . my bird. That's amazing. What did you do with the license?"

"I flew for the Los Angeles Police Department. I spent a year in the left seat as a copilot, on-the-job law enforcement, while learning what a police person does in a helo over that sprawling city. I stayed for nearly three years. We were recently flying over a neighborhood and my Black Hawk got hit by a drone. We made a hard landing, and we got lucky: we walked away from it."

Dev frowned. "Damned drones."

"Seriously. I decided to quit the police department and come home. I wasn't sure what I wanted to do, and my parents and I have been sussing out possibilities." She held up her briefcase. "I have a nine a.m. meeting with you, I guess. When I emailed my résumé for a job with the Lincoln sheriff as a law enforcement pilot, they referred my call to the assistant ops manager. I left my name and phone number. A woman called me back, a Jackie Turnbull, who scheduled me to meet with you. She never gave me your name."

"I see. Jackie works with both Pete and me. We've just gotten our office put together in the last week. And we're all running helter-skelter, organizing and getting up to speed. Either Jackie or Pete has your résumé because I haven't seen it yet."

Wryly, she said, "I'd probably faint if I went into your office and saw you, of all people, sitting there behind a desk," and she laughed, shaking her head. "What a weird, wild world we live in."

He joined her laughter. They were the next in line to get a booth. "We're still trying to get things in order at the airport. I'd noted on my calendar that a female applicant was coming in at nine a.m., but no name. Jackie's like a juggler with too many balls up in the air and trying to get our two offices online. It's hectic."

"I'm glad we met here, then," she admitted.

"I am, too."

"When I talked with Jackie, she said that the assistant ops manager would be my first interview, and that he would evaluate my skills and my résumé. If he found I was qualified, I'd get a second interview with Mr. Turner, who heads up the operation."

"That's right," Dev agreed. The waitress came up to him with two menus, gesturing for them to follow her. As luck would have it, a booth near the kitchen, off in a corner, was open for new occupants. It was less noisy. He gestured to Andy. "Ladies first," he said.

"Throwback," she accused, grinning and stepping ahead.

"Guilty as charged." They threaded through coming-and-going customers. Along the way to their booth, they halted three times because people who knew Andy stopped her and welcomed her home. When they got to the booth, the waitress gave them coffee and said she'd come back for their order in a few minutes.

Dev tried to keep his focus on keeping Andy at arm's

length, but he was finding that impossible. When she got to the booth, she shrugged out of her black nylon jacket and hooked the red scarf and knit cap beside it. He wanted to tell her that her shining red, gold and light brown hair gleamed beneath the overhead lights, accenting her pink cheeks. From the moment she'd seen him, she had flushed, and he wasn't sure what that meant. Wanting to drown in her light gray eyes with those huge black pupils, he knew he couldn't. If she was a potential employee of the sheriff's department, he'd be her boss. That deflated Dev as he opened the menu.

"I already know what I want," Andy said, pushing her menu aside.

"Because you grew up here and know the menu by heart?"

"Kassie has had the restaurant for nearly ten years. When I was in the Air Force and got sent stateside, my parents and I, and sometimes, my brothers or sister, would come here for breakfast."

"I see. Well? What do you recommend, Andy?"

"I love their Denver omelet. Kassie buys as much local produce from the farmers in the valley as she can. Instead of using cheddar cheese in it, there's a family here who raises goats and makes the most delicious feta cheese. So she puts the feta in the omelets, instead. It has green sweet peppers and onions in it, too."

"Sounds good."

The waitress came back and they ordered two omelets, plus hash browns and huge, light-brown sourdough biscuits, homemade by Kassie, to go with their meal.

"I just can't believe you're here," Andy admitted after the waitress left. She folded her hands on the table, studying him. "I always wondered what happened to you."

"I stayed in the Army for another year after our crash and then left. I still wanted to fly my Black Hawk, so I ended up with the Seattle Police Department. I flew for them after that."

"What got you here, though?" she wondered, sipping her coffee.

"Luck, I guess. Pete Turner had worked in operations for the Seattle Police Department. We were both getting tired of the big city. My folks live in Port Harbor, North Carolina, a very rural area, and I grew up by the ocean, fishing, swimming, doing some surfing and enjoying our small community. I wanted to get back to that."

"Pete told you about this job?"

"Yes, we've been friends since I worked in Seattle, and that's how I got this job as his assistant. We're a good team and he's an excellent boss."

"You and I were a good team under fire," she said, her voice tinged with emotion. "Without you, I know I wouldn't be here right now."

He gave her a humble look. "We all have strengths and weaknesses, Andy. What is important is that we both contributed to us getting behind the wire once more."

"I still have nightmares about that week," she admitted. "PTSD, they said."

"That's normal," he assured her. "I get it, too, even to this day. I had a therapist tell me that dreams were a way for us to work out the terror and other very human emotions of that trauma. Each time we dream about those terrifying events, the emotional and mental hold on us is loosened a little more. She said that someday I'd stop dreaming about it." Actually, that was half the truth. He'd dreamed about Andy from the time he left her outside the ER. And oddly enough, a week ago, when he'd arrived in the valley, he'd had a dream about her once more. At the time, when he'd awakened, he'd felt it was a good omen.

Little did he know he'd be meeting her in the flesh! He saw her face soften at his words.

"That's nice to know."

"Did you get therapy?"

Shrugging, she said, "No, not my style. I have a really good connection with my parents, and when I'm boxing myself in on something, I call them."

"Now that you're home, are you living with them?"

"I'm staying there for now, but if I get this job, I intend to rent a condo. Mom said there was a nice one at the end of town."

"I live there and it's well maintained."

"Good to know."

The waitress brought their food. Dev said to the waitress, "I'll take the bill."

Andy opened her mouth to protest.

"Business," he said. "I can write it off. You're coming to interview with me in a couple of hours."

"Okay," she said, cutting into the fragrant omelet, "this time. Thank you."

Dev hid his smile. She was independent, which he'd seen during their run for safety in Afghanistan. There was a quietness to Andy, but beneath it was a steel spine as far as he was concerned. She had the reserve that he'd seen in many pilots. They weren't loud and neither needed nor wanted other people's attention. "You're welcome."

It didn't seem like she was married or had kids. Dev was fairly sure she would have said something about it if she was. Why did he feel happy about that? He shouldn't. If she was hired, Andy would be an employee, not a lover. Was that what he wanted? Sophie, his wife, had died when she was twenty years old of a heart attack. They called it the "widow maker," and no one thought someone as young as she was could possibly keel over, dead. She'd been at the

University of North Carolina, where they were both working toward degrees. Even now, an old pain stirred in his heart. Gently, he put those memories away. They had no bearing on the present. Or did they?

"So," he murmured, holding Andy's gaze, trying to ignore that soft mouth of hers, "does this mean you're coming home for good?"

Dipping her head, she said firmly, "Yes. Let's put it this way, Dev: I've been around the world and I've seen a lot. I guess I was getting homesick. And as we dropped twenty feet to the ground and made a hard landing in Los Angeles, it sort of cinched that realization for me." She looked around the noisy but happy patrons in the café. "I grew up here. Now, all my friends are married and have kids. I have a lot of reconnecting to do with them, and I'm looking forward to it. Plus, I can drive to my folks' ranch, throw a leg over a good horse and ride. Riding always blew off my tension, worry or stress."

"I've not ridden horses very often, so I wouldn't know." He saw her give him an evil grin.

"You never know, Mitchell. Maybe I can introduce you to the Wild West. You're an Easterner."

"Guilty as charged." He chuckled. "I like all animals, so it would be interesting to get to know a horse."

"It could be a lot of fun. And that's what has been missing in my life. As a kid growing up here, my brothers and sister and I were miniwranglers. We all worked on the ranch to help out. I've missed that, too."

"I'm glad you came home," he said, meaning it.

"Would you have gone home to North Carolina if Pete hadn't hired you out here?" she wondered.

"I don't know. I've always had this thing for the West. Maybe I read too many cowboy books as a boy growing up," and he grinned bashfully, melting beneath her smile.

She was attractive, but it was that inner charisma that was part of her that beckoned so strongly to him. Andy's demeanor was a far cry from the pilot who got shot down in Afghanistan. They'd slept off and on during the daytime hours and moved at night, which was helped by their NVGs. And it was always under the threat of being captured, so they didn't talk about their past, their personal lives or even where they had come from.

Now? He had a chance to meet her all over again, and he warned himself to tread carefully. If Pete hired her, and Dev was sure he would, that made any thoughts he had about pursuing some kind of relationship with Andy a bad idea.

Rubbing his chest, he wondered why Andy had interested him even four years ago. At that time, he was fully focused on getting them to survive their crashes. To get back to a place of relative safety. He'd wanted to know about her on a personal level, but it hadn't happened.

More than anything, he was fascinated by her and what she was like when they weren't in dire straits and danger. Andy now was relaxed, the tension gone from her expression. She had an oval face with a strong chin and high cheekbones. She used her mouth to broadcast a lot of her feelings, and he liked that her lower lip was a bit fuller than her upper lip. It was her gray eyes that could go to a pewter color when she felt threatened to right now, a semi-transparent gray with those big, black pupils that held an intensity in them. This was a woman whose mind clicked along at Mach 3 with her hair on fire. And being a combat pilot, Dev understood her mind was like a bear trap, a mental computer weighing, visualizing and seeing flight strategies before they had to be initiated. Many men would be threatened by her, but he wasn't. Just the opposite: he was drawn to her, drawn to know her much better. His heart thumped in quiet joy over this unexpected meeting. He thought he'd never see Andy again. But here they were.

Glancing at his watch, he saw it was almost seven a.m.

"Our offices are located at the south end of the new regional airport building," he said. "Did Jackie give you directions on how to get there?"

"She did, bless her heart. I haven't even been over there yet. My parents want to show me around before the grand opening on July Fourth."

"It's a beautiful place, modern, with Wi-Fi and so much more. Very airy and light inside the main building."

"I'll be over there for the interview," she assured him.

"And I'll be waiting for the official sit-down with you. I'm sure it will go fine."

Andy had changed her clothes in favor of navy-blue linen slacks, a white silk tee with a dark blue blazer and a bright red scarf around her neck, the ends hanging just inside the opened coat. She wore a set of pearl earrings her mother had given her on her fourteenth birthday, saying all young women should have a set of them. On her eighteenth birthday, her graduation gift was a double strand of white saltwater pearls. She didn't wear those today but loved the warm feeling that came with the earrings.

Choosing flat white leather shoes that were comfortable yet professional looking, she also wore the gold Rolex she'd been given to her by her Grandmother Martha and Grandfather James to celebrate her college graduation. It was a very expensive gift and she rarely wore it, but today was a good day to do so. Because she was going to go on to be a pilot, the Rolex they had bought for her had all the bells and whistles she could use while flying. She dearly loved her very rich grandparents who never seemed to care that she and her siblings were adopted. Their affection was steadfast, and her heart warmed with such love in return for them.

She drove to the Nellie Tayloe Ross regional airport, which was getting its finishing touches for the July 4 opening. She liked that her parents had insisted that it be named after a Wyoming woman who was instrumental in the state's growth. Nellie was the first woman to be elected by voters to be governor of the state. Maud was very proud to have a woman's name on one of the major airports in the country. After all, the others were usually named after men, and her mother was a feminist of the first order. So was she.

The airport was white, long and gracefully shaped into an "S," the windows tinted almost a turquoise blue. Huge areas were already created with black asphalt, white parking lines marked on each rectangular area. Near the entrance, she saw the American flag flying next to the Wyoming one. What was nice was a recently created statue of Nellie that stood in an oval near the front entrance, bronze and gleaming in the sunlight. This was a donation from her Grandmother Martha, also a feminist. Grinning, Andy wondered if by some moment of kismet Maud and Steve had chosen her, not knowing just how much of a feminist she would grow up to become. Did genes somehow magically cross over to their adopted baby? She knew science would pooh-pooh such an idea. She had grown up with two terrific sets of grandparents. Steve's parents lived in Wind River since they had retired and handed over the reins to her parents.

For whatever reason, Andy wasn't terribly stressed about this interview. She parked in the day parking lot near the south end of the long complex and walked in a double set of doors that swung open for her.

Inside, there were workmen and women vacuuming,

painting and polishing metal here and there. She liked the light pouring in through the massive wall of windows. It had all the modern security machines necessary, the airline names above each area and long rows of counters that were ready to go. Thrilled that all the major carriers had leased space, it showed that the western part of Wyoming would finally have their own major airport, and it was going to be an important one economically for the area.

She followed the signs on the first floor, the pale-blue tiles waxed to perfection as she turned and walked down a shorter hall. The signage was excellent, and in no time, she saw the office Jackie Turnbull had told her about. Tucking the paper into a pocket of her blazer, she touched her hair, which she had put up in a thick knot at the nape of her neck. Jackie had given her the four numbers to press into the keypad that would open a security door that would lead her to the woman's office.

Inside, there was light slanting down the blue tile hall, all the glass-enclosed offices on her left. On the right was a wall that held many wooden frames for photos. None were displayed yet. She spotted Jackie at her desk, black-framed glasses down on her nose as she worked over some papers. Knocking lightly, she said, "Hi, Jackie."

"Oh, hi, Ms. Whitcomb!" She stood, pushing her glasses up on her nose and smiling. "Come in! May I get you some coffee or tea?" and she gestured to the corner, where the machines were situated.

"No, thank you."

"Have a seat. I'll let Mr. Mitchell know you're here." She beamed. "He's been waiting to talk with you. I gave him your résumé to read and he's ready for you."

Sitting on the comfortable light-blue upholstered chair in front of her desk, Andy nodded. "Great. Thank you."

Jackie picked up the phone and dialed a number.

In her briefcase were copies of all her certificates, permits, medical evaluations and other FAA-required information. Earlier, she had sent only her résumé. If Dev felt she was qualified, she'd hand over all these documents, which were necessary to a pilot's ongoing right to fly. Andy didn't try to fool herself: she'd been drawn to Dev Mitchell four years ago as she was right now. It bothered her because what if he was engaged or married? That would mean he was hands off and she had to shut down her personal interest in this man of mystery's life.

What surprised Andy the most was that upon seeing Dev again, that same yearning to be close to him, to hear what he thought and how he saw the world was even stronger than the first time they met. Oh, she'd had relationships off and on throughout her adult life, but none of them could be compared to the way her heart reacted to this enigma of a man. He was not giving her any signal other than that he was interested in her as a possible hire. That deflated her a bit because she knew she needed a job like this in order to stay in the valley. And right now, home was calling her strongly and that was where she had to focus, providing she got the job.

"Andy? Mr. Mitchell will see you now." Jackie pointed to her left. "Just go out this door and he's the next office down on the left." Then, she crossed her fingers for her. "Good luck! I already told those two guys I wanted to see some women pilots hired, not just men."

"I like your attitude. Let's see if that happens." She rose and gave Jackie a look of gratitude. Women had to stick together. As Andy left the office, her mind was on the strides women had taken in the twentieth and twenty-first centuries. But they still had far to go.

She saw Dev sitting behind his desk. He was on the phone, looked up and noticed her approaching, gesturing for her to come in and take a seat. Doing so, Andy saw a stack of what she assumed were résumés sitting on his desk. Behind his desk was a large color photo of him in his Army pilot uniform, looking toward the camera, seated in his Black Hawk. There was an expression of deviltry in Dev's eyes, and that cocky grin she'd seen at times was on his handsome face. He wasn't pretty-boy good-looking. Instead, he had a face that had seen good times and hard times. There were crinkles at the corners of his eyes, telling her he was a pilot. She had some herself. His mouth stirred her in womanly ways, and she quickly moved her gaze to his forest-green eyes, which were filled with laughter. She liked his reddish-brown hair, but most of all that blanket of coppery freckles across his cheeks and nose made him very attractive to her. He might be a man, but she liked seeing this side of him, that twist of his mouth, the glint in his eyes. The freckles double-checked her, showing that he might have to play adult when necessary, but she had a sense his little boy side was intact. Andy would like to meet his playful side; her life was too serious and she wanted to lighten up, play again herself, laugh and see the world through his eyes when he was in that kind of playful mood.

Dev hung up the phone. "Sorry for the interruption."

"No problem." She liked his smile. "Good news, I trust? You're smiling."

Chuckling, Dev got up and shut the door to the office. "My old crew chief in the military was Larry Fowler. He saw the ad and is applying for a job with us. We need two crew chiefs to rotate with the four pilots. He's a certified paramedic, and that makes him almost a shoo-in for this job. Besides," and he scratched his short hair, "Larry is always stirring up trouble with a big stick. We were talking about some of the times we got in to those types of missions.

He's got a helluva positive outlook on life and I always wanted him to fly with our crew. When things weren't serious, he was funny and a jokester." He sat down.

"I was thinking, as I saw you laughing and smiling, that it's going to be contagious. Flying an A-10 wasn't ever a joke. It was a heavy responsibility."

He grunted and opened her file. "Combat is never funny, as we well know."

It was her turn to grunt an answer. Words weren't necessary.

"I've had a chance to check out everything on your résumé, Andy. All I need now is for you to show me your flight certifications, FAA permits and your medical evaluations permitting you to fly. If all is in order, I'm recommending you to Pete Turner. I don't want to leave you hanging. I'd very much like to have you on our team." He opened his hands. "Let me give you the template for our working with the sheriff. We're hiring four pilots. You are the first one that I've recommended for hire." He thumbed toward the pile of résumés. "I've got two other potential hires, both women Black Hawk pilots like yourself. The fourth is a man. Pete and I learned a long time ago that women in combat are just as steady and can think through a crisis just like men can. You showed me what you were made of out there in the mountains of Afghanistan. You're rock solid. You don't get rattled and, most important, your focus was intense and didn't waver. That's the kind of pilot I want to fly with here."

Her heart thudded with relief. "That's good to hear."

"The group we hire is going to have forty-eight hours on duty and forty-eight hours off. We will have two sets of pilots plus one crew chief with each duty section. All of us are going to have to learn Wyoming laws and commit them to memory. You come from California, and their regulations for law enforcement flights are probably a little different from Wyoming's."

"I would expect that. It makes sense."

"We want to hire everyone in the next two weeks, if possible. We go online July fourth, after the Nellie Tayloe Ross Airport opens. I will have a schedule drawn up and everyone will get that monthly schedule as an email. There's a squadron room that is divided up between male and females. Each will have lockers, bunks, a shower and anything else we might need. There's also going to be a kitchen where we can cook, as well as a small dining room."

"That sounds plush," she said, pleased.

"It's a brand-new airport. It's going to have the latest of everything in it. We'll have our headquarters on the south end of the building. On the north end will be a wildfire unit that is similar in all ways to ours: offices, sleeping quarters, kitchen, showers and a dining room. It's pretty nice digs. I was over there the second day after I arrived and Pete Turner showed me around. So, for us, it's plush, a damned nice upgrade compared to Afghanistan."

"Sounds wonderful."

Dev got serious and folded his hands on the desk, holding her gaze. He went through what would be expected of her, the types of missions, the hours, the link training in Salt Lake City, Utah, mandatory for continued pilot upgrades and for keeping their skills refreshed for emergency flight situations. "And all pilots hired, regardless of gender, will make the same salary."

"That's really good to hear," Andy said, surprised.

"You'll have a medical exam from the state of Wyoming. I'm going to give your résumé my approval and Pete Turner, my boss, will make the final decision. I'm sure he'll hire you, so this is just a formality. I've asked Jackie to put together a file for you so you will have everything you need to know.

And if you come across something that needs an answer, see me. I'll be running the day-to-day missions and planning. And I'll also be on the flight roster. Part of my job is to give all of you FAM flights, familiarization of Lincoln County, which is where we're charged with enforcing the laws. Your flight uniforms will be ordered and paid for by the county, as will all your other flight gear, including your helmet, any radios or other necessities."

"Pretty much the way LA runs its helo unit," she said. "All good."

"Any questions?"

"When do I start?"

"Officially, June thirteenth. I'll give Pete my approval of you, and he'll need a couple of hours to go over everything in your personnel jacket."

"Was he a pilot in the military?"

"Yes. US Army. He flew Black Hawks until he lost an arm. He has a prosthesis now, and you can't tell the difference. He left the Army, headed to Seattle, Washington, law enforcement, which is where I met him. We worked together for almost four years. He was in upper management and I flew the Black Hawk."

"It's nice to have someone like him in your life. You don't have to start over with a new, unknown boss."

Dev smiled a little and rocked back in his chair. "You could say the same of us, Andy. We're a known quantity to each other. We know what to expect from each other."

Chapter Four

June 11

"That's an amazing coincidence," Steve Whitcomb said to Andy. They were having dinner together at seven o'clock at their log home.

"Synchronistic," Maud agreed. She cut into her pork chop, which was slathered with apricot sauce. She smiled across the rectangular oak table at her husband. "Don't you think it was rather a coincidence you and I met as we did?"

"You're right," Steve murmured. "Still, to meet Dev Mitchell four years after he disappeared from your life, Andy, is in a class by itself."

"The world of the architect," Maud teased, spooning some yams in melted butter onto her fork. "This falls outside your carefully constructed world. Synchronicity abounds."

Laughing with them, Andy murmured, "You two have very different brains, that's for sure. And yes, I'm stunned by meeting Dev once again. When I tried to find him and couldn't, I gave up and let it go."

"And you have a pilot's brain," Steve teased.

"Gotcha." Andy laughed. She finished off her pork chop

and paid attention to the fresh-cut green beans, which had almond slivers and petite white onions mixed in them. "I keep wondering if one of Sky and my unknown parents was a pilot."

Maud gave her a thoughtful look. "Steve and I have had conversations along that line from time to time, too. We wondered the same thing."

"I surmise that maybe your father was a pilot," Steve offered.

Maud snorted. "Why not her mother? Women fly just fine. They're just as good as any man at a stick or yoke."

Holding up his hand, Steve pleaded, "Peace, sweetheart. I'm not saying women can't fly, but Andy and Sky were given up by their mothers. Somehow, I don't see either of those women being pilots. Maybe I'm prejudiced, though."

"We'll never know," Andy said, sad. "Like you, Dad, I've often wondered if my father was a pilot." She slanted a look to Maud. "I guess I'm more like Dad than you," she apologized. "So often, women give up their babies because the father wasn't someone they knew that well, or maybe they were divorced from them. And, I'm guessing, because they were poor and didn't have much money."

Maud reached out, touching Andy's lower arm. "I wish we could find out, but we've run into dead ends that have stopped all of us from finding out about the biological parents of all four of you."

Andy didn't want the dinner to become maudlin. "Let's stick with the present. I'm shocked in a good kind of way that Dev is back in my life. Well, maybe he is. Pete Turner has to go over my résumé and he makes the final decision on whether I get hired or not."

"I met Pete last week," Steve said, "and he's an amputee vet. I liked his sense of humor and his kindness. There was a vet walking alongside the highway, just outside of town, and he was driving in from the airport and spotted him. Pete gave him a ride to Kassie's Café. He gave the guy money to buy a meal there. Kassie has a small apartment behind the café and she took him in, fed him and got him some new clothes from Charlie Becker's Hay and Feed store. In fact, Charlie and his wife, Pixie, donated three sets of work clothes, new boots and underwear for him, so he might be able to get a job in the area."

"They've done so much for our returning vets." Andy sighed, giving him a watery look.

"This valley is home to a lot of our returning men and women," Maud said. "Pixie called me later and asked if we needed any help at the ranch, said that the guy, Eric Davis, has some carpentry skills. And, as fate would have it, I'm going to be talking with him tomorrow at the office about becoming one of our carpenters. We really need a full-time person because we're building more tourist cabins."

"I hope he gets the job," Andy said.

"When do you think you'll hear about your job?" Steve asked her.

"Tomorrow."

"Are you on pins and needles?" Maud asked.

"No, because Dev said it was practically a done deal. I'm taking him at his word."

"He's not the type to hype," Maud said. "Not about a job as the number-two person in the department."

"Right," Andy agreed. She pushed her plate away. "I'm stuffed like the proverbial Christmas goose, Mom. That was a great meal. Thank you."

Maud said, "Thank Sally for this great meal. I don't know what we'd do without her cooking and cleaning for us."

Andy nodded. She was in her midteens when she realized that Maud's mother, Grandmother Martha, was one of the richest women in the world. Before that, it had never dawned on her that not everyone had a live-in cook like they did. Sally Fremont was a local, born in the valley. When her husband unexpectedly died of a heart attack, she had to go in search of a job. Maud was softhearted by nature and hired her. Growing up, Andy loved Sally fiercely for the care she always extended to all their adopted children. At the time, Andy was nine years old. Everyone in the family discovered very quickly that Sally was a wonderful cook, plus stepping in to become a part-time babysitter for them as well. Andy knew how lucky they were because Sally loved them as if they were her own children. Horror stories about being adopted weren't visited upon them, thank goodness. At that age, Andy knew just how fortunate they were. The four kids had been given a home with real love, with support, and their adopted parents urging them to fulfill their dreams. Maud and Steve had always stood in the background, cheerleaders for all of them, building their confidence and loving them in a hundred different ways that shaped them into the adults they were today.

There was a huge part of Andy that didn't want to know who her birth parents were. Maybe that was selfish, but she didn't care. She, of all the children, was the least interested in tracking down her biological parents. Giving Maud a loving look, she felt her heart burst open with affection for these two people who had taken them all in. There weren't a lot of people in the world like them.

"Listen," Maud said, finishing off the last of the green beans on her plate, "once you get the job, why don't you invite Dev Mitchell over here for dinner? We've never met him and we would love to thank him for helping save your life. What do you think of that?"

One of the many things Andy adored about her parents was that they always formed a question on anything they might want to do that involved one or all of them. It was never a statement or an order to obey. "I like the idea. I think he's a lot like us: a really tight family man, and that family is everything to him."

"Where's he from?" Steve asked.

"He said he was born in Port Harbor, North Carolina, a rural area near the Atlantic Ocean."

"So why did he take this job here in the West?" Maud wondered.

"He said he's always loved the West but had never gotten out here."

"That's a good sign," Steve said. "Your mother was born in New York City and is an Easterner through and through."

"Yes," Maud said, laughing and slanting Andy a humorous look, "and I guess I fall into Dev's world. I had always dreamed of going out West, too. It was a romantic place for me."

"And then you met me, wearing my black Stetson, my Levi's, and my cowboy boots at Princeton University."

Andy sighed. "I love hearing stories of how you met. Mom, did you mind leaving the East to marry Dad and come to live in the West with him?"

"Keep in mind we spent many years at Princeton," Steve said. "We'd come out here on some of the holidays and spend the others with her parents in New York City. We did spend our summers out here."

"That's where I really fell in love with the West," Maud said, smiling wistfully. "Steve taught me how to become a wrangler. Your Grandpa Sam taught me about being a rancher. Your Grandma Lydia taught me how to run a ranch as a business. I loved all of it. I do to this day."

"We kids are so lucky to have two sets of grandparents," Andy agreed. "Not everyone, because of distances, has them around much anymore."

"Oh, but you grew up with Sam and Lydia surrounding

you," Maud said. "They were terrific babysitters when I needed them, too. I was always grateful that they'd come over and care for you kids when I had to travel or go away on business. And your dad has been gone a lot more than me because of his global commitments."

"I remember," Andy murmured. "We loved when Grandma and Grandpa would come and live in the house, that they had their own guest bedroom here. Us kids always looked forward to it because Grandpa Sam would take us out in the hay wagon and we'd go up and down the dirt roads pulling it with his tractor. We found all kinds of things to do. He'd stop the wagon and we'd look for frogs in the ditch, or we'd spot wildlife. He always brought his binoculars along."

"He taught all of you to love and respect nature," Maud agreed.

"Most of all," Andy sighed, "remember when we turned eight years old? They bought each of us a pony. He wanted us to learn how to care, saddle and groom our horse. We loved it!"

"Yes," Steve chuckled, "they spoiled you in the best of ways."

"When I was running for my life with Dev in Afghanistan? I put a lot of what Grandpa taught us about being stealthy, about creating a back trail so if someone was following our footprints, we could confuse them and throw them off our tracks."

"Really?" Maud stared at her. "You usually don't talk about that time, Andy."

Shrugging, she said, "I know. I guess it's easier to speak about it now that it's four years later. It doesn't have the emotional impact on me it had before. I asked Dev one night, when we were resting in the darkness after climbing another ridge, if he knew what backtracking was. He did.

We were in an area where there was soil, not rock. We knew the Taliban were great trackers and they'd spot our footprints, so we spent an hour creating that false trail."

"You should share that story with Grandpa Sam," Steve urged. "I'm sure he'd appreciate knowing that."

Nodding, Andy said, "You're right. I will the next time I see him."

"Why not invite them to dinner to meet Dev, too?" Steve suggested to Maud. "Let him meet the whole Whitcomb family?"

"That's a great idea. Andy? You okay with that?"

"Sure. I think Dev misses his family, but he didn't say it in so many words. I feel he'd like being surrounded by everyone."

"Good," Maud said. "Let's wait for that phone call from Pete or him letting you know if you got the job or not. And even if you don't, Andy, we all would like to thank Dev for being a part of your getting back safely to us. The man deserves our thanks and then some."

June 13

Andy's cell phone buzzed. She was in her bedroom at her parents' home, and she saw it was Dev Mitchell ringing her. They had just finished breakfast; it was nine a.m.

"Andy here," she said, her heart beating a little faster.

"Hey, I just talked with Pete and he said to make you an offer you couldn't refuse."

Relief sheeted through her and her fingers relaxed around the cell phone. "Oh, that's great!" She listened to the offer and the generous state medical package, plus three weeks of vacation. It was more than she'd gotten in

California. "I'll take it," she told Dev. "Thanks for having my back on this one."

"We have a common bond," he agreed. "Are you free to come over and sign a gazillion papers so Jackie can get them posted to the governor's office and we can get you on board?"

"Absolutely. I'll be there in about thirty minutes. I'm coming in ranch clothes."

"Sounds good to me. See you then."

A special warmth flowed through her as she clicked off her cell phone. There was an emotional richness to his tone that hadn't been there before. Andy wondered if he was personally interested in her. It sounded like it, but she wouldn't put money on it. Giddy with excitement, she could feel her life changing in important but not yet revealed ways. Unable to explain the feeling, she hurriedly picked up her purse, throwing the strap across her shoulder.

Earlier, she'd been out in the broodmare barn, helping to clean stalls along with the wranglers. Wanting to get back into shape, plus jogging at least a mile every morning it wasn't raining or snowing, she had climbed into a pair of jeans, a lavender tee and comfy tennis shoes after taking a shower. Her hair hung around her shoulders, just washed and dried.

She had a job!

Hurrying out of her bedroom suite, she found her mother in the kitchen with Sally, talking over that night's dinner menu.

"I got the job, Mom!" she called, grinning widely.

Maud whooped at the news.

Sally threw her a thumbs-up at the door to the kitchen. "Told you that you'd get it, Andy."

"Yes," Andy said, laughing, "you sure did."

"Was that Pete who just called you?" Maud asked, giving her a bright smile of congratulations.

"No, it was Dev. Can you tell Dad the good news? I know he's out in the barn with the wranglers. I'm driving over to the airport to fill out a lot of paperwork and get officially on board. I don't know if I'll be back for lunch."

"No worries," Maud said. "Sally's making you a special dinner tonight, one of your favorites."

She stood at the door. "Really, Sally?"

"Yes, indeed," she said. "Tuna and noodles."

"Wow, this *is* a celebration day!" she whooped, opening the door. "Thank you, Sally! Mom, I'll call you later when I'm leaving the airport."

"See you then. Congratulations!"

Dev tried to avoid telling himself that hiring Andy had made his day, month and year. His heart warred with his head. His job position was at odds with his growing interest in her. He was attracted to her, but that was nothing new, was it? Those five days when they ran for their lives through enemy territory had shown him the grit and steel spine she had. And he'd known so little about her, until now.

In her personnel file, it showed she had been adopted at three months old by Maud and Steve Whitcomb. Her biological mother had dropped her off on the steps of the fire department station in Wind River, abandoning her. That was a rough first landing to take in her life and yet, as he mulled it over, Dev wondered if such a start, being given away, had made her the strong woman she was today. He had so many damned personal questions to ask her and yet, in his place as the assistant manager, he couldn't ask any of them. He did know she was single, but that didn't mean there wasn't a man in her life. That was none of his business either.

Andy wasn't an extrovert; she possessed a serious demeanor. Maybe it was because of what had happened to her early in life: she took nothing for granted, knowing that it was a struggle; even as a young child, she learned how serious life could be. He wanted to know what drove her to become a combat jet pilot. That wasn't exactly every little girl's dream, although he was fine with a woman using all her intelligence and skills to find a career she felt passionate about. And it was clear to Dev that Andy loved flying.

The knock on his door made him lift his head from the file in his lap. Andy was standing at the partially opened door, her gray eyes sparkling like diamonds, a cocky grin on her mouth that only a combat pilot had the right to wear, her chestnut hair in mild disarray around her shoulders making her look wild and untamable.

The picture she presented did nothing but make an ache of need settle in his chest. This was much more than about being sexually drawn to Andy. His need to connect with her on a much deeper and more important level stirred in him. "Hey," he called, gesturing for her to enter, "come on in. Can I get you some coffee, or have you had your fill this morning?"

Laughing, she came in and closed the door, sitting down in the chair at one corner of his desk. "I've had four cups. I was up at five a.m. to help the wranglers clean box stalls at our broodmare barn." She took off her lightweight denim jacket and laid it across her lap. "I need to get into better shape and there's nothing more physical than stall work."

"When I was in the Army, I was running two to five miles every morning at my firebase. Sitting your butt in the seat of a bird for hours at a time wasn't conducive to being in good shape. And I like to move around, as I suspect you do, too."

"Movement is healthy. Sitting is unhealthy. I'm wanting to get into some strength training as well." She held up her arm and flexed her fist, showing him her biceps. "See? Some progress."

"I'm impressed. Cleaning box stalls will do that." He set her file aside and nudged a group of papers in her direction.

"Sounds good. And after that?"

He stood and walked to the coffee table, pouring her a cup. "First, I'd like to take you to our conference room to get those forms filled out. Then, take you on a tour of our facility. Get your feet wet. Since you're our first hire aside from me, you'll be the first in the women's sleep quarters. You'll have your choice of the lockers, too." He pointed to the pile of papers. "These all have to be filled out. I'll take you back to our conference room down the hall. You might want a cup of coffee while you sign your life away. You'll probably get writer's cramp."

"Sounds great. Are you considering hiring other female pilots, then?"

"Pete and I agree we want at least fifty percent of our cadre to be female."

"That's good news. Do you have applicants?"

He sat down and pulled over the two top résumés. "I'm glad you asked that because these are two other pilots I'm considering. And I thought because you're a woman military pilot, you might know these women. They're both from the military." He handed the résumés to her.

Frowning, Andy instantly went into focus mode. She looked at them. "You aren't going to believe this."

"What?"

She held up one résumé. "I know Alma Lopez. She was a medevac pilot, an Army captain, and she was at Bagram. We became friends, but our missions and demands were different, so I lost track of her after I quit the Air Force." She held up the other résumé. "Grace Cameron is a dual citizen of the United States and Canada. She was a Night Stalker

Army captain with the 160th SOAR, Special Operations Aviation Regiment. She flew an MH-60L Black Hawk and saw a lot of action."

"More than likely," Dev said, "over in Pakistan." He held up his hand. "Yeah, I know Cameron was a top-secret DAP, Defensive Armed Penetrator, pilot, and I can confirm it, but I was operating out of Firebase Phoenix, the closest US outpost to the Pak border, so I saw my share of 60Ls, especially at night." He grinned. "Would you recommend these two pilots as possible hires?"

"Absolutely!" Andy told him, excitement in her tone. "Both are total professionals, they don't get rattled and they will always have your back."

"Good to know," he said as she handed the résumés back to him. "I'll be sure to put notes on their files for Pete, so he's aware there's a connection between all of you. Law enforcement is combat, too, and we want pilots who don't get shaken when bullets are coming their way."

"Totally understood," Andy said. "Show me around? I'm really excited about seeing the total facility here at the airport."

So was he. Sipping the last dregs of his coffee, he gestured to the door. "Make a left and go down the hall. It's the first right. I have the key to open it." Dev tried to tamp down the bubbling happiness in his chest as he followed her down the hall. He shouldn't be affected by the gentle sway of her hips, or that proud military carriage that signaled she was confident, something he'd always wanted in his women. The past leaked into his present, reminding him sadly of his young wife Sophie, who had died. Somehow, for whatever reason, the sadness and loneliness that had once cloaked him nonstop had lifted in Andy's presence. In its place, Dev felt hope flooding his heart. And the woman who came to a stop at the door to the conference room, giving him an expectant look, put his past in place. Dev didn't try to fool himself. He knew he craved Andy's closeness, her thoughts, her ideas and the way she saw her world.

He opened the door, pushing it open for her. "Come see me when you're done?"

"Promise," Andy said, moving past him and into the long, narrow room that had an oval oak table in the center of it.

Andy knocked on Dev's open office door. He was busy with paperwork. She liked the thaw she saw in his green eyes as he met her gaze. His brownish-red hair was clipped military short, and it made her feel like she was back in the place she'd called home for so many years. Holding up the papers, she said, "You weren't joking when you said there was a lot to fill out."

"It's eleven thirty," he agreed, rising and taking the sheaf from her hand. "It's almost lunchtime. Want to join me at Kassie's Café? And after that, I can give you the full tour, plus take a look at our Black Hawk out in the hangar."

A thrill moved through her, and Andy had to hide her pleasant surprise. She'd wanted quiet time with Dev, not business but personal. "Sure, sounds good." Understanding he was her boss, that five days in Afghanistan had given them an entrance to each other that would not normally be available. She decided to ask him instead of assuming anything about their old connection as he shut down his computer and came around the desk.

"Are you okay with us doing something like this?"

"Like what?"

"Going to lunch together? Off the clock?"

He gave her a thoughtful look. "I'm fine with it. But are you, Andy?"

She pulled the strap of her purse over her left shoulder.

"I was thinking earlier about that, Dev. We ran for our lives for five days, and there were many times when neither of us thought we'd live to see home or our loved ones again." She gave a small shrug, holding his intense green gaze, feeling care radiating from around him. "We have an odd relationship here because of it," she went on, lifting her hand and gesturing around the office. "We knew each other under some extreme circumstances."

"And we got to know each other in some ways that most people never will," he agreed quietly, searching her face. "I'm fine with our leading two different lives. It's just one of those things. You good with it?"

"Roger that," she murmured. "I can remember the hundreds of questions, personal ones, I wanted to ask you, but we couldn't talk much for fear of being heard by any nearby Taliban." One corner of his mouth hooked upward and she saw warmth enter his eyes. It made her feel good, but then, Dev had always been like the blankie she had as a child. As long as she carried her blankie around with her, she felt safe. He was like that to her. And it wasn't that she was the weak one on the team. She'd contributed just as much to their joint escape from the Taliban. He'd not been any more a white knight on his horse than she. How much she wanted to delve into the man she'd discovered back then. He was a stand-up guy. The kind she'd never run into before or since.

Dev had ducked into Jackie's office to let her know they'd be going to Kassie's. Her eyes had lit up, and he'd asked if he could bring her back a late lunch. She'd jumped at the offer, giving him money to buy her a hamburger and fries.

Andy smiled, liking his kindness and thoughtfulness toward others. She'd noticed it in him before. Not many men she'd met, except for her father and Grandfather Sam, had that same sensitivity. But Dev had that characteristic. She followed him out of the building.

"Hop in," he said, opening the door to his blue Ford pickup.

"Thanks," she said.

"I can't help myself," he admitted, giving her a gleeful look, "it's the officer and gentleman coming out in me. You okay with me opening doors for you from time to time, Ms. Whitcomb?"

Laughing, she said, "Only if you don't faint from shock if I do the same for you, Cowboy." She saw his cheeks grow ruddy. That was his handle from his Army days. He'd shared that with her the first night after the crash.

He managed a sheepish look. "Yeah, I'm okay with that. What was your handle in the Air Force? I never got to ask you that."

"Amazon." She saw his eyes light up and that boyish pale-green glint reappear. He was just too easy on the eyes. Maybe she'd find out if he was involved in a relationship. That would make him available or not.

"Good handle." He closed the door and walked around to the driver's side, sliding in and starting the truck.

Strapping in, she said, "I know you're from the East Coast, Dev, so how come your handle was Cowboy? There aren't any cowboys there, are there?"

He backed out the truck and headed it toward the nearby highway, which would lead them into Wind River. "My best friend, Chuck Gooding, was from Montana. His family owns a huge, sprawling ranch up near Billings. I used to go home with him when we'd come off deployment. He taught me just about everything about ranching: horses, riding, roping, branding and moving cattle. We'd gone through helicopter flight training, which is where we met, and it was like meeting my long-lost brother."

"That's nice. Are you still in touch?"

Sobering, he turned the truck onto the nearly empty highway. "He was the pilot on the flight you gave cover to."

Frowning, Andy said, "I'm so sorry. God, that's awful."

"I know I wasn't much of a partner when we met after that crash. Now you know why I wasn't very talkative."

"You were grieving. I can understand that."

"Yeah, well, I was pretty abrupt and impatient with you. Looking back on it, Andy, I felt really bad about that. But you took it in stride, like nothing was wrong."

"I know Black Hawks have at least three or four crew and you were the only survivor, so I chalked up your abruptness and curtness to just losing people you knew."

He slanted her a glance as he drove. "And I couldn't believe how flexible and easygoing you were under those circumstances. You'd just ejected and survived the landing. Not to mention losing your aircraft."

"I try to look through the lens of my beginning, when my biological mother dropped me off at the fire department when I was an infant. I can't think of too many other things worse than that, and I used that event as my measuring stick for everything else that has happened to me after that. And nothing, not even ejecting over enemy territory, was worse than that. I learned how to handle my emotions because my adopted parents were such wonderful people and teachers, and taught us with love. That's why I was probably less emotional or hysterical. The crash was bad and I lost my plane, but I was alive, and then you appeared out of the darkness, scaring the hell out of me. I hadn't expected that, but it was sure nice to have you show up. I'd been scared before, but you gave me a sense of calm in the midst of that craziness."

He nodded, his mouth compressing for a moment. The Wind River outskirts came up and there was more traffic in town. "I wasn't expecting a woman pilot. Wearing NVGs, I knew you were an American."

"You startled me, for sure, but I knew you were a friendly because you had those NVGs hanging around your neck, too. I just wasn't expecting you to walk out of the grove of trees, up that slope to meet me there. I thought the pilot who bailed might be outside the ravine."

"It was meant to be," he murmured. He parked in front of Kassie's Café. It wasn't filled up yet but would be in another half hour. "Come on, let's eat."

Andy nodded and climbed out of the cab, slinging her purse across her shoulder. There were a number of tourists visiting the area on the wooden sidewalk. She knew her parents had worked hard to make Wind River a place to stop rather than just drive through on the way to Grand Teton and Yellowstone Parks. "I'm a starving cow brute," she warned him, joining him on the sidewalk.

"That must be Old West slang," he teased, opening the door for her.

"It is." She saw Kassie at the counter and waved to her. Kassie broke out in a huge smile, waving back to her.

"Sit anywhere you want," she called. "You're early, so you've got a choice."

"In the back," Andy said, pointing toward the kitchen area.

Dev lifted his hand and told Kassie hello, too. Everyone knew Kassie and vice versa. The café was only about a quarter full. He followed Andy, who headed for one of three black leather booths that were set against the wall near the kitchen. It was an alcove of sorts and more private, quieter and lent itself to good conversation. He was looking forward to this lunch far more than he should, but the fact that Andy had already asked him about their odd relationship buoyed his heart. And his hope.

Chapter Five

"I just can't believe I'm seeing you again," Andy admitted after they ordered their lunch. She wrapped her hands around the thick, white ceramic mug of coffee, giving Dev a happy look. "The man I met on that Afghan mountain, I realize now, was in a really serious mode. You never smiled or looked relaxed, like you do now."

"Gotta admit," Dev murmured wryly, sipping his coffee, "it wasn't exactly a party spot out there where we crashed."

Giving him a sour grin, she said, "Touché."

"Which guy do you like better now that you've seen my two sides?"

"This one, for sure."

"I was a grouch," he admitted, his brows dipping.

"Because you lost good friends in that crash," she whispered sympathetically. "You told me they were dead right after we met and I wanted to cry, but I was too scared to."

"Same here. I know we both went through escape and evasion training, but it sure wasn't like what happened to us in real time. It's something I'll never forget."

"Same here," she said, her mouth twisting. "I got the

advanced training in E and E because I was a combat pilot."

"Lucky you."

"No, it was pretty awful. I got waterboarded. I hated it. And believe me, it is torture."

"Well," Dev soothed, "we're past all that, thank God."

She lifted her cup in toast. "Amen."

"I was thinking, we never had time to discuss much of anything about our personal lives, but I was wondering if your wife was horribly worried? I knew my parents would be once they were informed I was missing in action."

"I didn't have to worry about a spouse," he said. "My parents, Riana and Roanan, told me later they felt paralyzed with fear. Their world stopped. They couldn't do much of anything except sit in high anxiety, hoping against hope that I was alive and not dead."

"Same with my parents, Steve and Maud. When I got home, Mom confided that they were the worst days of their lives. My two brothers and sister put their lives on hold. Sky, my sister, had been in the military, and so had my brother, Gabe. She was in the Army and an Apache helicopter combat pilot. Luke was a sergeant in the Marine Corps. My other brother, Gabe, was in DEA and undercover, so he couldn't be reached. They told me later, after I got home, that because they knew what MIA meant, it was worse for them. They knew what could happen, whereas my parents didn't. Sometimes ignorance is bliss."

"My parents were in the same category as yours, and maybe it was a blessing in disguise. I was an only child."

"Well," she grumped, "it hadn't been lost on either of us what could happen if the Taliban found us. It would have been a nightmare. I was so damned scared."

"That's what kept me so serious. I wanted to ask if you

were married or had someone special in your life at home, but it never came up."

Shrugging, Andy said, "I was single then."

He studied her for a moment. "No special person in your life even now?"

"No," she admitted. "I'm not very good at relationships, if you want to know the truth."

"Coulda fooled me," he teased. "You were a strong, reliable partner out there in the mountains. You knew things I didn't and vice versa. We worked off our strengths against each other, Andy. That's a relationship of a sort. I thought you were incredible throughout the entire experience."

"Thanks . . . that's nice to know. I really felt bad after you left for the helo airport at Bagram and you had to leave immediately. I thought for sure you'd come back so I'd at least be able to thank you for your help in getting us behind the wire again."

"My squadron needed me at the firebase. I wasn't injured, so I was taken out on the next helo from Bagram. We were down a pilot, so I was covering for the situation. By the time I got break to check on you, it was three weeks later. I flew into Bagram to try to find you and that's when I found out you'd walked away and become a civilian shortly after arriving behind the wire."

"I had a lot of bad days after you left," she admitted. "I tried to find you, but I didn't even know your military ID number. Just your name. I kept hitting dead ends trying to find you."

"Well," he said, brightening, "it looks like karma wanted us back together again."

His smile drenched her and it felt good. Was Dev married? She couldn't conceive of someone who was as nice as he was being single. She was too cowardly to ask. Maybe he'd bring it up in conversation at some point.

"Dharma. Karma is bad and dharma is good." Dev had been a real hero in her eyes, and she wanted to tell him that.

"What we had was definitely good," he said.

The waitress returned with their lunches.

"Kassie makes the best chili," she told him, opening a pack of crackers and breaking them up over the steaming bowl.

"I'm still new here," and he pointed to his hamburger and French fries. "This is comfort food for me."

"She makes a lot of stews and soups during the winter, which is eight months out of the year. Her chili is Wyoming famous."

"I'll give it a try the next time I drop in here. That's the only thing I don't like about Wyoming: how long the winter lasts. I'm not sure I'll know what to do with myself other than getting cabin fever."

Grinning, Andy said, "You'll learn to love winter sports. Lots of people who live here ski and snowboard. We have a knitting circle, a quilting club and other hobbies to keep our minds off all the snow."

"What did you do, growing up here?"

"My brothers and sister and I loved snowboarding. My parents liked cross-country skiing."

"I was thinking about flying the helo in that kind of weather."

"Oh, there will be times when the wind is too powerful, or we won't be able to take off because of a blizzard coming through the area or the visibility is too low."

"Well, it was part of what we signed up for. Weather is always a factor."

"All of us kids, growing up, belonged to different clubs at school. We had our circle of friends, and that passed the time for us."

"Winter in North Carolina was pretty mild because we

lived close to the Atlantic Ocean. I loved flying, and Kitty Hawk wasn't that far away. I used to spend a lot of time as a kid daydreaming in the dunes near the shore, watching the gulls sailing on the wind currents, wondering how they felt while gliding along."

"You always wanted to fly?"

"Always," Dev said, giving a brusque nod and then biting into the huge hamburger stuffed with bacon. "How about you?" he asked between bites.

"I told you that I'm adopted and was dropped off by my mother at the Wind River Fire Department."

"How do you feel about that?"

"I feel good that I was adopted by such great parents. If a woman abandons her baby to be raised by strangers, it doesn't say much about her except that she's in a very bad place. I recognize single mothers constantly struggling to raise a child or children by themselves. It's hell. They're working two jobs, farming their kids out to day care or to their parents or grandparents. I admire them for sticking it out, keeping their child or kids and not giving them to strangers. But it's so damned hard on them. I don't want a life like that. Not ever."

He gave her a thoughtful look, picking up a French fry. "Has it, in some way, made you wary of getting married or having children?"

"It's no secret I want to stay single. I don't want children. I never did. Maybe because of what happened to me. Maybe I'm scared that if my life isn't in my control, I could end up like my biological mother did." She shook her head, her voice low, grim. "That's why I'm not good at relationships. I don't want to get serious. I don't want to give up who I am for a man. There's still too many demands on a woman. And that's not right. Or fair."

"I understand," he said. "My best friend, Kelly, was

adopted. He was greatly loved, like you were. And we were close. He'd often tell me when we were alone together, that he was afraid to make close ties with others."

"Yeah," she murmured, irony heavy in her voice. "I know that one. I had very few girlfriends growing up because I was afraid they'd drop me or leave me because they were moving away."

"I feel that every baby or child who is abandoned is going to have those kinds of issues. It's only logical."

"Terrible outcomes."

"No question."

"Are you still in touch with your childhood friend?"

He smiled a little. "Yes. To this day. We were like brothers, even though he wasn't of my blood."

"That's nice to hear. Is he still in North Carolina where you grew up?"

Shaking his head, he said, "No. Kelly went into the Navy after we went through college. He eventually became a SEAL, and he's still in. I think, in a way, because the SEALs are like a family of sorts, he found what he was looking for. He loves his life in black ops and he's in the Gold Team, the best of the best. We text a lot when he's not on a mission. And I try to see him, or vice versa, once a year for at least a week. That's when we can talk and really catch up with each other."

"Is he married?"

"No."

Grunting, she spooned the spicy, warm chili into her mouth. Swallowing, she asked, "Did you follow suit?" It was a bold thing to ask, but it felt like the right moment to ask. She saw his eyes darken and her gut tightened.

"I married Sophie, the girl I fell in love with in junior high. We married as soon as we graduated high school. We had our lives mapped out and went to the same university together." His voice lowered. "She died of a heart attack at twenty."

Stunned, Andy whispered, "Oh, no! I'm so sorry, Dev . . ." and now she felt bad for asking at all because she could see the grief in his expression.

"My parents told me that with time, the pain would dull." He looked away for a moment, and then held her sad gaze. "It happened over time."

"But that doesn't mean you will ever forget her."

"No, that won't happen. If you love someone, and I loved her with my life, it will never leave me. My mother told me that in time I would place Sophie in my heart and in a special memory file drawer in my brain, where she would stay. She was right." He wiped his mouth with a paper napkin and set it aside. "About a year ago, a lot of my past dissolved. Until then, I would look at any woman I thought I might be interested in and compare her to Sophie. I finally realized that was unfair. There will never be another woman like her. That's when I realized I was stuck living in the past, the grief supporting me emotionally so that I just screwed up every relationship I got into."

"Yet you know what love is."

"That was the gift that came out of it," he agreed, his voice raspy. "When you marry at eighteen, or any age, you don't expect your partner to die of a sudden heart attack two years later."

"No," she quietly agreed. "Well, we're a fine pair, aren't we? I avoid relationships because I'm afraid I'll be abandoned again. You avoid them because no woman can possibly stand in Sophie's shoes."

"Good analysis. As I've gotten older—maybe matured a bit more—I realized what I was doing. It took a lot of years to reach that point." He gave her a kind look. "Maybe someday you'll be able to move into a relationship and realize you aren't going to lose the guy."

"I don't know," she murmured, finishing off her bowl of chili. "I'm not there yet, or maybe I'm not as mature as you are."

"On another topic, you seemed really stoked when I showed you those two résumés, from Alma and Grace. They seemed like really good friends of yours."

"Oh, they are! We met in the military and became besties. We spent every day or week we could together. Part of it was because there weren't a lot of women pilots in fixed wing or helos. You learn to stick together if you're a female in the service."

"That's true, but the way you reacted, I thought they were really close buds with you."

"They are to this day. I text them at least a couple of times a week, keeping tabs on them. I'm surprised they didn't tell me they sent their résumés to you."

"It's been kind of short notice," he said, wiping his hands when he was finished with the juicy, thick hamburger. "We just circulated our employment ad this past week."

"Well, that's true," she said. "I hope you find them right for the tasks around here. I know they can do them all. But you and your boss have to decide that. Until then, I'm not saying anything to Grace or Alma. I don't want to get their hopes up if they might not be hired."

"Understood," Dev said, "and a wise idea."

She crossed her fingers. "It would be great if your boss thinks they're right for this type of employment, though."

"I think they are. But he's the one who has to decide. Ready to go?"

She smiled. "Yes. This was great, getting some down-time with you, Dev. I knew you were kind of a special guy out at the crash site, but I didn't have the chance to fully appreciate it then." She saw his cheeks turn ruddy. He looked vulnerable, and she'd rarely seen that in a man, and it drew her powerfully. The only other man in her life was her father, Steve. He was man enough to be vulnerable, and as a child, she'd desperately needed that. As a woman, he'd taught her as a role model to look for another man like him. Steve had drawn her out of her shell and she'd learn to trust again. And her trust wasn't something she gave to many. But looking at Dev as he rose and pulled his wallet out of his back pocket, she absorbed his vulnerability. Women were automatically vulnerable with each other, with children, but not always with men. Why couldn't all men be like her father and Dev?

June 18

"How do you like your new office?" Dev asked, walking into Andy's digs at nine o'clock that morning. Outside the window, he saw a lot of workmen putting the final touches on the airport hub. The place was like a busy beehive. Trying to ignore his yearning to have another personal talk with her, as they had at Kassie's Café less than a week before, he tucked it away like a precious jewel. Their single-piece blue flight suits had arrived just a few days before. They all wore one, at least those on duty. There was a patch above Andy's left pocket with her last name and first initial. Her gold wings shone just above it. They were all long-sleeved, but because it was summer, she had rolled the sleeves up to just below her elbows.

Flight boots—good, solid black leather and highly polished by hand—were the dress code for the pilots as well. Andy had her chestnut hair wrapped up in a ponytail. She wore no makeup or jewelry. She was beautiful in Dev's eyes. His heart swelled when she looked up from her desk and smiled hello, holding his gaze.

"Great. Just getting used to the PC, the program for missions and learning the ins and outs of the rest of the software."

"Sorta like the military, right? After action reports done in Ops?"

Nodding, she said, "Same old thing. But it's familiar and it feels good."

He held up some papers. "Just wanted to keep you updated on hiring. Pete has approved Alma and Grace to come in for final interviews with him."

Gasping, Andy said, "Really?"

"Yes. I approved them, passed the info that you knew them to Pete. He likes what he sees."

"When are they arriving?"

"Day after tomorrow. I'm sure you'd like some time with them?"

"Better believe it. Will they be staying overnight?"

"Yes, Pete's putting them up at a nice B and B just outside Wind River."

"I'll text them. Do they know the time they're to be here for each interview?"

"Yes. I purposely left eleven a.m. to one p.m. open so you three could go to Kassie's for lunch if you want." He grinned and felt his whole body respond to the happiness gleaming in her gray eyes. He wanted to make Andy smile. So often, the past few days, after she chose her office at the airport, he found ways to casually drop by to see her. She was new to the huge place and he liked helping her when she asked for it.

"You're a good person," Andy said, losing her smile, giving him a look of pleasure. "Thanks for doing that."

Heat rushed to his cheeks. He would never not blush.

He realized that when he was in junior high and a girl he liked said something nice to him. Shifting his boots, he said, "You're welcome."

"If they're hired, when would they start?"

"Three weeks. They have to tie up loose ends at their present employment, move here, find someplace to live and all that stuff."

"I can help them with where to live. The same condo building where you are? Did I tell you that I was assigned the condo across the hall from yours? Maybe I'll come over and beg, borrow or steal some sugar sometime?"

"I do have sugar." He laughed. "That's great news. Let me know when you want to move in and I'll help with the furniture. I'm sure Grace and Alma, if hired, will find that condo building a good place to rent."

"I'll let them know when the time's right."

He glanced at his watch. "Are you open to flying the Black Hawk? The mechanics just called me and they've finished their routine maintenance on it. It's ready to be air-tested."

"More than ready!" She shut down the computer. Standing, she said, "My FAM flight, right?"

"Yes, familiarizing yourself with the valley today. I'll be taking the left seat today."

"Music to my ears," she said, rubbing her hands together. Leaning down, she picked up her helmet bag and straightened. "Now I feel like I'm back in the military again." She saw his grin widen, his hands resting languidly on his narrow hips.

"Great. Follow me. We've got a golf cart at our disposal that will take the two pilots and crew chief to the hangar when there's an alarm bell ringing, alerting us we have a mission to perform."

Dev wanted to keep it impersonal with Andy, but it was

impossible. The way her eyes lit up with unabashed joy at getting to fly again grabbed his heart and didn't let it go. Her smile was winsome later, when they sat in the Black Hawk that had just been rolled out of the hangar and onto the tarmac. The morning sun was slanting across the valley, an emerald-green strip in the verdant flatlands of the area. Everything was lush and vibrant with life. Spring was something that really didn't come to this part of Wyoming until early June. They took the golf cart to where the helicopter was sitting with two mechanics nearby.

Once aboard, after the preflight walk around, Dev watched her fire-retardant Nomex gloves flying over the panel in front of them. Usually, they had a third person on board with them, the chief. He or she would handle the throttle handles up on the ceiling of the bird, but he would do that as copilot today. Whenever they went out on any mission, there would be a minimum of three people in the Hawk.

Today was a FAM flight, something quiet and undemanding. Andy had to familiarize herself with this helo. Even though she'd flown Black Hawks since leaving the military, every bird had its own idiosyncrasies. They went through the preflight procedure together.

The whine of the first engine went online, inching the overhead throttle forward a notch, and he absorbed the pleasure of Andy's profile as she pulled down the dark visor across her upper face, the eastern sunlight strong and blinding. He did the same. Outside the bird, one of the mechanics gave her hand signals, orange direction cones in his hands, taking the bird out to the nearest runway. Once the second engine came online, Dev called the tower for clearance, receiving a go and the number on the runway to take. It was actually a short runway for helos, with a large landing and takeoff area, well clear of all major buildings in case the bird ever crashed.

The mic was close to Andy's lips, her hands on the cyclic and collective, flight boots on the rudders beneath her feet. As copilot, he had his duties, so just the pleasure of watching her respond reminded him of the military. He liked the huskiness of her voice, low, in charge and stress-free. She would have been a great pilot to fly with in Afghanistan, but the number of women in that job was only around 15 percent of pilots who flew helos.

Braking, the Black Hawk sat shivering and shaking on its tripod landing gear. Andy ordered takeoff and he pushed forward, with the palm of his gloved hand, both throttles located in the ceiling between the seats. The blades swung faster and faster, the whole craft shivering, as if it could hardly wait to spring off its leash and get back into the blue arms of the sky above them.

In no time, with her butter-smooth flight ability, the helo lifted off, the vibration throbbing through him. It was a comforting feeling to Dev, and he absorbed it like breathing in oxygen. People who loved to fly, he'd discovered many years ago, always compared it to breathing in the air of life.

He told her to take the bird to three thousand feet, and she began a bank to the right, away from the airport, the dogleg, so that any other aircraft coming in for a landing would have full clearance. The people in the tower were learning their jobs, too. They were receiving more and more civilian plane traffic daily, getting used to the always changing weather conditions, the prevailing wind direction and so many other issues they had to stay on top of. The Ops people were hired and continuing to work and learn their jobs at this regional multiuse hub as well. By the time the Fourth of July came, the ceremony to officially open this airport, the Ops people would have a month of acclimation, which was good.

"Beautiful," Andy said, lifting her chin toward the sky outside their cockpit.

"Good takeoff," he congratulated. "And yes, it's a great day to fly."

Andy's mouth curved. "I do so love being in the air. When I was three years old, I used to fly around the house, my arms out, making buzzing noises. My parents knew then that flying might be something I'd pursue when I was grown up."

"Pretty astute on their part," Dev replied, impressed.

"When did the flying bug bite you?" she asked, slowly swiveling her head from right to left and then upward, always looking for aircraft in the vicinity.

"I wasn't as young as you were, but my dad bought me a model helicopter when I was ten and that's when I realized I wanted to fly one."

"Pretty astute on his part, too."

He laughed a little. "Yeah. We didn't have a whole lot of money, but my parents saved for me to go to college. I didn't get to learn to fly until after I joined the Army."

"It was different for me. My folks are very well off, and when they saw my love of flying wasn't going away as I grew up, they gave me flight lessons out of the Jackson Hole airport when I was fifteen."

"Wow," he murmured, continuing to check the skies around them, too, "what a great start."

"The Air Force was knocking at my door in my sophomore year," Andy admitted. "By the time I joined after graduation, I was taken into their combat jet program and got assigned the Warthog. I loved it."

"Until you crashed."

He saw her lips thin for a moment. "Yes, until then."

"Were you originally going to stay in for twenty?"

"Sure was. I guess," and she shrugged a bit, the harness firm around her shoulders, "I was romanticizing what I did. I didn't realize it at the time. I was so focused on saving lives, protecting the soldiers or Marines on the ground, that I didn't ever think about getting shot down. And when it happened? It shattered me in a way I can't explain."

"You lost the rose-colored glasses," he murmured sympathetically. "You probably saw yourself as the knight flying in on your white horse, saving others," and he glanced out of the corner of his eye at her.

He saw her lips soften. "I grew up on Harry Potter stories. I thought I could do everything. Plus, from the time I could remember, my mother read all of us fairy tales. I loved the idea that I could be one of King Arthur's knights even though I was a girl. I used to go out to one of the lush, green fields, lay down, tuck my hands behind my head and watch the white clouds move above me. I could see shapes in them sometimes. I always dreamed I had a white horse and I was the only woman knight from the Roundtable. I dreamed of amazing battles and winning," and she laughed.

"That's something we shared in common," he said. "As a kid there was a pretty tall sand dune nearby, close to the beach. I'd lay up there in the sea grass doing the same thing you did."

She slanted him a quick glance. "Were you one of the knights from the Roundtable, too?"

He felt his cheeks growing hot. "I was."

"Which one?"

"Oh, I imagined myself as Lancelot. How about you?"

"I modeled myself after Sir Gawain."

"Good choice. He was seen as formidable, always courteous to others and with a great heart. I'll bet you knew he loved herbs and was considered a healer, too?"

He saw her mouth curve and thought he saw pleasure in her expression, although all he could see was her profile.

"My mother loved Gawain. She read me his book, *Sir Gawain and the Green Knight*."

"Does your mother love herbs?"

"Very insightful of you," she praised, giving him a glance, her smile widening. "Mom has always had a love of herbs and spices."

"My father would read to me before I'd go to bed, too. You and I have some interesting commonalities."

"Truly."

He watched as they left the airport behind, going south. She moved the helo to about half a mile from the main highway that split the valley in half. It was an easy flight, the air still cold and, therefore, less turbulent than when the heat of the sun hit the land, warming it up and causing uprising currents. Flying was always done in the morning hours because no one liked hitting the air pockets that were formed by the heat radiating skyward. "I've been studying a lot of law enforcement arrests in the valley," he said. "I'll show you their maps and statistics when we get back. For now, I'll just point out certain areas and tell you where the hotbed of law entanglement with the locals is located."

"Oh," she said drily, "I was asking my dad yesterday about the Elson clan and whether they were still the bad guys of the valley. He said yes, but there was talk that they'd joined a Guatemalan drug lord, Pablo Gonzalez, and was making inroads into our valley."

"He's right. The Elson stronghold is in the southern part of the valley, just below a slope of the Salt River Range," and he pointed in a southeasterly direction.

"Gosh, that whole family has been a pox on the county."

"I read profiles on all of them," he said grimly. "It started with Brian, the father, who beat the hell out of his four sons, Hiram, Kaen, Cree and Elisha. He's dead. Roberta, the mother, lives in the main house. Hiram is in federal prison. Cree is dead. He kidnapped Tara, a local high school girl, and went to prison for it. When he got out and she came home from the military, he started stalking her again."

"Tara was one of my best friends," Andy said, her voice heavy. "My parents told me that when Cree kidnapped her a second time, he was caught and killed by Reese, a local rancher. Tara ended up alive, thank goodness. The Elson family is dark."

"Well, those who are left, Kaen and Elisha, are connecting with Gonzalez."

"In what way?"

"Take a slow left bank here. We're at the end of the valley. We'll fly near the Elson property, but I want you to climb and go upward on the mountain range. I'll direct you to where we're going."

"Uh-oh," she muttered. "Don't tell me there are drug drops up in mountain meadows."

"Yes, good call. Gonzalez is sending planes over in the dark of night to these meadows. Then the Elsons drive to either end of the trailhead, park their trucks and hike in to pick up the bales of drugs. Either that or they use an old dirt road at one end and drive where instructed to load the bales. If they're dropped closer to the parking lot, they carry them back to where they're parked, load them and take off. From there, they distribute them in a chain to the states around Wyoming."

She sucked air between her teeth. "Damn. That's a real escalation of drugs going through our area."

"Roger that. And it's our biggest law enforcement issue right now. Sarah, the sheriff of Lincoln County, is working with the FBI, DEA and ATF contingents."

"We'd need their help," Andy agreed. She nudged the helo toward the lower slopes of the mountain range that moved from north to south. It bracketed the east side of the one-hundred-mile-long valley. The Wilson Range, on the western side of the valley, also ran in a north-south direction.

Dev guided her up to six thousand feet, and for the next hour, he helped her identify six different meadows that were used for such drops. Andy had turned grim about it. In part, he thought, because this valley was her home. And she, like him, wanted to keep it and the people who lived here, safe. But could they?

Chapter Six

June 18

The 10:30 a.m. sunlight was bright through the Plexiglas, and Dev adjusted the air conditioning in the cockpit to keep them comfortable. Andy had just swung the helo north, beginning the flight home to the airport, when an emergency call came in from the Lincoln County Sheriff's Department. He picked up the radio, answering the call from the dispatcher.

Listening intently, he wrote on his kneeboard, scribbling the GPS location of the situation. Sliding a glance toward Andy in the right seat, he saw her lips purse, listening to the conversation.

Dev signed off and turned to her. "There's been a cell phone call from Rogers, a small town along Highway 89. A hiker has broken his ankle at Spring Creek. He called the Lincoln sheriff's office for help on his cell phone. Luckily, there was cell service near Rogers."

"I know that area," Andy said. "I've hiked there many times."

Nodding, Dev said, "We should check out landing near

the hiker to pick him up and take him to the hospital in Wind River. What's the landing area like?"

"There's a small lake at the end of the creek," she said, banking the helo after Dev punched in the new GPS location.

"We need official approval on this. I need to call Pete to get it."

"Good idea," she said drily. Swiveling her head, she was constantly scanning the instrument panel and the sky around them.

Within minutes, Dev had Pete's approval on the unexpected rescue operation. He said Dev could leave the Black Hawk to render aid, provided there was a safe landing area. Andy, who was the pilot-in-command, had to remain with the idling helicopter. Dev agreed with the plan. As they flew parallel to Highway 89, the only major road through Wind River Valley, he relayed the information to Andy.

"Do we have any medical supplies on board yet?"

Shaking his head, he said, "No. Next week. The two crew chiefs that Pete is going to interview are both paramedics." He held up his hands. "I'm not one, but I think I can help this hiker get on board and we'll fly him to the Wind River ER for help."

"It's better than nothing." She saw the meadow opening up around Spring Creek. To her left was the small lake. According to the map on her instrument panel, the GPS was about half a mile from the lake. The red "x" indicated where the hiker had given of his position. Squinting a little, she saw that the meadow was oblong and paralleled the path of the creek. About half a mile on either side of the flat, grassy area was a thick green carpet of Douglas fir.

Dev had taken the binoculars from the side of his seat and was studying the area. "Looks like a good, flat, grassy landing area, Andy."

"Only question is whether it's saturated with water from the creek or not. Do you see any dead trees nearby? Dead branches sticking up? Anything that would nick the blades as I descend?"

He liked her attention to detail. That came from being a combat pilot. "I see some downed trees, but nowhere near where the hiker's supposed to be located."

She grunted and gave a brief nod, her attention on her flying.

"No blanket in the back either?" she wondered.

Dev twisted around, studying the interior of the Black Hawk. "No . . . nothing. The whole cargo area is bare."

"Okay. Just wondering."

In ten minutes they were over the area. Andy spotted the hiker, who was sitting down, one leg stretched out in front of him, frantically waving his arms above his head. Her gaze swept the surrounding area. The man was sitting about ten feet from the creek. Land adjacent to water could be mushy, even swampy, making a landing dangerous. "I'm going to go about a hundred feet inward toward the meadow. It should be hard-packed ground, not soggy."

"Yes," Dev said, tucking the binoculars in a side pocket, "I agree. I worry the soil where that guy's at could be too soft for tripod landing gear. The tires could sink into muck, and then we'd be in double trouble."

"Roger that." She swung the Black Hawk farther into the grassy meadow filled with colorful wildflowers. Not seeing any overhead power lines or anything in the immediate area of the landing she'd chosen, she slowly eased the helo down. Not trusting the soil, she hovered inches over the meadow, the wheels grazing some of the taller wildflowers. Gently, she landed, feeling the tires bite into the soil, keeping the power up thanks to Dev on the throttles.

"Feels solid," she told him. "I'm landing."

"Roger," and he eased the throttles back once the bird was on the ground, surrounded with waving grass and flowers being buffeted by the whirling blades.

"I'll keep the blades moving, but we'll be on idle position," she told him. "I'll let Pete know we landed."

Dev set the throttles. "Roger that." He gave her a sharp look. "I'm going to unharness, slide open the starboard door behind your seat and egress. I'll leave the door open."

"Roger." Andy knew Dev wasn't only being copilot but behaving as a crew chief, talking to her and letting her know ahead of time what he was going to do next. That way, no surprises, no confusion or misunderstandings between them. He clapped her left shoulder with a pat as he left the cockpit. Her skin tightened beneath her uniform. She liked their teamwork. He was a seasoned helicopter pilot and it showed. She had less time in a helo, and not under combat circumstances, so she valued his insight and experience. It made the landing safer.

The blades moved lazily above her, the shadows dancing across the cockpit flooded with blinding morning sunshine. It was a good day for a rescue. Luckily, the weather cooperated, and because it was a morning flight, there was a lot less air turbulence when getting the injured hiker back to the ER.

This was their first rescue. It wasn't law-enforcement-related, but Andy knew they could be called out for lost or injured hikers, automobile accidents or the other issues that inevitably happened during the summer months in the valley and surrounding mountain ranges because the tourist population increased exponentially during that time.

She watched Dev's progress. The grass was lush, thick and tall, sometimes up to his knees. He walked alertly, lifting his hand to the hiker, who was about fifty feet ahead of him. How injured was he? He appeared to be in his late teens, with a knapsack on his back, wearing a black baseball cap and a bright, neon-orange jacket and blue jeans. She was too far away to see the hiker's expression, but she thought he must be relieved, if nothing else. There was no road or trail into this area. It was off the beaten path most tourist hikers took. Maybe he was a local. Usually tourists, from what Dev had told her in one of their familiarization meetings, stuck to trailheads that were marked with nice, oval asphalt parking lots that had restrooms. Out here? There were no restrooms. Just Mom Nature at one's disposal.

Dev's voice crackled in her ears. He was wearing a shoulder radio. He'd reached the hiker, shook his hand and knelt down, facing him. "Andy, call the ER. The guy's name is Justin Thatcher. He's a local, from Rogers, Wyoming. He's six foot tall and one hundred and seventy pounds. He fell into a badger hole he didn't see because of the grass, and there's part of a bone sticking out above his hiking boot. It's an open fracture. The doctors have to know that in advance. He's in a lot of pain."

"Roger," she said, turning her radio frequency to the ER's radio. In a minute, she relayed the information. It would take about twenty minutes to fly from where they were to the Wind River Hospital. Andy knew enough about injuries that a bone sticking out of the skin wasn't good. He'd taken a really bad fall.

Dev had left his radio on as he helped Justin stand. The kid was lanky, unsteady and had slipped his arm around Dev's broad shoulders. Pride in Dev drifted through Andy as she watched their slow progress in her direction. The hiker hopped on one leg, holding up the injured one. They reached the outskirt gusts kicked up by the whirling blades and bent their heads, crouching forward, heads down, a hand across their eyes. Dev's helmet with the dark visor was in place, protecting his vision, but the hiker was almost blinded.

Justin's face was pale, his blue eyes dark as Dev guided him to sit on the lip of the open door. Andy watched with sympathy. The kid looked like he was about to pass out from that exertion. Dev had taken a small towel out of his knapsack and wrapped it as best he could around the injured leg to give it some support. She saw blood leaking through the folds of the towel and wondered just how much he'd lost. Deciding to call the ER again, she reported what she saw.

"Ask him what his blood type is," the nurse on the other end said.

"Dev? What is Justin's blood type? Does he know?"

Dev got him inside with his injured leg spread out across the deck of the helicopter. He leaned over Justin, lips close to his ear.

"He says O positive."

"Roger that, I'll relay it to the ER."

Dev reached up and took down a pair of earphones, putting them on Justin, then explained how he could talk with them on the IC or intercabin connection. The kid nodded, relief on his etched, perspiring features as Dev slid the door shut and locked it.

Patting the kid on the shoulder, Dev said some comforting words to him and left him leaning against the rear bulkhead, his legs spread out in front of him. There was no way to strap him in at this point. Luckily, there would be few air pockets on their short flight to the hospital.

Dev eased into the cockpit, sitting down and pulling the harness over his shoulders, locking it in place. "Okay," he said, "ready for ascent," and he placed the palm of his hand on the handles of the two throttles above his head, awaiting her orders.

"Roger that," Andy said. She sat forward, her full attention on the takeoff.

Once in the sky, the vibration feeling comforting to Andy, she turned to a private channel to speak only with Dev and said, "This is a helluva way for me to make my first real landing at the hospital." It had a large asphalt circle outside the ER area.

Grimacing, Dev said, "Yes, I was just thinking about that. Want me to do the landing? I've practiced doing it about ten times since I've arrived."

"No, I'll be fine, but you can be my other pair of eyes and spot for me. Any suggestions are welcome."

He liked her confidence. There was a ghost of a smile on her lips. "I'm sure you've been in far more serious pickles than landing for the first time at a hospital."

"You could say that."

Chuckling, he twisted around, checking on their patient. Justin had stretched out now, his hands across his belly. He had his eyes closed. At least he hadn't passed out—yet. For that, Dev was grateful. He lamented not having more of a medical background.

Within twenty minutes, Andy had them hovering over the large, black asphalt landing pad with a white circle around its edges, near the hospital. He guided her in because there were power lines to the south. They weren't that close to the landing area, but it was something she needed to tuck away in her mind for future reference. Just as before, her landing was light and gentle. She asked him to bring the blades to idle and he followed her request.

Andy watched as a team with a gurney rolled rapidly toward them. Two male aides, a nurse and a doctor came to the side door. Dev slid the door open for them and helped Justin slowly sit up. The two orderlies entered the cargo hold, maneuvered the hiker to the lip and positioned him gently onto the gurney, getting him comfortable. Within moments, they had whisked him back into the open doors of the ER and disappeared inside.

Dev slid the door shut, locked it, turned and threw her a gloved thumbs-up.

"Nice landing," he congratulated her, sliding into his copilot seat. Pulling the wide nylon harness across his shoulders, he added, "Ready to go home to the airport?"

"Better believe it," she murmured. "Been a pretty interesting day so far."

Powering up the throttles by easing them forward, Dev warmed to her smile. "I think Pete will be more than impressed with your impromptu performance," he said.

Lifting off, a dance between the cyclic, collective and rudders beneath her flight boots, she said, "Thanks."

"I'll buy you a mocha latte to celebrate."

Laughing heartily, Andy eased the Black Hawk toward the airport after reaching a particular altitude. "You're on, Cowboy."

"Mmm," Andy said between sips of her mocha latte at Kassie's Café, "this tastes great! Perfect end to my first FAM flight."

Lifting his Americano, Dev murmured, "Let's celebrate. A good day was had by all. We accomplished a lot, much more than was required."

It was nearly two p.m., and the place was about half full, mostly tourists dropping by, which was great for Kassie's business. Andy studied Dev across the booth table from her. "Were you on 'good behavior' with me today?" Giving him a wolfish grin, she saw him sit back, brows raised in surprise, giving her a confused look.

"What? Why, no."

"Just wondering. I've seen some bosses be 'nice' at first and then, later, within a couple of weeks, their mask comes off and you meet the real guy you have to work with." Shrugging, she said, "Sometimes, it's okay. But I had to quit one firefighting company because of that change between the dude who was one way in the beginning and, within two weeks, a bully and arrogant jerk thereafter, trying to push and order me around. It didn't work."

"I had some of that in the service," he said. "But as for me? What you see is what you get. I'm not PC per se. I do try to be diplomatic, but that's something I'm learning to do. It doesn't come easy."

"Because you call the shots as you see them."

His mouth twisted. "For better or worse, yes."

"My parents would love to meet you, Dev. They've asked me to invite you over for dinner at their home sometime soon."

His brows rose again. "That's nice of them. But are we clear on the first issue? That I'm not putting on a game face now and then later will turn out to be an ogre boss?"

Laughing a little, she said, "I had that coming. Yes, it's settled. I'm glad I'll be working with the guy I worked with today. No surprises down the road is good to hear."

"I've been wanting to meet your parents anyway."

"Oh?"

He sipped his Americano. "Just to thank them for all the years, probably over a decade of concentrated work, to bring this regional multihub airport to this little valley. That's a huge, unrelenting vision to get running. I'm impressed with them."

"My mother, especially, knows how the lobbyists of Washington, DC, work. And not all lobbyists are ogres either. She works with several outstanding firms that have true ethics, good morals, values and integrity. They work toward what she terms 'compassionate humanitarian goals.'"

"She sounds pretty compassionate herself."

Dipping her head, Andy said, "My mom and dad gave the four of us something money couldn't buy: the understanding that there is a right and a wrong. There might be gray areas, but they guided us to always do the right things for the right reasons. I saw them, every week, dealing with lobbyists, making phone calls, and my mom flying to the capitol to speak to senators and congresspeople. When I was older, because I had an interest in what she was doing, I'd go in and sit with her at some of those meetings. I learned a lot."

"She knows the system, then."

"Because my grandmother, her mother, knew it. My mother grew up doing the same thing with Grandma Martha, and she made it part of her life, utilizing that knowledge and experience to bring this amazing gift of an airport to Wind River Valley."

"They should erect a statue to your parents," Dev said, meaning it.

"Oh, no!" Andy laughed. "My parents are very low key. They'll sing the praises of so many others around them who have helped bring this vision about, but never would they take personal credit for anything. They're great leaders, in my opinion."

"Well, something should be done for them. This valley isn't going to be the same once the airport opens up for business."

"They'll take quiet pride in it, and privately congratulate each other. It's their way."

"They're like a pair of Stealth bombers. You don't see them coming until afterward," he said.

Andy grinned, finishing off her latte. "That's a terrific way to put it. Yes. Our parents have taught us to walk quietly— no drama, no histrionics, no arrogance, only humbleness because everyone can teach us something if we're open to hearing and learning from them."

"In some ways," he murmured, putting out a bill to pay for the drinks, "they're a lot like my parents in the way they see the world."

"I'd love to hear about them. Mom wanted to know if you could come over for Sunday dinner. She has a family meal every Sunday at three p.m. It's a tradition. She usually invites friends and folks from around the valley. But this time, it would be just the four of us. Interested?"

Hell yes! Dev told himself he shouldn't be excited, but he was. "I'd like that. What's the dress code?"

"Oh, come as you are. It's nothing fancy. Just pretend you're sitting down at your own family's dinner table."

"Can I bring anything?"

"Just yourself."

"I can do that."

June 23
Sunday

"Tell us about your family," Maud Whitcomb urged Dev as they ate Sunday dinner.

"Yes," Steve said, passing the mashed potatoes to his wife. "It takes a certain kind of person to do what you did—helping to rescue Andy and then keeping her safe from the Taliban for five days."

Feeling heat crawling up his cheeks, he murmured, "My

parents taught me that nothing is ever done alone, that it takes another person, or people, to get the best ideas or plans."

Maud gave him a nod, studying him from where she sat at one end of the table. Cutting into a buffalo steak, she said, "That's the way I was raised. My mother and father always acknowledged other people, defining what they accomplished. One might have an idea, but it takes a team to fully envision the dream and then get it up and running."

Steve gave her a grin from the other end of the table. "Like the airport multihub idea. But enough of that. We'd like to know about your growing-up years, Dev. They define who you are today, and Andy has a very high respect for you."

"I think that's true of any family." He pushed the peas with pearl onions around with his fork. "My parents are first-generation Irish. They got their green cards and became citizens of the US. Then I came along. My family is very close to our Irish roots and relatives to this day."

"What part of Ireland?" Maud asked. "I love that country and its people."

"Galway Bay," he murmured.

"Ohhh," Maud murmured, pressing her hand over her heart, "that is one of my favorite places in Ireland! Steve, you've been there, too."

"Yes," he said with a nod, "I work with an architectural firm based in New York City." He lifted his chin, holding Dev's gaze. "Where on the Bay are your relatives?"

"Barna, just outside of Galway on the bay," he said. "My father's family owns several bed and breakfasts in the village. My mother's had a childcare service there."

"How did your parents meet?" Andy asked, sitting opposite him.

"They were born in Barna, went to school together and

were the best of friends. My father wanted to move to America and become a citizen because there was more work here. My mother agreed. Both were risk-takers."

"Which explains why you were chosen to be a Night Stalker pilot," Andy said, giving him a look of pride.

"I suppose," he muttered, embarrassed, not used to being the center of attention of three people who were sincere about getting to know him. It was enough that they'd made a huge fuss over him earlier for saving Andy's life. She didn't help matters, saying he was a hero, when he didn't feel that way at all. If the tables had been turned, she'd have done the same for him. After telling his parents about those five days, at least the nonstop-secret version of their escape, they, too, were upset. They hadn't realized just how much danger he'd been in. To say the least, they were grateful he was safe and had called them as soon as he got to Bagram.

"I remember Barna," Steve said, enthusiastic, smiling. "In fact, I've got photos of it and Silverstrand Beach, which is famous in its own right."

"It is famous," Dev agreed.

"Have you been back to see your relatives?" Andy asked.

"I try to go to Ireland every couple of years to visit them."

"I imagine you really enjoy your time there?" Maud asked, opening up another biscuit and drizzling some honey across it.

"Very much so." Dev looked over at Steve. "Silverstrand Beach is one of my favorite places to go. It's beautiful, and there aren't a lot of tourists in the winter, which is when I visit."

Steve laughed. "I visited in the summer and it was packed with tourists and locals alike."

"Which is why," Dev said, finishing the last of his steak,

"I go in the winter. Rains a lot and tourists only want the sunshine and clear blue skies of summer."

"Smart," Andy said.

"Have you been to Ireland?" Dev asked her.

"Yes, with my mom. I'm familiar with Galway, the city, but I don't remember Barna."

"It's a small village. You may have been distracted at the time," and Maud smiled benignly.

"I remember Silverstrand, though. You took me there for a picnic."

Dev smiled. "I wonder if you met some of my relatives in the course of your stay in the area."

Andy shrugged. "I don't know. It would be neat to find out. You can take a photo of all of us to Ireland when you visit next and see if anyone recognizes us."

"Good idea. I'm slated to visit this November."

"It's so green over there, like in Wyoming in summer," Maud said wistfully. "I loved the Princeton area, where Steve and I lived while chasing our master's degrees, because it was out in rural New Jersey. Green and grassy, with lots of trees."

"And it's the same here from what I can see," Dev said, gesturing toward the large picture window.

"Pretty much," Steve chuckled, "but we get a heck of a lot more snow than Ireland ever does."

"That's why I loved growing up in North Carolina, near the ocean. It reminds me a lot of where my relatives live."

"Do you think your parents chose Port Harbor because it's closer to Ireland than the West Coast?" Andy wondered.

Dev warmed to her insights and logic. "Yes, exactly. Doesn't get as much rain, and hurricanes are worries for them, but they loved it."

"I imagine," Maud entertained drily, "that it was a lot warmer than Galway Bay in the winter."

"You're right about that," Dev agreed, smiling. Ever since stepping in the door to their fabulously constructed, two-story cedar log home, he'd felt at ease. The Whitcombs treated him as if he were a natural extension of their family. The kitchen and dining room, plus the living room, were beneath a cathedral cedar ceiling far above them. The fireplace was made of the natural sedimentary stones found in central Wyoming. They were created out of ancient sea creatures, floating to the bottom of the shallow ocean that had been in the center of the country during prehistoric times. Steve had shown him some of the slabs that contained fossils, which made the past come alive. Dev appreciated Steve's connection with the past and his talent for incorporating it into the present. Even more, there were framed photographs of their four children, plus a wedding picture of Steve and Maud. He warmed to the fact that this was a tight family that appeared not to be in a spiraling state of dysfunction, making him relax even more.

Dev frowned for a moment, listening to Steve talk about some of the fossils. He was well versed, no question. It was true he missed being close to his family. Being here, this afternoon, seemed . . . well, so right. Why?

Steve handed his empty plate to Sally Fremont, the housekeeper and cook. He thanked her for another wonderful meal.

Sally beamed, her blue eyes sparkling. "And we have your favorite dessert, Steve."

Steve glowed. "Yeah?" He slid a look to his wife, who was smiling broadly.

"Yes," Maud said. "Bread pudding with caramel sauce."

Dev made a sound of pleasure.

Andy laughed. "What? You're a bread pudding lover, too, Dev?"

Rubbing his belly, Dev said, "Absolutely."

Steve gripped his upper arm. "Man after my own heart. We have a lot more in common than I thought."

Sally picked up the rest of the plates and flatware. "I suspect Steve and Dev want twice as much as usual? Ladies?"

"Oh," Andy said, holding up her hand, "I love your bread pudding, but I'm stuffed like a Christmas goose already. How about you, Mom?"

"Standard amount, Sally, please?"

"You got it!" and Sally turned, hurrying through the kitchen to the service area, where the dishwasher and refrigerator were hidden behind a pocket door.

Steve leaned over and whispered, "Sally will pile on the whipped cream, too, Dev."

Andy giggled. "Oh, you guys are all alike!"

Maud joined in, nodding sagely, her eyes glistening with laughter. She reached out, squeezing Andy's hand. "See? While you were gone, nothing changed."

Squeezing her hand in return, Andy gave her mother a loving look. "It's really nice to be home, Mom. I always missed you two and the ranch. But lately, I felt such a deep, deep yearning to be home with you that it astounded me."

Maud released her hand and looked proudly at her. "You grew up here, Andy. This is your real home and it always will be." Her voice went husky, emotion choking her words.

In Dev's opinion, Andy might be adopted, but truly, she was their daughter whether she was their blood or not. That took a huge heart; not everyone was able to adopt a baby or young child. He was beginning to realize just how special these two people were. They knew who they were. They knew how to dream big and how to bring that dream to fruition. They'd adopted four children and, according to what Andy had said about her three adopted siblings, they were just as fiercely loved as she was. That was amazing. It was heart melting. He was so glad Andy had had a soft landing after being abandoned. Because life didn't usually happen as it had for her.

Dev sat with a huge dessert in front of him as Sally finished serving the pudding. Steve murmured his thanks to her as she placed a plate in front of him with the steaming bread pudding on it, drizzled thickly with butterscotch-scented caramel awash in thick, real whipped cream. The pleasure in Steve's face was something to behold. This was a family who didn't hide their feelings from one another. His family was like that, too. He had found out during his years in the military that not all families were the same. Dev had learned to truly appreciate his parents.

Stealing a glance across the table, he watched the joy on Andy's face. Earlier, her cheeks had pinked up over her mother's loving praise. Her words about that yearning to come home told him she was probably home for good. And what a home it was. Already, she had pleaded with him to go for a ride next week, to see the ranch from the back of a horse. And because he'd always dreamed of coming to this state, he felt like he was in some kind of great dream come true. When Andy lifted her chin, her gaze touching his, he saw her gray eyes widen, those black pupils enlarging. Yes, there was no question there was something good, something he wanted to continue to explore, between them.

Chapter Seven

June 23

Andy covertly watched Dev throughout their Sunday afternoon meal. He wasn't a show-off, he wasn't a braggart, nor did he ignore her and her mother in favor of her father, the other male at the table. Those were all boxes that needed to be checked off before she allowed her romantic and idealistic side, which she kept carefully closeted, to look at him on a personal level. All the other men in her life had turned out to be exactly what she couldn't stomach. It was tough finding a man who treated her like an equal. There was unconscious bias, something every human being had, but the smart men discovered it and worked to stop that kind of behavior. Whether it was bias over skin color, gender or anything else, she wouldn't put up with such an attitude in her life. She didn't want to think about the many mistakes she'd made through the years, trying to weed out the Neanderthal males from the "real men." Looking for a man who saw women as his equal in every way. Full stop.

There was no question her parents liked Dev. He was easygoing, a good listener, fully engaged with them. On that five-day run for their lives, though, he was anything but laid-back. She decided she had seen his warrior and survival side. What had attracted her from the first hour they'd met on that cold, wind-whipped mountain slope was his genuine care and concern for her. He'd put her first, not second. He hadn't viewed her as an irritating addendum. Not as some pain-in-the-ass woman he had to protect or put up with. She'd seen too much of that as a Warthog pilot with male pilots in her squadron. She wasn't wanted. She was taking up a slot where a man should have been. And on and on until she wanted to throw up. It was male bias against women, of course. She'd gone through flight school like every man and was top in her class. To the flight instructors, who were more interested in who had the skill sets and goods to be combat pilots, that was all that mattered, not gender. They could care less whether she was a female in the cockpit. They wanted combat-hungry pilots who flew by the seat of their pants to protect the troops below.

After dinner, she joined Dev on the dark green outdoor swing at one end of the wraparound porch. The sun was low on the western horizon on the opposite side of the house. It was shady where he sat in the swing, watching her languid progress toward him. Andy didn't make the mistake of thinking Dev was like all the other men she'd been attracted to. He was very different, and that caused her to hesitate, even though she wanted to connect with him. That push-pull was driving her crazy.

"Come sit down," he invited, patting the lime-green cushion.

"Thanks, I will." She held a cup of coffee in her hand, and she saw that he had one in the cupholder on the end of the swing's polished cedar arm.

"I imagine you used this swing a lot as a little girl growing up?"

She liked his insight and sat down. Taking the other end, she lifted her feet, which were bare now, and placed them up on the cushion, tucking her toes into the lumpy material, her back against the thick pillow behind her. Holding her coffee in both hands, balanced on her stomach, she said, "This was one of my favorite places as a kid." She looked up at the roof above them. "I daydreamed a lot out here."

Cocking his head, he gently nudged the swing just a little with the toe of his boot, liking the movement but not wanting to spill anyone's coffee. "What did you daydream about?" He knew it was a personal question, but the mellow energy between them had inspired him to ask.

He saw her features sadden a little. "I don't normally admit this, but when I found out that all us kids were adopted—and I was the first to be told—I needed this swing. I needed the privacy, quiet and solitude so I could think and feel my way through it all."

"I was wondering when Maud and Steve told you."

"They wanted to adopt us, and they did. Neither of them wanted to keep that fact from us. I was twelve when they sat me down out here, in this swing, one on each side of me, their arms around my shoulders, and they told me I wasn't their child by blood."

"I'm sure they weren't looking forward to it any more than you wanted to hear something like that."

One corner of her mouth lifted momentarily. "At the time they told me, I'm afraid I was pretty selfish and self-centered. It hurt a lot to know I wasn't their daughter by birth. They tried their best to make me believe that they loved me and, in their eyes and heart, considered me the oldest daughter in their family. I believed them, but I felt this huge hole open up inside me, inside my heart. Afterward, all I could do was cry because they were the only parents I knew and I'd loved them all my life. I wanted to know why my real mother threw me away. I wrestled with that the longest, but as I got older, around eighteen, I just let it go. I realized that Maud and Steve loved all of us, fiercely and forever."

His mouth tightened. "I wish I could put myself in your shoes, Andy, but I can't."

"You're doing a pretty good job of trying," she joked sadly. "Most men never ask sensitive questions like you're doing, except for my dad. He's ruined my outlook on men, pretty much. None of the guys I've ever met, with the exception of you, had unselfishness in their worldview."

Grimacing, he said wryly, "Yeah, we're a pretty thick-headed bunch sometimes. I discovered early on that even young girls in grade school were a lot more mature than any boys. My mother was and is, to this day, my icon of maturity."

"And your father?" She tilted her head, catching the amusement dancing in his eyes. It struck her in that moment that Dev wasn't afraid to drop that man shield, as she referred to it, and become vulnerable with a woman or child or baby. That was the most pleasant of shocks, and her heart opened with that discovery.

"My father was a risk-taker, like my mom. They shared the same dream of making more money, going somewhere to take advantage of a larger country, like the US. He idolizes my mother, has always respected her intelligence and ideas. They work as a team."

"Kind of like my parents? Ahead of their time? They treat each other as equals and there's a boatload of respect between them."

"I was struck by that very thing," he admitted, ruefully shaking his head. "It made me miss my parents a lot after I left home. I didn't see it often in the world. It was then that I began to realize just how lucky I had been."

"You see them every two years or so? Or do you go home once a year and then travel to Ireland and see your relatives the year after that?"

"Caught me," he said, smiling, giving her an admiring look. "That's exactly what I do. Since becoming a civilian, I can only spend two weeks with them, not thirty days like I did when I was in the military."

"I'm sure everyone loves to have you visit."

He sipped his coffee. "My dad has a lot of health issues, so when I come home, I try to do a lot of inside and outside repair on their home and around the property. It's pretty much the same in Ireland. I'm young, big and strong."

She smiled softly. "Well, you're a greatly loved son, and I'm sure your dad is grateful for your help."

"It's an act of love as far as I'm concerned."

"You're right, it is."

"What about you, Andy? Did you come home on leave when you were in the military?"

"Sure did," and she planted an index finger into the cushion. "I don't think I put 'wrangler' on my résumé when I applied for a job with you. My dad took the four of us, as soon as we could throw a leg over a saddle, around with him and his wranglers, keeping this ranch going. I think I was three when I sat on my first horse. I loved it. I loved the old mare's mane and how soft and sleek her shoulder was."

"You're a cowgirl." And he grinned lopsidedly. "It's a shame you didn't note that on your résumé. I think that's a good addition." His smile dissolved and he frowned. "When we were running for our lives out there?"

"Yes?"

"I never got to tell you how courageous, strong and tough you were. When I realized you were a woman and not a male pilot, I thought we were screwed." He gave her a look of apology. "I thought you were going to slow us down and that you wouldn't have the stamina that run was going to require of both of us."

Her eyes gleamed. "Fooled you, didn't I?"

"Yes." He held up his hand. "Honest to God, you surprised the living daylights out of me, Andy. But now that I realize you were a wrangler, I'm sure your background played a key part in your keeping up the pace with me."

"Sure did."

"You never once slowed us down. You were a trooper. I was so damned worried we'd get caught. I knew how good Taliban soldiers are at tracking. I was scared. But at the same time, I was grateful that you were tough, strong and your head was in the game. You never wavered, never gave up and kept up even though you must have been whipped."

"Oh, every day was like that for me, Dev. But I trusted you because you told me about your time in the Sandbox and that you were flying black ops, so you really knew the lay of the land. It was easy to follow you. I felt so lucky in that way, and you did not disappoint me either." She laughed a little. "I was afraid I was going to disappoint you on that run."

"You never did." He rubbed his chin, studying her. "Tell me if I've gone a step too far with you. I didn't know you were adopted. We had no time to talk about our lives. If I'd known that, plus from childhood until eighteen you'd been a wrangler, it would have explained to me why you were so resilient out there in the bush. You didn't act like some of the women behind the wire at the firebase where I was assigned."

"I was a combat pilot, Dev. I'm not like most other women."

"I realize that. Honestly? My assignment was with men only in my squadron. The women at the firebase were civilian workers."

Nodding, she murmured, "Understood. Pilots are a different and separate breed."

"You mean you don't put all men into the Neanderthal category? That pilots are in another one?"

Giving him an evil look, she said, "Male pilots were more Neanderthal than the normal guys were at my air base."

"But you don't see me that way?" he challenged.

"You're the first pilot I've met who wasn't arrogant, thought he was God's gift to women and was utterly self-absorbed. So far, I don't see any of those traits in you. Maybe it was the parents you grew up with, great role models where you saw your mother being treated as an equal, so you saw other women in the same way."

He drew in a deep breath, old pain stirring in his chest. "My mother is all of those things."

"I thought so." She wiped her brow, giving him a silly look. "Phew! I know it's probably off-limits, but I was hoping to hear about my two helo girlfriends who were applying for jobs here. Did either of them make the cut?"

"Pete's close to making a decision. As soon as I hear, I'll let you know. I approved both of them, but he's the boss."

"Understood," she said. "It would be nice, because we worked well together."

"In Pete's world, that's worth considering. Be patient, eh?"

Snorting, Andy muttered, "You *know* I'm not that patient sometimes. I was headstrong occasionally on that run for our lives."

"Yeah, you were, but in the end, you were right, too. If they're both like you, I can't see why Pete wouldn't hire them." He crossed his fingers and saw her glow with hope. There were no filters on Andy or him. What you saw was what you got. Just like Sophie was. His heart twinged, the past rising up once more. If only . . .

June 25
Tuesday

Dev heard the screech of women's voices outside his office. Grinning, he knew what it was about. On Monday, Pete had informed him that Grace Cameron and Alma Lopez had been hired. He decided to call the two ladies and ask them to come in at eleven a.m. to see Andy, who knew nothing about it—yet. The shrieks, the laughter and joking floating down the hall told him the three women were having a good time in Andy's office. He'd told Jackie earlier, on the phone, to take the three of them for a long lunch and come back at one p.m. to fill out all the mandatory paperwork.

He'd ask Andy to squire them around the women's sleeping and locker quarters in their part of the terminal. It did his heart good to hear the raucous laughter of the pilots. He understood that tight, military, hivelike community forged by pilots in general, no matter what their gender. His mouth continued to curve upward as he worked on a shitload of paperwork involving the two crew chiefs who had been hired, as well as the last pilot to come on board, Tucker Johnson. His afternoon was filled with getting the three men through the paper chase, the sleeping and locker quarters arrangement. Yes, it was a busy day, but not stressful. It was good to see the crews who would be saving lives in the valley finally coming together.

"Dev!"

He looked up, seeing Andy smiling broadly, her cheeks a bright red. "Yeah? Did you like your surprise?" His heart opened as she stepped in and closed the door behind her. She was in the dark-blue, one-piece flight suit they were all wearing. Her expression was one of gratitude.

"You didn't have to do this. Grace just told me that you're paying for our lunch."

"Hey, some things should be celebrated, don't you think? Getting to see pilot buddies once again? And that you'll all be working together again? Just like old military times."

"Well," she said, her voice soft with feeling, "you didn't have to buy all of us lunch."

"Pete was in on it, too."

"And I bet you're the one who thought of it and engineered it," she insisted, shaking her head, giving him a smile of pure thanks.

Heat flooded his chest. It was startling to him. The errant thought that he'd been alone too long, without a woman to share his life. Andy was perfect for him.

It was true he hadn't known her long, but hell, he *knew* her. She was the one for him. Andy standing here, her hands on her hips, grinning at him, her gray eyes like shining diamonds connecting with his gaze, suffused him with wonderment. Clearing his throat, he said a bit gruffly, "Hey, take off with your friends, okay? I've got a ton of work here to get ready for two just-hired crew chiefs and our fourth pilot."

"Oh," Andy gasped, surprised, "then we're a whole unit! We're mission ready!"

"Not yet," he counseled her, pulling over another filled-out form. "It's going to take us a good month to get up to speed, to get that seamless teamwork thing going."

She laughed and turned, opening the door. "I think it will come together faster than that. Military people are easy to train. They're used to the demands of the organization. Can I bring anything back from Kassie's Café for you?"

Her thoughtfulness struck him deeply. "No, I bought a

sack lunch from home. Thanks, though. Go have some fun and catch up with one another's lives, eh?"

Lifting her hand, she murmured, "I owe you, Dev."

"Nah. Get outta here, Whitcomb."

Laughing, she wagged her finger at him. "I'll let you get away with it this time. *This one time*."

He leaned back in his chair, liking her baiting. "Am I supposed to be shivering in my boots?"

She held the door open and stepped out. "I'll get even. That's all I'll say. Ciao."

"Ciao, bella."

Her brow raised. "So? You know some Italian?"

"Just enough to get myself in trouble."

The door closed and Dev heard her walk down the hallway toward her office, making him go hot with longing. Andy Whitcomb didn't take any prisoners. That was the combat pilot coming out in her. That titanium confidence earned in the heat of facing the enemy twenty feet off the ground, bullets flying all around her. Damn, but she was the whole package, at least for him. Sophie had been a confident young woman, too, and it had beckoned to him then, as well. He had always been drawn to strong women.

Sighing, he wished he could let the paperwork go, but he couldn't. Bringing in the last three employees was important. He, like Pete, wanted this chaotic part of a startup business over and done with. He longed for the quieter times when, like the military, the routines would work like a good timepiece, faithfully and with no bumps in the road causing issues.

Still, as he focused on Tucker Johnson's papers in front of him, Dev wished he could go with the ladies. He was very sure they would have a high old time with one another.

* * *

"I can't believe this," Grace Cameron whispered as they sat in a booth at Kassie's Café. "The three of us together! Again!" She swept her shoulder-length, wheat-colored hair away from her red tee, giving Andy and Alma, who sat together on the other side of the table from her, an evil look of pure glee.

A waitress came over, giving them iced water and menus, taking their drink orders before leaving.

"I feel like I'm in a never-ending dream," Alma confessed. She moved her single shining black braid, long enough to hang halfway down her back, across her shoulder. "Don't you, Andy?"

"It's a little different for me," and she explained her life for the last year in about ten sentences to her girlfriends.

"I remember getting an email from you about that," Alma said, shaking her head. "I don't blame you for taking a quiet, backwater job compared to LA law enforcement. That is brutal work."

Grace cocked her head and studied Andy. "I think the call of home brought you here after that?"

Andy nodded and closed the menu. "Right, as always. You're half shrink, Grace, I swear you are."

Tittering, Grace moved her long, spare hands, palm down across her Levi-clad thighs. "I'm just a highly clairvoyant mystic who rides the invisible wings of air currents," she teased them.

Alma laughed heartily. "My mother is a *curandera*, and she comes from a line of mystic women."

"That's okay," Andy reassured the pilot, who had gorgeous gold-brown eyes, "you were a medevac pilot and put that magic to work saving lives."

Grace nodded, folding her hands on the table. "It's nice to be back together again. This time we're in the same squadron, so to speak."

"But no one is shooting at us," Alma joked.

"That's one of the reasons I came home," Andy admitted. "Not the first one, but a close second. I've had enough war to last me a lifetime."

"Haven't we all?" Grace said with a grimace.

The waitress returned and they gave their orders.

Andy rolled her eyes at her American-Canadian, blond-haired friend. "Flying DAPs meant you were flying Black Hawks with heavy weapons. You *were* the war!"

All three women laughed and grinned at one another.

"Well," Grace said drily, pointing a long finger in Andy's direction, "you were a Warthog pilot. If anyone was in the center of battle, it was you."

"We aren't exactly wilting lilies," Alma agreed, growing somber. "I'm hoping this job will last me a long, long time. I've never been to Wyoming before and I'm a little bit concerned about the eight months of winter."

"Yeah, I would be, too, if I had tropical blood in my body," Andy teased, hooting.

Alma gave her a good-natured dig with her elbow. "You were born and raised here. You know how cold it gets."

"Freeze-your-ass-off cold," Andy promised, barely able to stop grinning.

"When I was growing up in Toronto, my American mother was always wanting to go back to the US."

"Yeah," Andy said, "but she was born in La Jolla, California. That's desert-rat blood."

"My father could never figure out why she'd want to leave our six months of snow and ice," Grace said, chuckling.

"So, this winter stuff isn't gonna bother you, Grace?" Alma asked.

"Not in the least. I think my Canadian father's snow genes are in my blood."

"I'm pretty much like you, Grace. Our parents made fun

of our eight months of winter. I'm sure you and I will be skiing in Jackson Hole come winter. They've got great ski conditions."

Alma wrinkled her nose. "I'll need to adjust."

"Just put a sun lamp in your living room," Grace deadpanned, barely able to keep a straight face.

"No mercy from you two, I can see," Alma grumped, her full lips edging upward.

"Nada," Andy said, "you just have to remember how bad it was in the Sandbox and then a Wyoming winter won't look so dismal."

"Tell me," Alma said, "are there any other good-looking guys like Dev around? Is this a hot spot for hunks or what?"

"I hope so!" Grace said. "And you're right, our boss is to drool over."

"He's a nice guy," Andy told them, becoming serious. "Very sensitive, and he's one of the very few men, aside from my father, who can be vulnerable around a woman. He doesn't play tough guy, thank goodness."

Wrinkling her nose, Grace muttered, "I'm so sick of Neanderthals that I could barf."

Groaning, Alma said, "I've had my fill, too."

"So, the three of us are single? No guys in our lives?" Andy pried. She saw the waitress coming with their orders. They had, to a woman, ordered hamburgers, French fries and a chocolate milkshake.

Grace muttered, "I'd rather be single than hitch up with one of those last-century jerks. I'm over them, but they aren't over themselves."

"What we need," Alma opined as the waitress distributed their platters of food, "is a twenty-first-century male who adores us, knows we're kick-ass and we can hold our own with any male on the planet."

Laughing, Andy put the straw into her thick milkshake

after thanking the waitress. "You know? When you're as good or better than the other guy in the cockpit? Men don't understand that we see them very differently than how they see us."

"I'm sick of being looked at like ass and breasts on two legs," Alma griped, pouring the ketchup on her fries.

"Ditto," Grace said, nodding sagely.

"You two always had a gaggle of guys hanging around you," Andy said.

"And we hated it," Grace said, biting with gusto into her juicy, thick, bison burger.

The booth quieted as they hungrily dove into their meal. After coming up for air, Andy said, "This valley is full of cowboys."

"Are they as full of themselves as pilots are?" Alma demanded, giving her a one-eyebrow raised look.

"There are a lot of military vets coming home here," Andy said. "But most of them are ground pounders, not pilots, insofar as I know. For instance? The Bar C is owned by Shaylene Crawford-Lockhart, who was in the Marine Corps. She came home to take over her family's ranch because her father, at forty-five, had a stroke. Reese, who had been a company commander and Marine, found her ranch and went to ask if they had any jobs for someone like him. Shay, who is a good friend of mine—we grew up together and went to the same school—had decided to make the Bar C a haven for returning vets."

"She gave them a place to heal up and reorient?" Grace asked, popping a French fry into her mouth.

"Exactly," Andy said. "Everyone working at the ranch, man or woman wrangler, is ex-military. It's a real success story."

"Any single male wranglers over there?" Alma wondered, giving her a playful look.

"Well," Andy said, "there's a way to find out."

"Oh?" Grace said, perking up. "Tell us how."

"On July Fourth, my parents have invited anyone who wants to come to a barbecue celebrating Independence Day, plus the opening of the regional hub. The people of this valley never miss a ranch invite like that. I think every single military vet will be there in his best duds. You'll get a good look at all of them."

"Hmm," Alma said, "sounds cool. I'd sure like to find a guy who's nice and treats a woman like his equal. I'm so over how we've been treated."

"The #metoo movement has fixed that."

"I like the #timesup one," Andy said. "I'm so over the last ten thousand years of men running this planet and putting women down and always telling us we're only good for one thing: being barefoot and pregnant."

Grace lifted her upper lip in a snarl. "I haven't ever had any patience with that type of dude."

"Which is why," Alma said crisply, "we're all single and hitting thirty years old."

Grumpily, Grace muttered, "I'd rather be an old maid, as my mother is worried I'll become, than deal with a jerk who never sees me as a human being, just something to screw."

"#Timesup," Andy said lightly, grinning. "Well, hey, Shay is one of us and look at her: She met Reese Lockhart, they fell in love and married. Now they have a beautiful baby daughter."

"You've met Reese?" Alma demanded.

"Not yet. I've barely been home two weeks, but I intend to meet him at the barbecue."

"Are all the good ones taken?" Grace worried.

"Haven't a clue. Mom was saying, in the last decade,

the valley has really changed because so many of the men coming here are ex-military."

"Yeah," Alma said, "and not all of them have their shit together either."

"Granted," Andy agreed. "But Dev is ex-military. Look at him."

"Yeah, but it's the guys who got their brains clobbered by IEDs and have permanent brain trauma as a result who worry me," Grace said. "That's not what I want in my life."

"Dair Wilson, one of the Bar C wranglers, had her foot blown off by an IED and her dog killed," Andy told them, sadness in her tone.

"Women can get hit with those pressure waves from the IED explosions, too," Grace agreed grimly. "I'm sure she has some residual from that."

"I'm sure she does," Andy agreed sympathetically. "Mom gave me a list of military men and women and I intend to meet all of them. I'm living here now, and I want to know the people of the valley."

"That's not a bad idea," Alma said, munching on her hamburger. "We should meet them, too."

Grace threw a thumbs-up, sucking happily on her milkshake.

"Well," Alma said, "Pete Turner and Dev are decent men. I think that's a good sign that maybe there are other guys in the valley like them."

"I sure hope you're right," Grace murmured, raising her eyes upward.

Andy said nothing, her heart resting on Dev and their slowly developing relationship. There was no question in her mind that he was interested in her, just as she was in him. Yet he was her boss. She knew that relationships usually died when two people who worked together fell for each other. Still, she didn't want to curse the possibility because he truly was, from all appearances, that rare twenty-first-century male every woman wanted as a lifelong partner. What would the coming weeks bring?

Chapter Eight

June 29

"Hey," Andy called to Dev, who was in his office, "want to do something really cool tomorrow? It's Saturday. You and I aren't on the schedule to fly. We have the day off!" She gave him an impish grin and stood in the doorway. It was quitting time around the busy, harried office.

He looked up. Andy was tall and beautiful, her chestnut hair in a ponytail, tendrils touching her flushed cheeks. He liked that she didn't wear any makeup, comfortable with who she was. Seeing the hope burning in her gray eyes that he'd agree to her offer, he said, "Sure, I'm open. What's up?"

She slipped inside the office, leaning back against the doorframe. "I'm starting my weekly wrangling again at the ranch. I told Mom and Dad that I wanted to devote at least one day a week to it, get back into shape and be of some help to them."

"Sounds like fun. Do I get to come along and watch?"

She wagged her finger at him. "Oh, no, tenderfoot. You're gonna help me by throwing your leg over a good horse, and I'll get you all the gear you need to ride fence with me. I'll teach you the ropes as we go. There's no 'watching' here. Just doing. We'll be a wrangler team out on the ranch. How does that sound?"

"Well," he murmured, leaning back in his creaky chair, "I've been trying to get over to Wind River to pick up a gym membership and start lifting weights like I did when I was in the military."

"Oh, wrangling will give you the best workout in the world! You'll love it. And you don't have to pay for a gym membership either."

"So? You think I can do this? An East Coast tender-foot?" he teased, smiling. His heart opened swiftly when she laughed huskily, her eyes dancing with mischief.

"I'm positive. We're both living at the condo, right across the hall from each other. How about you come over at 0700 and I'll drive us to the ranch? We'll spend the day there, have dinner with my folks and then I'll drop your weary butt off at your condo."

"Don't take such delight in my being out of shape," he grumped good-naturedly.

"Wear jeans, work boots, and a cap of some sort. I'll have a pair of half chaps and good elkskin gloves waiting for you in the tack room."

"Sounds like fun."

She snorted derisively, pushing away from the door-frame. "Wrangling is many things, but I'd never say it was 'fun,' Mitchell. You're gonna be sore as hell and your joints will creak by the time we're finished with our day riding fence line."

"Won't you be, too?"

"Oh yeah." She chuckled. "Misery loves company, you know?" And she swung out of the office, heading down the hall.

Shaking his head, he felt a thrill of joy move through him. At last! Time alone with Andy. The past week had been long, stressful and yet rewarding. They had all their employees and everyone was either spending time in Salt Lake City, Utah, undergoing link trainer instructions on the Black Hawk, or getting their helicopter properly outfitted with cots and medications. It was known that sometimes a nurse or doctor, or both, might be on board on a call to take care of the patients they were flying in to rescue and bring back to the hospital. Yes, everything was falling into place. He liked the crews. Tucker was the only male pilot, and the three women razzed the hell out of him, but he took it in stride, giving as good as he got. There was a respect among the four pilots, and that was the glue that held this whole thing together. Pete had done a good job of finding the right mix of people. He, himself, would be the fifth pilot, the standby should one of the pilots on the mission roster get sick or have vacay or not be able to come out due to another life emergency. And he would fly on the roster schedule as well. That way, each pilot would get seventy-two hours off, which was necessary to life demands in turn. Plus, pilots could only fly a certain number of hours within the FAA regulations, and five on the roster met those guidelines.

Wrapping up the day, putting the last file away in a side drawer, Dev looked forward to the weekend. The thought of a whole day with Andy was like a dream come true for him. What would unfold? He was still just as interested in her as before. And she appeared to be also. A part of him, the impatient part, wanted more time with her, but under the circumstances that wasn't going to happen. His mother had told him while growing up that patience paid off. He hoped it would now. But what did he really want out of this if their relationship moved forward? Sophie was still a deeply rooted part of him and would remain so. Had he finally worked through the grief and loss of her?

Dev had heard, once again from his wise Irish mother,

that grief had its own way with people, that it didn't last just a year. It could last a decade or decades, depending upon the individual and the love they had for the person who passed over. Sophie had died suddenly at age twenty. He was twenty-nine now. Nine years. There was no question he had loved her and she, him. He'd had so many dreams for them after they graduated from college, but she died in their sophomore year. His life was shattered. Joining the Army, making it through helicopter flight school, had distracted him greatly from his grief. Maybe that was why it had taken so long for him to work through it. He honestly didn't know. Most people in their early twenties didn't have to go through a powerful and life-changing event like that. Dying was for old people, not someone in their twenties.

As he rose, fishing out the key from his pocket to lock his office as he left, Dev pondered what lay ahead for him. How was Andy viewing what they tentatively had? She was the same age as he was. He didn't know how she felt about settling down, if it was even on her life radar. So many questions. Maybe he'd get some of them answered tomorrow.

June 30
Saturday

"Do your legs feel like a wishbone that's ready to split in half?" Andy teased as they sat down under a line of cottonwood trees that comprised one of the grass lease pasture fences. She watched him walk with bowed legs and grinned with understanding. Her legs felt the same. If one didn't ride at least three or four times a week, one always got bowed legs and stress on the inner thighs.

"Seriously," he muttered, bringing along the leather

saddlebag that contained their lunch. Handing it to her, she settled her back against the tree. Earlier, she'd said of this line of cottonwoods that it stretched for a mile and they were nearly 150 years old. They gave the cattle shade during the day, although it rarely got to eighty degrees in the valley during the summer.

Andy patted the grass next to where she sat. "Sit with me? It's always nice to relax your back against a tree. Stretching out your legs before you will help those poor, screaming adductor muscles on the insides of your thighs."

He grunted and slowly sat down, the sensation that his inner thighs were stretched and were protesting mightily was number one on his list for immediate attention. "This feels good," he admitted. Their elbows were about six inches from each other. Moving his boot heels around, he smoothed out a place to rest them on instead of letting the toes tangle in the thick, long strands of grass. "We've spent the whole morning on just this one pasture."

Opening the flap of the saddlebag, Andy said, "I warned you, working as a wrangler is far better exercise than any gym." She chuckled when she heard him groan his reply. He took off his elkskin gloves and then removed his black baseball cap since they were in the shade of the tree. His hair was still military short, and she saw the sheen of sweat on his brow. They had been working hard, with few breaks. He was handsome in her eyes, with a face that had some lines, some character, and she liked that.

He gestured upward. "At least we don't have to worry about this side of the leased pasture. These cottonwoods aren't going to rot like a four-by-four will."

"That's true," Andy said, pulling out one of the beef sandwiches she'd made for them. "When my dad's relatives bought land in this valley, they tried to plant young cottonwood trees everywhere to use as 'posts' for the pastures.

Unfortunately," she said, handing him a sandwich, "the long, hard winters killed all but this line. And these survived because they wrapped them in gunnysacks to protect them from the freezing conditions when they were young saplings."

"Thanks," he said, taking it. "I guess no one knows how much hard work goes into a ranch until they hear the rest of the story from those who came before you."

Setting the saddlebag aside, she smoothed out a place on her leather chaps and opened up the other foil-wrapped sandwich. "You said it all." She grimaced and slowly moved her knees, then stretched out her legs once more. "I'm sore myself. This is my first day at it since I've been here. I'm sure both of us will have sore biceps and sore thighs before we're done this evening."

Looking around, appreciating the brown and white Herefords in a pasture opposite the one they were working on, he said, "No question. I don't know about you, but I'm going to take advantage of the spa room at our condo. Twenty minutes of very warm water on my body will take a lot of the aches and pains away."

"Roger that," Andy said. "I'll be joining you."

He munched contentedly on the sandwich, the lettuce crisp, the mayonnaise tasty with a tang of curry spices in it. "Kinda nice to spend the day with you, though."

Her heart pinged once at his words. "Yes, I like it, too."

"Are you up for twenty questions?" he teased, slanting a glance toward her.

"With you, I am," she said. "I have twenty questions for you, too."

"Okay, that's fair." He wiped the corner of his mouth with one of the paper napkins she had put in the bags. "You go first."

"Tell me about your life as a kid growing up in North Carolina."

"My parents would say that I was a wild kid, a risk-taker, curious and a strong swimmer. I liked swimming in the ocean when I could get there."

"Surfing?"

"No, never had an interest in it. I liked swimming."

"And yet you're a pilot. How did that happen?"

Grinning, he said, "Kill Devil Hills was near where we lived. That changed my life."

"The Wright Brothers took their first flight in that area," she noted.

"Yes. Nowadays, very few people know much history."

"Oh, my dad told all us kids from six years old onward that we needed to read a lot of biographies of famous women and men, that history was the most important thing in our lives."

"Because if you don't know your history, you're doomed to repeat the same patterns from the past all over again."

"Dad said that many times." She wiped her fingers on a paper napkin. "He's a history nut. He compiled a yearly list of history books for us to read. And since civics was no longer taught in schools, he taught us himself. He said it was important to know how our government worked and functioned, that voting was a privilege."

"My parents were green card people, so once they became citizens, they really hammered into me that I was to vote in every election, that I had to pay attention to local politics, as well as state and federal politics. They'd sit down with me and show me the inner workings of running for office, about polling places and voting, how vital they were for a strong, healthy democracy. They made me realize that what we have here in America should never be taken for granted. That democracy lives because people everywhere votes, gets involved in what their politicians are doing and are proactive in local politics."

"I think," Andy said drily, "that your parents and mine would see eye-to-eye on a lot of issues, things that are important as I came to discover as I matured."

Nodding, he finished off his beef sandwich. "Got another one?" he asked, pointing at the bag.

"Sure do. Two for each of us." She picked them up and handed them to Dev. "Get me my second one? I'm still starving."

"We've burned up a lot of calories," Dev agreed, giving her a beef sandwich and setting his on his lap. Looking into the depths of the bag, he asked, "Any dessert in there?" and he grinned.

"Of course. I made a pineapple upside-down cake last night. Two big pieces in the other bag."

"Good to know. Thanks for making it. And thanks for sharing it."

She liked the gleam in his eyes. "It's nice to be thanked. Most dudes wouldn't think of it at all."

Setting the other bag down between them on the grass, Dev said, "I come from a family where nothing is ever taken for granted. My dad thanks my mother for her cooking. And nothing is ever thrown away and *everything* was eaten that was put on your plate."

"Wise," Andy agreed. She unwrapped the foil. "When did you first see the Wright Brothers' National Memorial at Kill Devil Hills?"

"I was nine. My parents were big believers in history, too, but in a different way. They wanted me to learn and appreciate the local history that surrounded us. When I saw the biplane, my parents bought me a book on the Wright Brothers, and that was the beginning of my love of flight."

"Before that, did you dream of flying?"

"No, not really. But I always enjoyed the seagulls sailing in the air above my head. I always wondered what they saw when they looked below at me or other people on the beach."

She frowned. "Maybe I'm getting too personal with you, Dev, but what pushed you into Army aviation?"

Finishing off his sandwich, he tossed the wrapper back into the saddlebag. He wiped his hands on the lush grass. "By the time I was a junior in college, I had joined an Army ROTC program and got accepted into aviation."

"You must have aced a lot of tests to get that promise out of the Army."

"I had a four-0 average," he admitted humbly.

Andy gave a low whistle. "That's impressive."

"I don't let it go to my head."

She laughed heartily, trading a warm glance with him. "I like your humility."

"That means something to you?"

"Sure. I think it does with most women. I don't like dudes who are braggarts or think they're God's gift to women. Because they aren't. At least, not in my world."

"I'm kind of picking up that you like men who are . . . well, for lack of a better word, vulnerable?" and he studied her.

"Very much so," she answered, stuffing the trash into one bag. Opening the flap on the second one she pulled out the cake, some napkins and two white cardboard forks that wouldn't harm the environment. "When I was in my teens, I used to wonder what my real father was like and why he abandoned me. I tried to create him in my thirteen-year-old mind."

"Did you succeed?"

"Naw," she said, opening up the tinfoil. "Too young, too immature and still a kid. But my adopted dad was, as I found out much later, very different from most of the men I've run into since I left home."

He cocked his head, giving her an incisive glance. "How is he different?"

"He is, as you used the word, vulnerable, and was always like that. There were times when my folks would cry. I always thought men cried until I got out into the world and men called other men sissies if they cried. My dad is my hero. I liked that he could cry. I mean, he didn't do it all the time, but when our dog, Blackie, died, he cried. We all cried. Blackie was a member of our family. He wasn't just a dog. And he loved us, too. The six of us stood out at Blackie's grave and we held one another and bawled our eyes out. It hurt so much, but I remember clinging to my dad and his arm around me and the others, crying with us. I just didn't realize how wonderful and important it was that he could cry with us. When I got into the military, of course, those guys were so jammed up and had been taught not to show emotion or cry, if they did, they'd be razzed to death."

"Men have usually been taught not to cry or be emotional," he agreed, savoring the pineapple upside-down cake.

Her eyes narrowed. "Can you cry, Dev? Or are you one of them?"

Chuckling, he said, "Yeah, I can cry. Your dad is like mine. He cried from time to time, too. I grew up knowing it was okay to let it all go. But going into the military, I had to shut it down, or find a place where I was alone and couldn't be heard."

"Same here," she muttered, shaking her head. "I hate that men think crying is a sign of weakness. It really isn't. Maybe society thought it was weak, but thankfully, those times are changing. Besides, men own hearts and have tear ducts just like women do. Crying isn't a sin. I think it's healthy."

"Do you cry?" he wondered, watching the sorrel quarter horse he had ridden happily up to his knees in grass.

Her mouth twisted. "As you know, you can't fly in combat and be an emotional mess."

"Right."

"I remember when I was about six years old and my mom saw me stub my toe and fall out near one of the barns. I sat there trying not to cry. She picked me up, sat on a nearby bench, held me in her arms and rocked me. And then? The tears really came."

"Did you always fight crying?"

"Yes, I did. I guess," and she sighed, watching the horses content and eating. "I was probably stuffing the fact that my biological mother abandoned me. I didn't even know I was adopted at that age, but I remember that day. I remember all this hurt bubbling up inside me, and I had no idea where it had come from. I mean, I did stub my toe, but my shoe protected it. It happened in July, and I had a pair of coveralls on. My mom pulled up each leg and saw that I had redness on my knees. She kissed each one of them. And I cried even more." She halted, confusion in her low tone. "I didn't forget that day because I cried so hard and for so long."

"Maybe six years' worth of tears you'd hidden inside of yourself without ever realizing it?"

She finished the cake. "I've come to the conclusion there isn't one single human being on the face of this earth who isn't badly wounded in some way, shape or form. And some of us have more than one wound. I've talked to my parents about this observation and they agree with me. This is such a planet of pain and suffering, Dev. On most days I let that go because it's just too much to carry by myself. On other days, when I have one of those depression-like times, that's when I cry. My mom taught me: better out than in."

"Well, if it's of any support," he said wryly, finishing his cake, "I grew up seeing my parents struggle every day.

It wasn't easy for them. Plus, getting a green card was just the beginning of their travels toward citizenship. They had to study a lot. I remember one night my parents were at the kitchen table, ten at night, working over their books on government. I could see and feel their confusion about some things. My dad finally hired a tutor, even though they couldn't really afford it. I think, as a ten-year-old, you don't understand the pressures on your parents."

"That's true. Being parents is the toughest job I know." She wadded up the foil and shoved it into the bag. Dev reached over and put his in there as well.

"So?" he teased, "did we solve the woes of the world over lunch?"

Andy snorted. "Hardly. But I think we've got bigger fish to fry from that Friday afternoon update we got from Sheriff Carter on the Elson gang. That was damned scary, if you ask me."

Sobering, Dev nodded. "I'm glad she's giving us updates on the known players around the valley. Having color photos of the three sons who are left in that snake pit of a family are good."

"From what Sarah said, Kaen, whose thirty-one, has taken over since Brian, the father, was shot and killed by her last year. He's lethal-looking," she whispered, getting up on her knees and putting everything away in the saddlebag and strapping it shut. "Scary."

"Sometimes looks match what the person really is," Dev said. He slowly stood up and held out his hand to her. "Come on, we gotta get back to work."

She gripped his hand, liking the warm strength of it as he gently pulled her to her feet. "Thanks," she said, releasing it. Lifting her chin, she met his gaze. "I like our talks, Dev. I really do."

"Then can we keep having them? Whenever we get a window of opportunity to do it?"

She smiled and carried the bag over to Goldy, her palomino mare, throwing it across the rear of the saddle and strapping it on. "Yes. Operative word here is 'opportunity.' July Fourth is coming up soon enough; we've got a lot more flying and work to do between us and the hospitals here and in Jackson Hole as well as in Salt Lake City."

He brushed his chaps and headed for the sorrel known as Prince. "We are busy and it's going to stay that way. I think most of our medevac trips are going to be during the summer months. As soon as the snow flies, most of the tourists leave."

"Except for the skiers who come in. The mountains above Jackson Hole are well known. We get in a whole different set of tourists at that time."

"True," he said, mounting the horse.

Andy saw a grimace come briefly to Dev's mouth as he swung his long leg across the saddle and settled in. "Thighs screaming?" she asked, mounting Goldy.

"Better believe it. I can hardly wait until we get back to the condo. I'm looking forward to that hot tub."

She nudged Goldy forward, aiming her toward another line of fence posts where the cottonwood line ended. "Remember, you wanted to learn to be a wrangler."

He rode up alongside her, their boots brushing from time to time. "I'm beginning to have a new appreciation for you doing this as a young girl growing up on this ranch."

"Yes, we all did it. Our summer vacations from school meant about three months of wrangling here on the ranch."

Shaking his head, Dev muttered, "That's brutal."

Laughing, she looked around in appreciation of their long, narrow valley bracketed by two mountain ranges that had snow on all their peaks. "We loved it! None of us were good at sitting still all day long in classes. We were all highly athletic and loved pitting ourselves physically against the world." Drily, she added, "Or, in this case, it was us against rotting four-by-fours, cutting off the six strands of barbed wire and then throwing a lasso over it and hauling it out of the ground, thanks to the strength of the horse we rode. No," she said, smiling over at him, "we all loved it."

"Do Sky, Luke and Gabe, when they come for a visit, go out and help the wranglers?"

"They sure do. You'll get to meet them soon enough. Luckily, they all got some days off from their jobs and they'll be flying in at different times and staying here to celebrate the opening of the airport. We're all so proud of our mom and dad in getting this wonderful hub into Wind River Valley. This is a game changer for the people eking out a living here. So many of them are going to be hired by the airport. They'll finally get a decent, living wage. Lincoln County will no longer be the poorest one in Wyoming."

He rested one hand on his chap-covered thigh after pulling the black baseball cap bill down a little more to keep the sun from hitting his eyes. "I hope I'm going to be able to meet them at some point. I'm helping Pete with all the celebration events."

"Oh, not to worry. I was asking my mom the other day about just that."

"What?"

"Well, I really wanted my siblings to meet you. My mother wants to invite you to a quiet family dinner the day before the festivities."

"Wow, that's an honor," he murmured.

"You're in the good graces of my parents," she teased. "They really like you, Dev."

He felt his cheeks heat up. "I'd like to accept that dinner invite."

"Good, it's a date, then." Andy realized what she'd just said and saw a sharpening look in his eyes over the use of that word. Flustered, because she felt herself growing closer and closer to Dev, she stammered, "W-well, maybe 'date' was the wrong word."

"No, I'm fine with it, no matter what you want to call it," he soothed, giving her a warm look.

"Really?" Her heart sped up. Chiding herself because she sounded like a breathless teenager, she saw amusement come to his gaze.

"It's nice to talk to a woman whose got intelligence, maturity and was in the military," he offered. "I'm not saying all other women aren't smart and aren't mature, but in your case, I was seeing you differently because you were in the military. Plus, we shared five days of life-and-death hell, and we lived through it—together." He opened his gloved hand. "I guess I feel we already have a bond, Andy. Now that fate has thrown us together again, I see it as a second chance with you. I liked you when we were running for our lives. You had courage, a steel spine and you were a fighter."

"Just like you," she whispered, suddenly choked up by his unexpected admission. "There were hundreds of questions I had about you, too."

"I didn't know that." He smiled a little.

"I feel comfortable around you, Dev. I did even out on that rugged, damned-cold mountain we crashed on."

"Funny, when I realized you were a woman, I felt okay about it. The way you handled yourself and all, I suppose. You always conveyed an air of calm and confidence. Do you know that?"

"No, I didn't. You had that same kind of demeanor yourself."

"I think being a combat pilot shaped us like that. We can't let our emotions get the better of us. Whether we want to or not, we have to stay focused through the fray and make good, tactical decisions."

The breeze picked up, and she drew that green-grass scent she loved so much into her lungs. For Andy, it was a perfect day with a man she'd longed to know on a much more personal level, and now he was revealing himself to her. It was exciting. Scary. But good. "That calm in the storm will be with us, I'll bet, for the rest of our lives."

"Not a bad attribute to have when a crisis is whirling around us," he agreed. He pointed down the line of fencing. "See that sixth post down there?"

"Yeah," she grumbled, "it's leaning like the Tower of Pisa."

"Amazing what five to six feet of snow will do to a line of fence," he said. "You get snow dumped by the foot here in northwestern Wyoming."

"True," she said, wanting to stay on their original subject—themselves—but knowing that work on the fence post was going to interrupt them for the next twenty minutes or so.

"Hey," he said, standing up in the stirrups for a moment and stretching his aching thighs, "how about a rain check on what we started out here at lunch?"

"What?" she asked, frowning, not sure what he was proposing.

"We don't have a lot of time to get to know each other like we wanted when we met in Afghanistan. I'd like to take you to Kassie's Café for dinner, and then we can drive to the condo and have that hot tub together. Sound like a plan?"

"I like the idea." She wasn't sure if Dev would have had

enough of her, but apparently not. Her heart lifted. Where was this going? He was far more likable, a man's man in her eyes. Most of all, it truly was his humbleness and vulnerability that drew her powerfully. Well, that wasn't exactly true, Andy admitted. She couldn't deny the pleasure she felt at watching his well-shaped mouth change and then show that Irish smile of his. She wondered what it would be like to kiss this man, her own experience telling her he would be a wonderful lover. *Whoa! Double whoa!*

Inwardly, Andy scrambled like a wild mustang that had suddenly felt a loop settle over its head. Where was this going? Dev was her boss. She desperately wanted this job she's just gotten. Office romances were not on the table. Wanting to stay home, to be close to her parents and do some part-time wrangling, because she missed it so much, hung in the balance.

As she searched his gaze, she saw a man who was interested in her. What she didn't see were signs of lust and sex in his expression. No, there was something more here, and Andy moved uncomfortably in the saddle. What did Dev want out of this burgeoning relationship? How did he see her? That was key. As a partner for a one-night stand? Something more serious? Befuddled, she didn't know and was dying to ask him. But better to let things unfurl magically between them, like what had happened today. Her heart felt lifted; she felt hope and happiness. Dev was good for her. But the question was: what did that mean?

Chapter Nine

June 30
Saturday

Skylar Whitcomb's heart raced as she hurried from her rental car toward Kassie's Café. She was home once again and it felt so damned good. The only home she'd ever known, at least consciously. At two months old, she had been adopted by Maud and Steve. They had flown into Phoenix, Arizona, picked her up from a foster family, and brought her home to Wind River, Wyoming. She'd found out from Maud after driving to the family ranch, that her older sister, Andy, was going to the café for dinner. That she and her new boss, Dev Mitchell, had been out on the ranch earlier, digging out rotted posts from lease pastures. The air had a rich scent of newly sprouted grass, and she inhaled it deeply. She was home.

That word meant so much to her, body and soul. At twenty-eight years old, she had come to appreciate it so much more than ever before. She couldn't explain why. But it didn't matter to her as she threw her purse with its long strap across her shoulder. It was 1700, five p.m. civilian time, and the wooden sidewalk was crowded with tourists

who were stopping to eat at the busy, popular café. Hoping
that Andy was in there already, she quickly smoothed the
wrinkles out of her light tan slacks, pulled the white collar
of her three-quarter-sleeve cotton blouse into alignment
once more, and hurried through the ambling people toward
the café.

She hadn't seen Andy in over two years because of her
duties with the Montana aeronautical company that rented
out the air tankers she flew to put out fires all across North
America. Lately, even in the winter, places like Arizona
and California had huge fires because of prolonged
drought conditions and climate change. Normally, she took
the winter off and came home, taking over her old bedroom
at the main ranch house, slumming and relaxing. She
turned into a wrangler for three months out of the year,
despite the snow and winter conditions. There was lots to
do in the barns and buildings, from repair of structures,
saddles and bridles to cleaning out box stalls. All part of
the job she loved. Even now, the fragrant scent of alfalfa
hay up on the second floor of the red barn was like heaven
to her. She might be a Latina by blood and the brown color
of her skin, but in her heart, she was a Wyoming cowgirl
and one helluva pilot on the front lines of wildfires.

Oh, how she missed seeing her older sister! They were
so tight growing up. Nervously, she pulled at the long,
black ponytail that fell between her shoulder blades, brushing at her temples for flyaway hair and hoping she looked
presentable. Taking one more look before she went in, she
thought her light brown flats went well with her slacks.
She'd always dressed down, like her mother. Sky had never
been a frilly, feminine female. It just wasn't her.

Gulping in a deep breath of air, she went to the door and
stepped into the diner. It was early for dinner, so there were
empty booths. Instantly, her gaze went to the one nearest

the kitchen. It had walls on two sides and it was near an exit, the kitchen itself, and away from all windows. A grin tugged at her lips. There was Andy! And OMG! The guy across the table from her was a hunk. Lucky her! A boss with those rugged good looks was like a storybook hero coming to life. Her grin widened into a smile as they caught sight of each other.

"Sky!" Andy's voice was a shriek of joy. She slid out of the booth, arms open, walking swiftly toward her.

A warmth filled Sky's heart as her sister, who was two inches taller than she was, grabbed her and hugged the hell out of her.

"Oh!" Andy whispered fiercely, holding her tight, "it's so good to see you, Sky!"

Kissing her sister's cheek, Sky stepped out of the mutual embrace, looking up into Andy's wide gray eyes, filled with utter happiness. She gripped her hand and squeezed it before releasing it. "Mom told me you'd be here with your new boss. I just got in and was dying to see you."

Andy's face crumpled with so many emotions. "Two years, Sky. It's been two years since we last saw each other. I've missed you so much!" and she hugged her fiercely again.

Laughing, Sky's heart burst open with the love she'd always had for her adopted sister. Andy was easy to like and to love, unlike herself. She'd been locked up emotionally and still was to a large extent because she feared life in general. Her birth mother, whoever she was, had abandoned her on the steps of a Catholic church with a note, begging the local priest to take care of her, that she couldn't. She asked forgiveness and asked that Sky be given to a loving family where she would have the opportunities she could never give her. And the last sentences of the note, which were burned into her soul were: *"Take care of my beautiful* niña. *I will always love her with all my heart. I want only good things for her. I can only give her pain and bad memories. I am a bad person. My daughter deserves so much more than that. Thank you, Father, for taking in and protecting my* niña. *Bless you."*

It was signed Maria L. A name Sky had often tried to chase down in her efforts to locate her birth mother. Why had her mother left her that clue, that her last name started with an "L"? Did she want her to find her? How often had she dreamed of just that? Sky had lost count over the years, that same, recurring dream haunting her life, always in the background but there. Tearing away from the past that hovered around her like a thick, heavy coat, she smiled at Andy.

"You look wonderful! How are you feeling, Andy?"

"Oh, I'm fine, fine, Sky. And you? Mom said you've been busy in all four seasons, which was why you haven't been home in the winter for the last two years."

Sky slid her arm around Andy's waist as they walked toward the booth. "Wildfires, because of climate change, occur in all four seasons, not just three. I've missed coming home, too."

"How long can you stay?"

"I managed a month off. I'll be staying at our home, helping out and doing some wrangling. I really miss throwing a leg over a good horse and riding fence line." She gave Andy an evil smile, seeing her sister nod and then laugh with her.

"Hey," Andy said, pointing at her legs, "I feel like a dude. One day of fence repair and Dev and I are walking bowlegged!"

"He's easy on the eyes, Andy. Lucky you. He's your boss, right?"

"Yes. He's as nice as he looks, Sky. Come on, let me introduce him to you."

Sky saw the man slide out of the booth and stand. It was the Old West at its best. She liked that cowboys held some respect for women, standing when they were introduced, opening doors, tipping their hats in respect. All good in her book.

"Dev, this is my sister, Sky Whitcomb. She's a year younger than me. Sky, meet Dev Mitchell."

"Nice to meet you, Sky," he said, holding out his hand to her.

Sky shook his large, warm hand. "Nice to meet you, Mr. Mitchell."

"Call me Dev, will you?"

Andy tugged at her hand, motioning for her to slide into the booth on the side she was sitting on. Her sister slid in, too, giving her a happy look. This was easy, Sky thought, giving her plenty of room so Andy could sit exactly opposite Dev. She saw something in his eyes, sensing he really liked her sister. Neither of them were any good at relationships, and Sky often wondered if it was because they had been abandoned. Trust was hard to come by in their world; she'd seen it play out over and over again in all four of them. She'd often discussed it with her sister when they were in the military and managed to get thirty days' leave to come home and be together with their parents.

A waitress came over, giving Sky a glass of water and a menu.

"Have you guys ordered yet?" she asked them.

"Yes," Andy said.

"We're having hamburgers and fries," Dev offered.

Sky nodded, handing the menu back to the waitress. "I'll have the same, but I'd like a large, thick chocolate milkshake, please?"

The waitress smiled and wrote it down. "You got it. Any coffee?"

"Oh, definitely," Sky murmured.

"She likes cream and sugar," Andy volunteered, pulling over a container filled with different types of sugar packets. At Kassie's, they always brought over a fresh pitcher of milk or cream to each table, but this one was empty.

"I'll make it happen," the waitress promised, tucking the menu beneath her arm and leaving.

Happily, Andy turned toward her. "So, you can stay here a whole month?"

"Yep. I got my boss to give me the time off because last year I was due two weeks of vacay, but he needed me and the other wildfire pilots to move on to Southern California."

"This is so wonderful!" Andy whispered, suddenly emotional. She turned her gaze to Dev. "Sky and I are thick as thieves. We've loved each other since I can remember."

"That's good," Dev said. "I can tell you two spell trouble with a capital 'T.'"

Both of them giggled and nodded.

"You're pretty astute, Dev," Sky congratulated him.

"I'd like to think good managers develop an awareness of their employees."

Snorting, Sky muttered, "That's all well and good, but it isn't always the case. When I got out of the Army, I went through two wildfire companies, trying to find just that."

Groaning, Andy said, "She went through two really bad bosses. The first was a womanizer and the second one told her if she didn't sleep with him, she'd never get a raise."

Dev's mouth tightened and he met and held Sky's gaze. "It's a story that happens too often to women."

"Not any more, not after #metoo and #timesup," she parried.

"A long time coming," Dev agreed. "Far too long."

Giving him a one-eyebrow raised look, Sky said wryly, "What? Are you the figment of women's imagination? The twenty-first-century man? The dude who respects women?"

Andy cut her a pleading glance.

"Okay, okay," Sky muttered, "I'm sorry, Dev."

"No, don't be. I've seen my mother taken advantage of by men. I've seen what it's done to her, so no need for apologies."

Andy patted her forearm. "Don't go off on him, Sky. You can't put Dev in the same box that Neanderthal-trained men live in."

"So?" Sky challenged, "What happened to you?" and she drilled a hard look into Dev's gaze.

"I was raised by a set of parents who respected each other," he offered. "My dad always treated my mother like an equal, because she was just as smart and usually smarter than he was. I grew up in that household believing women were human beings."

A grudging corner of her mouth lifted. "I like what I'm hearing. We need billions of parents to teach their children just like you were. Women are sick and tired of being seen as something to be used and not respected."

"Hey," Andy begged her, "can we table this, Sky? Dev is one of us. Not them."

Her nostrils flared. "I'm sick to death of them."

Andy laughed and looked at Dev. "Which probably explains why the two of us never married, never wanted to get into relationships. All the men we run into are Neanderthals."

"I don't blame you," Dev said, remaining serious. "If you don't have equality, the relationship is one-sided, not fair."

Sky sat back, a sudden grin blossoming across her mouth. She slanted a gaze at her sister. "Is there a clone of him somewhere? Maybe we can make a 3D out of him?"

She saw pink touch Andy's cheeks and realized there was something between those two. Not meaning to make her uncomfortable, Sky said, "Just teasing, sis."

"I wish I could clone Dev," Andy admitted.

The waitress brought Sky's coffee and a pitcher of cream. Sky thanked her.

"So, Dev Mitchell, I understand from Mom that you were working at becoming a wrangler out there riding fence today. How did you like it?"

Dev's mouth twitched. "Let's just say it feels good to sit still for a while."

Laughing, Sky gave them an amused look. "Well, for the next month I'm going to go through the pain of getting my horse legs back, just like you're doing."

"Sky used to come home for five months out of every year, starting in November through April, and stay at the family ranch. She's a wrangler like I am."

"You traded in your pilot hat for a cowgirl's hat?" Dev teased Sky.

"Yep, and after piloting in bumpy-as-hell water tankers, getting my teeth jarred out of my head, dealing with up-drafts and downdrafts large enough to throw my plane into a nosedive flat spin or ripping a wing off the fuselage, I was more than ready to do hands-on work. At least moving hay bales, and cleaning and repairing leather, won't do that to you. Feet on the ground. I always loved coming home for those months, but the last two years I haven't been able to do it."

"And before that? Andy said you were in the military. What branch?" Dev asked, sipping his coffee.

After stirring in cream to her coffee, Sky took a quick sip and said, "The Army. I flew Apache combat helos over in Afghanistan." She saw admiration and respect instantly come to his face. "How about you? Were you in the military, too?"

"I was in the Army, like you. Went in as an officer, took flight training and ended up with Black Hawk helicopters. Later, I flew MH-60L DAPs (Defensive Armed Penetrators) and then was invited to fly with the Night Stalkers."

"Oh, you flew those hot and lethal DAPs. You're a black ops pilot."

He nodded. "Yeah, that's what I did. Now? I like flying medevac. That's enough excitement for me today."

"Andy was a combat Warthog pilot. And you're the guy who helped rescue her?"

"Well," Dev hedged, "we saved one another. Both our craft crashed."

Andy became serious and told her, "He did most of the saving."

Sky saw their food coming. "Hey, chow's here. Tell me about how you two met here in Wind River while we eat, okay?"

"Sure," she said.

"It wasn't exactly boy meets girl," Dev teased, giving Andy a smile.

Sky didn't miss the look that passed between them, now convinced that Andy wasn't "just an employee" and he wasn't "just her boss." Nope. She sensed a positive and yearning energy between them, and that made her feel good. "I'm all ears, Andy. Tell me."

"Are you sure you won't join us over at the condo hot tub?" Andy pleaded with Sky as they emerged from Kassie's Café an hour later. The sun was heading toward the west, the heat of the day over.

"Nah," she said. "I'm really tired and I want to get a good

night's sleep. Mom needs help with all the airport celebration details and I told her I'd be her gofer until this shindig kicks off on the Fourth of July."

"I've got forty-eight hours on and off duty," Andy explained as they walked toward the parking lot in back of Kassie's. "On my days off, I'll be helping, too."

"Good," Sky murmured, walking with them across the gravel between the buildings.

"And Dev, plus some of the other employees, are going to be getting their stuff ready for the celebration. He gave me the time off to help Mom and her team."

Giving Dev a pleased look, she could see why Andy liked him. Not wanting to further embarrass her sister, she decided to hold her questions until they were alone. Just how far were they in to their relationship? Andy was smart enough not to have an office romance. She knew better. But then, Dev Mitchell wasn't the average guy either. Throughout their meal, she was pleased with his sensitivity and ability to read people, as well as to ask good, insightful questions of each of them. Sure that Dev knew all of Maud and Steve's children were adopted, Sky didn't want to bring it up at the table. Did Dev know Andy was adopted? Unsure, Sky wasn't going to cause a stir between them by asking questions. She knew when to keep her mouth shut. That, and she realized timing was everything.

"This hot tub is doing wonders for my sore backside," Andy groaned to Dev. They were in the spa room, which was empty at this time of day. There was a large swimming pool that took up most of the room, the hot tub off to one side in the corner of the facility. She sat across from him, the warm water up to her shoulders, bubbling and working its miracle of easing her tight leg muscles. She tried not to

stare at Dev, who wore a pair of black trunks that fell
halfway down his thick, curved and hairy thighs. The man
was in very good shape. Drooling inwardly, she tried to
pretend not to be attracted to him. The carpet of dark chest
hair only emphasized his masculinity. The five o'clock
shadow on his face gave him a look of someone not to
tangle with in a gun or knife fight. From her perspective,
though, it only made him look like a risk worth taking.

She cautioned herself that the biggest hurdle was that he
was her boss. And she wanted this job more than anything
else. Being home, making a quieter life for herself, was her
number-one priority. That, and being with her family. Still,
the way a lock of brown hair glinting with strands of red
beneath the lights made her want to go over and use her
fingers to gently move them off his brow. Andy knew that
was a nonverbal signal of the strongest kind, letting Dev
know in no uncertain terms that she wanted more, much
more from him.

"It feels so damned good," he muttered, closing his
eyes, sinking his naked back against the smooth blue tiles
in the tub. "I think I'll sleep in here tonight."

Laughing, Andy understood. "You were in the saddle off
and on for seven hours today. That's a lot to ask of your legs
when they aren't used to being wrapped around a horse."

He pried one eye open, a loose grin coming to his mouth.
"I was thinking that very same thing. Are you a mind
reader, too?"

"Naw," she said, "I'm experiencing the same thing. I
lost my riding legs when I left home at eighteen."

"How long?"

"How long, what?"

He pointed to his legs sprawled out in front of him.
"Until I get riding legs?"

"Oh," she said, shrugging. "Depends upon whether you

want to learn how to be a wrangler. Wrangling is hard, physical work, with brawn mixed into it."

"And," he said, studying the redwood rafters of the ceiling, "all my romantic ideas that cowboys were an iconic symbol of the wild, untamed West and such."

"I'm curious. Did you have an interest in being one when you were a kid?" She liked the amusement glimmering in his green eyes. Truly, he was Irish. The way his sculpted lips shaped into that teasing grin made her yearn for him even more.

"Yeah, growing up I wanted books on cowboys, on Kitty Hawk and the Wright Brothers and stories about flying in general. I remember when I was seven telling my mom one day that I knew I'd be a cowboy when I grew up."

Brows raising, Andy sat up. "Really?"

"It almost makes me look clairvoyant about my future, doesn't it?" He gave her a wry look. "Now don't be too impressed, okay? The Irish are well known to have the sight, the ability to see, hear or know things before they happen."

"Wow."

He held up his hand. "My mother really does have the sight."

"So maybe you inherited it from her?"

Giving her a mirthless grin, he said, "My grandmother Betha was an astrologer, and everyone in Barna, and the rich folks from Galway, came to her for readings. She was rarely wrong and was a very well-known, loved and revered woman. Everyone said she was half fairy because so many of our tales are about the magical fairies of Ireland."

"I love myths, legends and stories. Growing up, I read every Harry Potter book I could get my hands on. And another children's author, Darcy Deming, who wrote a fabulous Native American series about a set of twins, Sage Stone and his sister, Rachel, just inspired me so much. To this day, some of the books I read as a young girl and teen influenced me far more than I realized. And look at you! You read cowboy books!"

"My dad is a huge fan of William W. Johnstone. He's a prolific writer, nearly a hundred books so far. For his birthday, every year, I'd go to his publisher's website and order the latest books he's written and send them to him. And he saves them in a special bookcase, and when I'd come home, I'd read them and we'd have some great discussions about the West."

"Imagine, your dad loved cowboy books," Andy said, giving him an awed look. "I don't suppose they have anything in Ireland that's an equivalent to a cowboy?"

Laughing, he said, "No, not even close."

"So, you got your cowboy leanings through your dad and his love of cowboy books. That was a great influence. Have you told him yet that you're studying to become a wrangler?"

"Not yet," he deadpanned. "I wanted to see if I could survive today."

The laughter between them floated throughout the empty facility.

"Well, since you have, Dev, are you going to share with him your little secret?" she teased him. Andy had never seen him as relaxed as right now. It served to tell her that when his face was unreadable, he was tense and focused on something. Right now? He smiled often, the glint in his evergreen-colored eyes truly reminding her of him being a genuine Irishman. As if there wasn't enough to like about him, she realized the tension he carried on his shoulders was gone, too. Feeling that he was like a delicious box of chocolates she could never have, it tempered her need to dig more deeply into his fascinating Irish background. Surely he had a woman in his life? He had to have! This man was so many cuts above the usual men out there that it left her wanting him all over again. Dev was a one-of-a-kind type of man. Her type.

Panning the bubbling water in front of him with his large hand, he said, "I try to call them on the weekends. When I get back to my condo, I intend to chat with them."

"I wish I could eavesdrop," she said.

"When we can get together again, I'll fill you in."

"I imagine your dad will be surprised and excited."

"He'll blame it on the Johnstone books I've read over the years."

"I wonder if writers know how much influence they wield on us."

"Good question. My dad has always wanted to write."

"Well, aren't the Irish storytellers?"

"We do have a gene for storytelling, that's true."

"Have you ever wanted to write?" she wondered.

"Not really, but I do like reading books. It's downtime for me. It destresses me. Are you an avid reader?"

She shook her head. "No, I've always been a risk-taker, a Type A personality and restless. I had to be doing something all the time. That's how I got into wrangling at the ranch: because I was bored out of my skull. Sky was a lot like me. My two brothers were geeky. They liked playing computer games by the hour, but Mom laid down the law to them, told them one hour a day. And that was after they got their homework finished. And on weekends, like Sky and me, from age twelve onward, we learned the art of wrangling."

"Did all of you want to do it?"

"Yes. We all loved horseback riding, loved working with the men and women who were real wranglers on the ranch. Face it, Dev, when you wrangle there's something new every day. You just don't get bored."

He gave her a thoughtful look. "You and Sky are pilots. Tell me about your two brothers."

She gave him a wistful smile. "Luke will be here tomorrow but he said he might be coming in late. He's number three out of four. My father was in Boise, Idaho, on some architectural business when he found out Luke, who was two at the time, was up for adoption. Our mother wanted four kids, and Luke seemed like a good fit. She'd dreamed of having two girls and two boys."

"And what kind of work is he in? Married? Kids of his own?"

"Luke is like me: a risk-taker, easily bored and a Type A. We were really close growing up because he was just as bold as I was about taking challenges. It drove my poor mother crazy. He did two years at the community college in Boise, and then became a Hotshot. When it was spring and summer in the Northern Hemisphere, he would be working wildfires in Canada and here in the US. In our wintertime, he was hired by the Australian government and spent six months fighting wildfires in the Southern Hemisphere."

"He must be really good, then."

"Luke is twenty-eight and respected in the firefighting world. He's single still because he doesn't want to get tied down. He likes traveling and he usually drops in for about a month every March and stays here at the ranch, catching up with Mom and Dad, plus doing indoor wrangling duties with the employees."

"No moss grows under his feet," Dev agreed. "I'd almost say he had Irish blood in him, because we're a wandering genotype."

Growing sad, Andy said, "Well, like me, we're all adopted. And I know it bothers him and my other brother, Gabe, like it does all of us, wondering who our birth parents were and why they abandoned us."

He became serious. "I was thinking about that."

"There's a year's difference between each of us. Gabe is the youngest, twenty-six this year. He, like Sky, has Hispanic blood. He doesn't know what country he comes from either. Gabe and Sky were always close, I think, in part, because they shared that background."

She wrinkled her nose. "My dad was in San Diego on a job when he checked in with a local adoption agency, and Gabe was three years old. He'd been given back to the agency because of emotional issues. My dad saw him, took photos of him, sent them to my mom, who said he would be number four."

"Did either of them worry about his behavior issues?" Dev wondered.

"Gabe had anger issues. When my dad looked into the foster family he was with, he felt it just wasn't a good fit for Gabe. He was restless, bored, wanting to be outdoors all the time, and the family he lived with wasn't outdoorsy at all. Plus, they were older, in their forties, so there was a huge generation gap."

"As you get older, you get more fixed," Dev agreed. "Did Gabe's anger simmer down, then?"

"It took about two years," Andy recalled. "Sky had a huge influence over him. She became his sounding board, which was really positive. And once he learned he could trust Mom and Dad, he settled down. But it was a rocky start for him, for all of us. He had terrible rages, almost uncontrollable when they hit. I remember my parents sitting the three of us down, explaining why Gabe was raging. It's not uncommon for anyone who is thrown away by their parents to be angry. Gabe held a grudge. He hated his parents for deep-sixing him."

"Did Gabe ever find them?"

"Not yet. But he's in DEA, and they're privy to a lot of information because they are in federal law enforcement. If he's that interested in finding them, he probably could."

"If," Dev stressed gently, "he really wants to find them."

Her mouth twisted, "Yes, but growing up with him, all we heard was his hatred for what they'd done to him: thrown him away. When you meet him, I'll bet you'll feel that tightly held rage he buries deep inside him."

"Did he ever take it out on any of you?"

"No," she said firmly, shaking her head. "He felt we'd been thrown away, too, so he treated us with nothing but kindness, patience and was always there to support us. We supported Gabe, too. Sky, Luke and I wanted so much to help him get rid of that rage. But he never did. He just buried it."

"Did he get angry with Steve and Maud?"

"Not usually. Gabe was headstrong, but they never were hard or dictatorial with him. My dad would often go for walks with him, find out how his day at school went, and if something upset him, he'd spill it to him."

"Sounds like Steve was a good father to him, then."

"They're wonderful people." She sighed. "I'm so hoping that someday Gabe will see how lucky all of us were to be adopted by them. Each of us had a hole in our hearts from being given away. I can't speak for anyone but myself, but my parents healed me with their incredible love and acceptance. They were teachers as much as they were parents. And I've often heard them say that we four are the best things that ever happened to them. My dad is a world-renowned architect. My mother comes from one of the richest families in the world. And yet, we kids knew they loved us with all they had to give. My dad never missed anything important in school for any of us. My mother was very active in parent-teacher meetings. And they were always working with the people of the county to make Lincoln a place where everyone could get a good-paying job."

"They're overachievers," he agreed, "in the best of ways. They give you love, they support you and they've taught you morals, values and integrity. Not all kids get those things. I'm lucky in that I got those same, basic teachings and support."

Giving him a happy smile, she said, "Maybe that's why we work like the good team we are, because we have terrific parents and were given lots of love." She held up her hands, palms out toward him. "Look, my fingers have turned into wrinkled prunes. I think it's time to get out."

He sat up, running his long fingers through his military-short hair. "Better get out now or I'll start calling you Ms. Prune."

Giggling, she stood and pulled the bottom of her black bathing suit downward. "At least it isn't Ms. Prude."

Standing, he laughed. "Big difference in words, eh? Prude and prune."

She took the five steps, picking up her thick yellow towel off a nearby lounge chair. "Well, don't you dare call me 'prune' in front of anyone."

"I promise I won't," he said, following her out and reaching for his dark blue towel.

She pulled the towel across her shoulders.

"Because?" she teased.

"DAP pilots are the arsenal in the sky for black ops missions, including the use of Hellfire missiles." He gave her a studied look. "I rarely missed what I aimed at and I can keep secrets."

"Good to know," she murmured. "I trust you, and I know you're good for your word. Thank you."

"I'll always have your back," he said, rubbing the towel across his gleaming shoulders, "Like you, I'm glad to be settling for a quiet backwater in my life now."

"What? Thinking of settling down?" There was joking in her tone.

"Oh, possibly," he admitted, leaning down and wiping the beads of water from his long, powerful legs. "Maybe a do-over. Maybe life is going to give me a second chance. I just don't know yet . . ."

Chapter Ten

"Excuse me, I'm looking for Andy Whitcomb."

Dev looked up from his messy desk covered with paperwork. A stranger, someone he didn't know, stood in the doorway, dressed as a wrangler. He wore a black Stetson on his military-short black hair. He appeared to be Hispanic, his skin a golden tone. Dev creatively tagged the stranger as a predatory wolf on the prowl for his next meal. He often compared humans to the animal world.

"Andy's out on a flight right now," he replied, not knowing who the man was or what business he had with her. The feeling of tension within the stranger, although not obvious, hit his senses. The cowboy might appear relaxed, but he wasn't. Guessing he was probably in his midtwenties, the man was dressed presentably in a blue-and-white cowboy shirt, the sleeves rolled up to just below his elbows, a clean pair of Levi's and scuffed-looking boots, indicating he wasn't some dude playing a part. "And you are?"

"Gabe Whitcomb. I'm her baby brother." He managed a twist of his lips, this a family joke he was sharing with Dev as he leaned his shoulder against the doorjamb. "I just flew in a few hours ago, traded in my wardrobe for cowboy gear while I'm home visiting our folks."

Dev instantly relaxed. Andy had mentioned Gabe as being a DEA agent. Well, that sure as hell fit. If he hadn't come from a black ops background himself, he probably wouldn't have picked up on Gabe for who he really was. Standing, he came around the desk, offering Gabe his hand. "I'm Dev Mitchell. Andy mentioned good things about you, and she was excited that you were going to be here for the opening of our airport. Welcome home."

Gabe came out of his slouched position, giving his hand to shake Dev's firmly. "Good to know you. Every time my sister mentioned you, she got breathless. That isn't like her." He released Dev's hand, giving him a thorough once-over.

Chuckling, Dev said, "We share a common experience from years back."

"Yeah, I remember the incident, the crash. Thanks for saving her life over in Afghanistan. I was undercover at the time and knew nothing about it. My dad put in an emergency call to the DEA to reach me about it, but I was out of the country and unavailable. I learned about it a month later."

"That's hardcore work," Dev said, admiring the man. "And damned dangerous. Andy is due to return in about an hour. If you're not doing anything else, would you like to join me at Kassie's Café and jaw a little? Interested?"

"Yes," Gabe said, "I'm very interested. When Andy survived that crash, she left the Air Force."

"It was a pretty harrowing time for her."

"For both of you," he said, giving him a look of respect. "Let's talk over coffee at Kassie's."

Dev nodded. He grabbed his black baseball cap and

settled it on his head. "Let me tell Pete, my boss, where I'll be and then we'll go over."

Gabe nodded, removing himself from the doorway. "Sounds good."

Sensing Gabe was putting himself out a lot more than he would with a stranger like himself, Dev knew undercover work was a hundred times more stressful than any other job he could name. Dipping his head into Pete's office door, which was always open, he told him where he'd be and for how long.

"How about," Pete said, "I tell Andy where you two are when she gets in? I know she said her brothers were coming in on the second and third of July. I'm sure she'd like to see Gabe."

"Good idea," Dev said. "Let her know."

"Roger that," Pete said, lifting his hand and waving goodbye.

Gabe was glad to see Dev Mitchell chose a booth toward the rear of the diner, where he could have his back to the wall, away from the windows and near an exit through the kitchen if things went south. As they sat down, a waitress came over with water and menus. Dev told her that someone else would be joining them in about an hour.

Kassie's was just getting done with the lunch crowd. Gabe knew all the locals and didn't see any. The town was overwhelmed with people coming in for the regional airport celebration and opening. Not that Wind River had that many hotels. He'd heard from his mother that 90 percent of the bigwigs coming had already gone fifty miles north to Jackson Hole, taking up residence in the five-star hotels with which they were accustomed.

Gabe liked the laid-back quality of Mitchell, and his sincere friendliness. There had been a distinct change in his attitude when he learned Gabe's identity. Dev protected Andy almost fiercely, with that low growl of his, a warning buried in it to any stranger. Andy had more or less admitted she liked her boss a lot more than she should. Now Gabe saw why. The man was ruggedly handsome, in top athletic shape like himself. Dev Mitchell missed nothing.

Taking off his hat, he hung it on a nearby wall peg, pushed his fingers through his short hair and sat back, forcing himself to at least look relaxed, even if he wasn't. He'd been undercover with a major drug ring in Tijuana for a year, working his way into the organization and taking the names of the soldiers and the cartel bosses, identifying them, getting photos and sending them back to the San Diego DEA office. If he was ever caught, they'd kill him after days or weeks of torture. No, he wasn't able to relax hardly at all.

The waitress returned with mugs of steaming coffee.

"This is on me," Dev said. "Have you had lunch?"

"No, not yet. I just flew in, rented a car at the Jackson Hole airport and drove to the ranch, said hello to my parents, changed clothes and went to see Andy."

"Go ahead and order," Dev urged.

Gabe chose a hamburger and French fries. The waitress took the order and left.

Warming to the man whose face was unreadable, but with a voice filled with emotion, Dev said, "Andy will be happy to see you. Did you know Sky was here, too?"

"Yes," he said, pulling the thick white ceramic mug toward himself. "I saw her at the ranch. She and my parents were having lunch when I walked in on them unannounced." Shrugging he added, "I should have texted them, but I'm so used to not having electronics on me, I figured I'd surprise them instead."

Grinning, Dev murmured, "I'm sure you did, but it was a good kind of surprise. The best kind." He took a sip of his coffee.

"In my business? I don't like surprises at all."

Chuckling, Dev nodded. "For damned sure. How long can you stay? Andy was hoping you could hang with the family for a month."

"The only reason I'm here is because I'm being sent somewhere else in the drug ring food chain," Gabe said. "I have five days, is all. I know Andy and Sky are going to be unhappy, not to mention my parents, but it's the most I can give them."

"I wouldn't like undercover work."

"Andy told me you were a Night Stalker, a DAP pilot, over in the Sandbox."

"Yes."

"That's undercover work, too. Just a different kind."

Dev leaned back, liking Gabe a lot. He knew the man was revealing far more than he ever would to a stranger. "That's true, it is. But I didn't have to change my persona, my name, and pretend to be someone I wasn't," he pointed out.

Gabe raised his brow momentarily and then nodded. "Yeah, takes a special kind of chameleon to pull that off," he said, derision in his tone.

Understanding that Gabe trusted him because he came from the world of the military and black ops, he asked, "Normally? I don't think you're this loose with details about your undercover life. Did Andy say something to you about my background?"

He saw Gabe's mouth pull in a wry position. "My sister told me a lot about you."

Stunned momentarily, Dev managed, "Oh . . ." He saw amusement dancing in Gabe's eyes, but he didn't supply anything further. "The fact we're both military, worked in the black ops world? That creates a bond of trust, for sure."

Nodding, Gabe assessed him for a moment. "Do you like Andy?"

Dev was surprised by the question but regarded him levelly. "Very much."

His fingers relaxed around the mug. "Good to know. Andy, as well as the other three of us, has never trusted anyone easily because of our background. That has nothing to do with the love Maud and Steve gave all of us. That was real and it was binding. But with anyone other than them? We don't trust nearly as easily as kids who weren't jettisoned out into the world, not knowing where they were going to land. Trust has to be earned."

Hearing the bitterness in Gabe's tone, the censure in his look, Dev offered, "Our trust was forged in a life-and-death, five-day run to escape the Taliban after the crashes. That's our connection. We never got personal with each other out there because we were being hunted down like animals."

"Did you know that when Andy returned home to us, her biggest regret was never seeing you after you got air-lifted back to Bagram? She wanted to thank you for saving her skin. And then, when she couldn't locate you, it was really hard on her. She desperately wanted to find you, and at that time, she felt there was something more between you that she never got to follow up on. That's why I asked if you liked her. There was something in her voice that tipped me off that there was more to this than gratitude for saving her hide." He managed a wry, one-cornered smile.

Uncomfortably, Dev moved around. He didn't know the family that well, or the dynamic among them, except for what Andy had shared with him, plus one dinner with her parents. "From my perspective, it's because of our escape from the crash sites."

"That's true. When you survive an event in which you think you might die, two things happen. First, you're surprised you made it out against overwhelming odds. Second, the realization that you were part of the reason you're alive becomes very important."

"No question about that," Dev agreed, somber. "I was the one with the Boy Scout and nature ability, knew about tracking, had a compass and all that. Andy brought in a lot of details I overlooked."

"And it's the details that will get you killed or get you out alive. Every time."

Dev began to understand the strain Gabe was under. He wasn't sure the man's family knew about his stress, and sensing he was highly protective of those he loved, he'd probably kept all his secrets from them. Parents tended to worry about their children, so he was sure Maud and Steve worried about all their kids, all the time. All four children had gone into high-risk careers. "You're right about that."

"Andy being a Warthog pilot, working twenty to a hundred feet above the enemy, just her in that cockpit, was always in danger of being shot down. Even though our parents weren't in the military, they understood clearly that Andy was a prime target of the enemy."

"And finally, one night, she did get shot down."

"Did you see it happen?" Gabe wondered, eyes narrowing a bit.

"Yes. I'd just left my crashed helo when I saw her eject. I was wearing my NVGs and saw it happen. At the time, I didn't know she was a female. I automatically assumed it was a male bailing out."

A sour smile crossed Gabe's mouth. "Bet you were surprised when you found out otherwise."

Laughing, Dev said, "Yes, I was."

"You seem like someone who protects people who aren't capable of doing it for themselves."

Dev knew undercover agents were peerless in evaluating other human beings. They had to be because their lives depended upon that skill. "I am." And then he grimaced. "With #metoo, men are having to reevaluate how they interact with women, how they see them. But four years ago, I was having knee-jerk reactions to Andy having been a combat pilot, surviving an ejection, and I was on the ground in the dead of night realizing all that. That was another shock. She's always been a survivor, but she showed it in spades."

Gabe looked up and saw the waitress coming with his food. He moved his coffee mug aside and nodded thanks in her direction as she set the platter down in front of him. She refilled their cups and left. Pouring ketchup on those fries, he said in jest, "Bet you'd never met a woman like Andy before."

"In some ways," Dev said, "you're right. But in others, over those five days, I saw a lot of my Irish mother in Andy. She was strong, confident, resilient, a leader."

"Bingo," Gabe said, biting with relish into the half-pound hamburger.

Dev saw the pleasure come to Gabe's face as he slowly chewed the burger that had lettuce, tomato, onions and crispy bacon with cheddar cheese melted between the buns. "I guess where you're at, there's not a hamburger stand nearby."

Wiping his mouth with a napkin, Gabe shot him a sardonic look. Setting the napkin aside, he said, "I was in Guatemala. It's nothing but a green hell filled with poisonous insects, snakes and drug soldiers. If bullets don't end your life, there's always that deadly centipede crawling around on the floor of the jungle, or a Fer-de-Lance pit viper who'd like to finish you off with their venom. And where I was, getting antivenom was impossible. I'd die from the bite. We call this viper *terciopelo*, which means velvet in Spanish."

"Why velvet?"

"Because once those one-inch fangs sink through the leather of your boot and inject their poison into your foot, it's all over. Most people die within hours of being bit. The venom is so powerful and you don't realize it until it's too late. It's like drinking whiskey: goes down smooth and velvety in your mouth but burns a hole in your belly at the other end. We lost at least a dozen drug soldiers where I was in Guatemala to that viper."

"And I'm sure what you're telling me isn't something your family knows about."

Giving him a mirthful look, Gabe muttered, "No way in hell. My family worries more about me than they do themselves."

"They know you're undercover?"

"Yes, but that's all. They don't know I've been in Tijuana for a while."

Frowning, Dev said in a soft voice, "We were briefed by Sheriff Sarah Carter and the FBI that there's a new drug ring moving into our area in the southern part of our valley."

"Yeah, the cartel I'm working undercover with."

Swallowing his surprise, Dev couldn't help but stare at him. "And you know this?"

"Yes," he said abruptly, picking up a fry slathered with ketchup. "I've worked my way up to what I term middle management in the cartel. I was sent into Tijuana to head up a small ring that's forming. My job is to link with the drug soldiers on the American side of the border."

Shaking his head, Dev said, "Your family would go nuts if they knew that."

"I'm telling you for a reason," he said, locking onto Dev's gaze. "Andy has never spoken about a man the way she speaks about you. I think she likes you more than a little. And that's new for her; she's never allowed herself to get close to anyone." He grimaced. "Being abandoned puts a hole in your heart that will never be healed. She doesn't allow herself, nor does Sky, to get to really trust a man, let a relationship not only blossom but deepen. They keep everyone at arm's length." He hesitated. "I'm very protective of Andy and Sky. I grew up with them. I watched them struggle with the fact that they were thrown away like milk cartons, that they meant nothing to the women who birthed them. Living is damned painful down here on this planet of ours. I can't tell you how many times Andy would start to trust a boy in high school, and then he'd try to take advantage of her, breaking what little trust she'd given him." He flexed his fist. "I got into a number of confrontations with the so-called boyfriends of my two sisters. They're both very attractive, and they had gaggles of boys following them around, wanting to take something from them but never giving anything to them in return. That's what they learned the hard way, over and over again."

"Reinforcing the same pattern of being thrown away, or at least, by those boys not seeing them as human beings. Just something to be used."

Gabe stared hard at Dev. "You get it."

"Andy's said I'm the first twenty-first-century man she's ever met. She told me she hoped there was one out there, despite the billions of Neanderthal males around."

Giving a dry laugh, Gabe said, "That's my sister Andy all right. She doesn't suffer fools gladly, especially not any guy whose approach is just about sex. She nails them."

"I sensed that, but on our run to save our hides, there

wasn't time to explore the personal side of ourselves with each other."

"Well, you have time now. Are you married?"

"No." Dev gave him an amused look. "But I have a feeling you're going to check me out very thoroughly in the DEA office, and run a background check on me."

"Roger that," he said, taking another big bite of his hamburger.

Dev sat back, smiling to himself, liking Gabe a helluva lot. While Andy could handle herself with any man now, it was okay that her younger brother was protective of her. And he had a hunch that if he were home, like the rest of the grown children wanted to be, Gabe would certainly be checking out any male who showed an active interest in her. But he was out in the field, undercover and in a dangerous cat-and-mouse game where his life was on the line every day without fail.

"Gabe!"

Andy's call floated across Kassie's Café as she practically ran across the long room toward her youngest brother. When Pete had told her, as she dismounted the Black Hawk, that Gabe had just dropped by forty-five minutes earlier, Andy practically ran to her car to drive over here. She was in her one-piece, dark-blue flight suit and flight boots and didn't care. She saw Gabe's handsome, brooding features light up. He rarely smiled, but as he scooted out of the booth and turned in her direction, he had the biggest, most loving smile on his face for her alone. Her heart burst wide open. It had been two years since she'd last seen him. Of all the children, his life wasn't his own. Working for the DEA, he couldn't take two weeks or a month off, even though he wanted to. She'd missed him so much!

"Oh, Gabe!" and she threw herself into his open arms, drowning in the love glistening in his gray eyes. Of all the kids, he was the one who had been silent, buried deep within himself, his thoughts to himself, but despite his Scorpio demeanor, Gabe had been her and Sky's chivalrous knight in shining armor throughout high school. He'd been their big, bad guard dog. Throwing her arms around his broad shoulders, he whispered her name, choking up, crushing her against him, burying his head beside hers. Tears leaked from her eyes, but she couldn't help herself, even knowing Gabe hated to see a girl or woman cry. He had such a soft spot for babies, young children and women. The air whooshed out of her, and she felt him kissing her hair and then her wet cheek.

"Ah, *mi hermana*, my sister, don't cry, don't cry . . ."

Smothering Gabe's face with kiss after kiss, her hands bracketing his high, sharp cheekbones, Andy heard him begin to laugh. It was a light, joyful laugh, and she began to laugh with him. They stood sagging against each other, hugging, holding, kissing each other's cheeks, a Latino custom for those within a family or a best friend.

Dev stepped up and offered the white linen handkerchief he always carried in his back pocket. Gabe gave him a grateful look. Andy was sobbing and couldn't stop. He pulled his sister beneath his arm and held her close as she buried her face against his chest, her arm tight around his narrow waist. Gently, he daubed one of Andy's reddened and damp cheeks, the other pressed against his shirt, wetting it, but he didn't care. He wished this hadn't happened in a public place; several tourists were staring at them with odd, questioning looks. He urged Andy toward their booth.

"I-I'm sorry, Gabe," she whispered, sliding into the black leather booth.

"It's okay," he whispered, his voice off-key. He handed

her Dev's handkerchief. "Here . . ." he said awkwardly, sliding in after she gave him room to sit down next to her.

Taking it, Andy gave Dev a look of thanks as he moved into the booth opposite them. Pressing it to her eyes, she felt like so much jelly inside. When Gabe slid his arm around her shoulders, it was the best feeling, one of safety. Only Dev's near proximity gave her that same kind of sense of protection, of profound and sincere care. Sniffing, she blew her nose several times.

Kassie, the owner, came over. "Andy, are you okay? Is there anything I can do?"

Looking up through tear-beaded lashes, she choked out in a whisper, "I haven't seen Gabe in two years, Kassie. That's a long, long time . . ." She gave Gabe a loving look. "I've missed you so much. I've missed our talks. I could tell you anything and you were like a rock to me, Gabe."

Kassie smiled softly. "Can I get you some water, Andy? Anything?"

"Thanks, I'd love some water." She gave Kassie a fragile smile. "I'm sorry if I upset your customers or you."

She lifted her hand and shook her head. "Don't worry about it. I just wanted to make sure nothing bad had happened to you or your family. We're all in this together, you know."

Daubing the last of her tears away, Andy whispered, "Isn't that the truth?"

"Something we can all count on," Kassie agreed. "I'll send the waitress over with water."

"Thanks," Andy said. She started to give the handkerchief to Gabe.

"Not mine," he said, giving a nod toward Dev. "He gave it to me to give to you."

Andy handed it across the table. "Thanks, Dev. Sorry I broke down. Hope I didn't embarrass you tough warriors."

Dev refolded the damp fabric and leaned over, sliding it into his back pocket. "Even warriors cry," he told her.

"I like this guy of yours," Gabe teased Andy.

Feeling heat rush into her face, Andy gave her youngest brother a playful elbow in his ribs. She absorbed his love for her, his arm resting on the back of the booth, so close she could feel the heat of his skin against her. "I know you don't like tears."

"One of my faults," he agreed, apology in his tone.

"Tears are healthy," she said, giving him a firm look. "I feel better now that I cried. I haven't seen you in two years."

"I know," he answered. "It wasn't on purpose, Andy. It really wasn't. I missed you, too."

"I don't know what the hell you're doing in DEA, but their vacation time sucks. Tell your boss that, will you?"

His lips lifted and he ruffled her chestnut-colored hair, which was drawn back into a ponytail. "I'll do that."

"I'm home for good, Gabe. Why can't you be, too? Sky is looking into coming home, too."

"What about Luke?"

"Him, too," Andy said.

The waitress came over and gave her a glass of water filled with ice cubes, and Andy thanked her. She took several sips to clear her throat, feeling Gabe's gaze lovingly embracing her. He had always been her favorite. Of all of them, Gabe was the "dark one." The kid who was closed up, withdrawn and untalkative. Andy had reached out to him first by holding him, rocking him and being at his side, not wanting to leave him by himself. Now, at age twenty-nine, Andy understood that being left on the doorstep of a Catholic church in Yuma, Arizona, had hurt him the most deeply of all of them. But as a young child, she hadn't understood all the psychological wounds that being given away by their mothers would change in them forever.

Sometimes she wondered what all of them might have been like if their mothers hadn't given them up for adoption.

She lifted her chin, seeing softness in Dev's eyes, just sitting quietly, watching them and giving them time together. "How long have you been here?"

"Almost an hour," he told her. "Are you hungry, Andy?"

Wrinkling her nose, she said, "No. Hey, I got two out of the four nicest guys, aside from our father and Luke, with me."

"That's a nice compliment," Dev said. "I don't know that I've earned that accolade, but I'll take it."

"Oh, you earned it years ago," she said.

"I think fate brought you two together once more," Gabe told her, holding her watery gray gaze. "What started years ago must come full circle."

Snorting a little, Andy said as she gave Dev a wry look, "Half a circle? Don't you think just seeing Dev again is enough?"

Patting her shoulder, Gabe's mouth lifted. "Hardly, dear sister. This time, you'll have a chance to see what might have been or what might be."

Her cheeks blazed red again and she was at a loss for words.

Dev said, "Well, at least we'll have more than five days to find out, won't we, Andy?"

Grateful that he was digging her out of a place she didn't want to go yet, she said, "Yes, more than five days."

"That's how many days I can be here," Gabe told Andy. Her face crumpled and tears welled up in her eyes again. "I can't help it. I'm sorry," and he smoothed some tendrils of her hair that had become mussed when she buried her face into his chest. "Five is better than nothing, right?"

Trying to be strong for him, she whispered unsteadily, "If it's five days, Gabe, we'll make the most of it." She gripped his hand, squeezing it hard, giving him a look that told him how much she loved him.

Gabe leaned over, kissing her cheek, and repeated, "Five days is better than nothing." Andy swallowed her disappointment, so glad to see her quiet, deep, dark brother with his heart of gold. A heart that had never known love until Maud and Steve had chosen him.

"Listen, I've got to get back to the office," Dev told them apologetically. "Why don't you two stay here? I'll pay our bill, Gabe."

"Wait," Andy said in a pleading voice as he stood up, "did anyone tell you that you're invited to our family dinner on July third? The night before the ceremony? Please say you'll come, Dev."

He grinned. "Yes, I'll be there."

Andy saw something in his eyes, something wonderful but unspoken, and she felt showered by his eager reply, happiness mirroring in his features at the thought of being with her family. "Wonderful!"

"Do I dress up," he teased, smiling into her shining eyes.

Her heart burst all over again. There weren't many men she loved . . . Or even liked. Her father, Luke, Gabe and now Dev. Finding herself wanting to say the word "love" when it came to him, Andy tried to caution herself. Yet the look that Gabe gave her and then the one he turned to Dev, showed her that her brother had given Dev his blessing. That meant so much to Andy.

"Luke's going to be delayed coming home," Gabe told her. "Are you off the flight roster? We could meet him at the new airport. The first regional airline is coming in for its first time. Mom said he hitched a ride on it. They'll be landing at eight a.m."

"I didn't know that," Andy gasped. "That will save us

driving to Jackson Hole airport to pick him up, or him renting a car there and coming down here."

"Right on. Luke is a Gemini. He can talk himself into and out of anything," and Gabe laughed.

Andy laughed with him, nodding vigorously. She reached out, gripping Dev's hand for a moment, an intimate, non-verbal sign that she liked him. "Be there at five p.m.?"

"I will," Dev promised.

Never had Andy felt so happy. She allowed her love to flow toward Dev. After fighting it for so long, Andy at last felt it was right to finally acknowledge what he meant to her. She hadn't given it voice yet, but she saw his eyes soften, his expression change when she reached out and gripped his hand. And he'd returned that squeeze of caring. A long, wonderful handholding. Was she ready for the next step?

Chapter Eleven

Dev had brought a bottle of good red wine with him when he showed up at the Whitcomb Ranch at five p.m. His heart lifted when he saw Andy come down the hall to the large foyer. The screen door allowed the eighty-degree breeze to filter into the house. Where he was standing, he could hear the family laughing heartily. It was a good sound to hear.

"Hey, Dev! I'm glad you made it," Andy said, opening the door and standing aside. "Come on in! We're all in the living room. My whole family is here and I want you to meet them."

Her smile and buoyancy were infectious and he smiled, handing her the bottle of wine. "Sounds good. I wasn't sure you were going to have wine, but here's some, just in case."

"That's so thoughtful," she said, taking it. "I'll give it to Sally, who's busy in the kitchen whipping up a wonderful meal for all of us."

Automatically, his heart swelled with silent happiness as she took the bottle, their fingers touching. "Whatever she's cooking," he said, testing the air with his nose, "it smells great."

"Mom's favorite meal is prime rib with all the trimmings. Follow me to the kitchen, and then we'll introduce you to my family."

The air was alive with quiet excitement that Dev could palpably feel. The joy was infectious. Tomorrow at noon, the Nellie Tayloe Ross Regional Airport would officially be open for business. "Have your grandparents from New York City arrived yet?" he wondered. They were Maud's über-rich parents.

"They're coming in tomorrow morning." Her face glowed. "And they're landing in their private jet. We'll all meet them at nine a.m. and come back here for brunch."

"You can feel the excitement everywhere. I've never seen the people who live in Wind River Valley be so high. Everyone's smiling. Over at Kassie's Café, it's crowded, full of happy noise and laughter. Everyone is celebrating what this means for your valley."

She went into the large kitchen through a swinging door. "It's your valley now, too, Dev."

Sally Fremont greeted him. She was busy at the granite counter. The blue-eyed woman dried her hands, turned and shook his hand, smiling up at him. Her black and gray hair was up in a topknot, and she was dressed in a pair of simple blue slacks with a white blouse. She had an assistant, Judy, helping her with today's menu. She was thrilled to have the wine and thanked him.

Catching his hand, Andy said, "Come on, let's go out to the main living room."

He was caught off-guard by the warm greetings when he entered the massive room with its floor-to-ceiling river-rock fireplace. There were three long, dark brown leather couches placed in a U-shape toward it, so that everyone had a place to sit and could make eye contact with one another. In the center was a black, red, gray and white hand-woven Navajo rug, and a large cedar coffee table with glass, so the beautiful rug could be seen through it.

"Luke," Andy called, gesturing for him to come over to where they stood at the opening of the couches, "come and meet my boss, Dev Mitchell."

Dev saw Luke, who had short brown hair, dark blue eyes, and a six-foot frame unwind, a grin on his oval face. None of the adopted children looked anything like the others. He put his hand forward. "Nice to meet you, Luke."

"Same here," he said, gripping Dev's hand and shaking it. "Andy told me all about you."

Rolling his eyes, he said, "Oh, no . . ."

The room burst into laughter.

Andy gave Dev a playful punch in the upper arm. "It was all good, Dev!"

Luke released his hand and gestured to the couch. "We've saved you a place. Come and sit down?"

Quietly in awe of this multicultural family, the obvious love in everyone's eyes for one another, made him feel good. The Whitcombs had men and women of all colors working on their ranch. That, to him, was a good sign. It didn't matter the color of a person's skin or their religion or gender. He'd been around Maud and Steve enough now to realize they were looking at a person's heart, his or her actions; not what they said, but what they did. He did the same thing, feeling at home with this group.

Luke grabbed Andy's hand as they approached the couch. "Sis, you can sit between us. A rose between two thorns," he jested, guiding her over so she could sit down.

"Only for you, Luke," she threatened.

"Oh, I forgot, you're the combat pilot in the family," he

teased her mercilessly, giving her a quick, hard hug and kissing the top of her head.

Dev sat next to her, liking the fire in her eyes as her brother teased her. Everyone was chuckling and trading glances.

"We're glad to have you back with us," Maud said. "Would you like some coffee or tea?"

"No, thanks, Maud. I had a mocha latte before driving out here." He saw several large plates of appetizers spread across the gold-and-red cedar coffee table. "Besides, Andy just took me to the kitchen and said Sally was making prime rib." He touched his stomach. "I want to save room for that."

Pleased, Maud asked, "You like prime rib?"

"Corned beef is my first fav, but prime rib is my second."

"Good thing you said that." Steve chuckled. "Maud's favorite meal is prime rib."

"I think he's psychic, Mom," Andy spoke up.

"Oh? How do you mean?"

"Dev brought a really nice burgundy wine with him. That's your favorite red wine."

"Wow," Maud said, giving Dev an awed look, "you really are psychic."

Steve, who sat next to his wife, turned and whispered loudly, "And he likes prime rib. Think we'll keep him?"

Dev noticed the sparkle in Maud's eyes. And then he noticed Andy was blushing fiercely, her cheeks a bright red.

Luke gave Dev a look of appraisal. "My Wonder Woman–sister thinks you're a real hero, and we all agree with her. She's told us the story of how you met and how you led Andy out of harm's way in Afghanistan."

Holding up his hand, Dev demurred, "Andy had just as much say as I did in that five-day run to escape the Taliban."

"Yeah," Luke said slyly, "but you were the Boy Scout."

"Well," Dev said, giving her a tender glance and then devoting his attention to Luke, "she's being too humble. It took both of us to get out of that situation. We each brought certain skills and knowledge, not to mention intuition. We were a team and we worked off each other's strengths, not our weaknesses."

"I like him, Andy. He's a team player."

"Yes," Sky spoke up, "and the military has trained us for that: helping one another."

All heads nodded somberly, agreeing.

"Did Andy tell you anything about me?" Luke wanted to know, placing his arm around her shoulders, giving her a quick hug.

"No," Dev said. He saw Luke was far more outgoing than Gabe. And Andy obviously had a very loving relationship with her younger brother.

Sky snickered. "Luke isn't one to hold back. He's the true extrovert of our family."

"He's a Gemini," Maud said, her smile growing. "Anyone who meets Luke has a new friend in him."

"Actually," Luke said, giving Dev an amused look, "my family is being very kind because you're here. I was adopted by them when I was two years old. I don't have any memories until about three." He pointed at Andy. "I remember Andy being stressed and asking our mother why I always talked so much."

The whole family burst into laughter.

"Gabe and Sky were the quiet ones," Andy said.

"What were you?" Dev wondered, teasing her.

"She was the oldest one of the kids," Gabe told him, "the queen bee in the house."

"I helped the other three get around when they were young," Andy admitted good-naturedly. "Mom and Dad relied on me to round up the herd and get them where they needed to go."

"Head wrangler?" Dev asked, watching the grins broaden, heads bobbing in unison.

"Yep," Steve chimed in, "and because I was out of country so much, Maud did rely on Andy's help a great deal. Later on, we hired a nanny so that Andy didn't have to take on that much responsibility at such a young age."

Gabe gave Andy an evil look. "By then, it was too late. Andy was the boss. The poor nanny, Mrs. Jones, always asked for her help with the three of us."

"Partly true," Andy agreed. "She was a sweet older woman, and we four were truly a handful."

"You see," Gabe said to Dev, "our parents believed in allowing us to unfold without trying to brand us into what they wanted us to be. As a consequence, we were four highly independent children very early on. We ran circles around poor Mrs. Jones. Looking back on that time, we were wild children to contend with."

"But to give Mrs. Jones credit," Andy said, "she agreed with our parents that we should be given a lot of independence."

"That didn't mean," Sky said, "we were unsupervised; we were. Mrs. Jones happened to have the same philosophy about children, so she acted like a benign dictator, stepping in only when we might hurt ourselves."

"Or stopping us from doing really stupid things like swinging on a rope in the barn, pretending we were Tarzan and Jane in the jungle," Luke chortled.

Slapping her thigh, Sky laughed and said, "The poor woman went white as a sheet when Andy leaped off the second floor of the barn hay mow window, hanging on to that rope and swinging to the other side of it where the hay was kept."

Dev's brows rose and he stared at Andy. "Really? You did that?"

"I sure did," Andy said. "Mrs. Jones came out after the other three had already done it. I was the one who got caught."

"Yes," Gabe said, pleased. "Andy took the heat on that for all of us. Mrs. Jones let my mother, who was in her office, know what we were doing."

Andy grumped, "Yeah, and I was the one who had to go to her room and think about what could have happened."

Gabe sat up, buttonholing Dev's gaze. "Our parents didn't believe in hitting or spanking us. We had time-outs to go think about the choices we'd made."

"Yeah," Luke hooted, "and you were in your room about as much as Andy was. They were the two risk-takers."

"Oh," Andy said archly, "and you're a Hotshot, Luke. Like you aren't a risk-taker, too? And so is Sky. We're all in the same category. We're always testing life."

"Still curious, aren't we?" Gabe said, giving her an affectionate glance. "That's not going to change. Ever."

"Yeah. Mrs. Jones caught me playing with a lighter when I was eight years old. Luckily, it was outside and not in the barn or the house. That got me an audience with my parents immediately."

Andy gave a wry laugh. "Yes, and you had hours to think about what you did."

"It worked, kind of," Luke admitted. "Our dad suggested I read up on fires, firefighting and things like that."

"As I recall," Andy said, "Dad bought you about four books on firefighting."

Luke gave his father a proud look. "He did. And the rest

was history. I knew right then, Dev, that I wanted to be a Hotshot."

"He did," Steve agreed. "And he was a junior volunteer fireman at the Wind River Fire Department at ten years of age."

"It honed his love of firefighting," Maud told Dev.

"And I wouldn't have found out if Mrs. Jones hadn't caught me with that lighter," Luke said, giving them a Cheshire cat smile.

"Maybe," Steve cautioned. "But we channeled your interest in fire into something positive."

"Instead of burning the house down around our ears," Gabe deadpanned.

"I wouldn't have done that!" Luke protested.

"Mrs. Jones, on that particular day," Andy said archly, "sure thought you were going to burn *everything* down."

"As I recall," Sky put in, snickering, "it was July and you went around building little piles of straw outdoors and had them all in a row about two hundred feet long down by one of the corrals. You had them all lit when she discovered them, and you at work."

"Lucky on that day there wasn't a lot of wind," Gabe said, barely able to squelch his grin.

"And," Andy said in defense of Luke, "he did build those teepees out of sticks and straw in the dirt, not in the grass or inside a building. You have to give him some credit for doing that."

"You sound like you were the mad scientist of the group," Dev teased.

"You think the fire experiment was over the top? We're lucky he didn't blow the house up," Gabe offered. "He wanted a science set he saw on TV and our parents bought it for him. The one experiment he wanted to replicate was the explosion."

"Even then," Luke defended himself proudly, "I liked explosions." He turned to Dev. "When you're out on a wildfire, you'll get all kinds of trees or groves exploding, so that fulfilled some of my need to take risks."

"Mom took your chemistry set away from you," Sky reminded him. "She was afraid you'd blow up the house."

The room rocked with laughter. Dev could see Luke preening over all the attention, even if it was at his expense. He took it in good-natured stride. A lot of men had too much pride and arrogance to laugh at themselves, but Luke wasn't one of them. He gave everyone a bashful smile as the family remembered his growing-up antics.

"Now," Sky ragged on Dev, "aren't you sorry you came to dinner with all of us here at one time?"

His lips twitched. "I was an only child. This is new to me, but I really am enjoying it."

The family traded proud looks with one another, bathed in the glow of Dev's sincere words.

"Are you married?" Luke asked him.

He hesitated. "I was, but my wife died of a sudden heart attack in our second year of college."

Quiet settled over the jocular group. An uncomfortable silence.

Dev saw Andy's eyes widen, and then he saw sadness come to her expression. This wasn't the way he wanted to tell her about his past. "Sorry," he offered everyone. "I probably should have been a politician and changed the topic."

Andy reached out, putting her hand on his thigh. "I like you just the way you are, Dev: honest. Politicians lie for a living. I hate that. You can never trust them or what they say." Her gaze grew intense. "But I trust you."

"Hey, dude," Luke muttered, looking chastened, "this was my fault, not yours."

"Yeah," Gabe intoned darkly, "your Gemini mouth gets ahead of your brain sometimes."

"Guilty," Luke offered quietly. "I'm sorry to hear that about your wife."

"It's okay. Over the years, I've worked through the shock and loss. Life goes on," Dev quietly offered Luke. "You just do the best you can."

"Luke is a love-'em-and-leave-'em type," Gabe said, giving his brother a serious look.

"That's true," Luke said. "I just haven't settled down, is all. I'm only twenty-eight."

"None of us have settled down," Sky muttered darkly. "I think it's because we were all abandoned, left to die."

The room grew quiet again.

Dev struggled to say something healing for all of them because he could see the truth of Sky's embittered words slam into the other siblings. "Being an only child, but never abandoned, I couldn't know how it felt. It had to be tough and heartbreaking for all of you when you realized it later on."

"It's like," Gabe said, "losing the person you loved."

"Only you can make that statement," Dev said. "I was never abandoned, nor would I ever do that to someone else."

Andy kept her hand on his, fingers tightening around his. "You proved that when you didn't leave me at the crash site in Afghanistan. You were there for me in every way possible. You never quit on me, you never said I was too slow or slowing us down."

"It's nice to be with all of you," Dev said quietly, making eye contact with every one of them. "I miss times like this at home with my parents. You were fortunate that Maud and Steve took all of you in. From my standpoint? They chose each of you because they loved you. And I know from having a lot of friends in the military that no family is ever perfect. Many are dysfunctional. Being able to come here and meet all of you has really helped me in ways I didn't even realize I needed to keep healing up from my own past."

"I'm sorry I asked you that personal question," Luke offered, his hands clasped between his knees, watching him for a reaction.

"It was bound to come up sooner or later," Dev said. "The people at our medevac facility are all ex-military. And you naturally become personal with those people. They aren't employees. We see one another as a team. And when you're a team, you open up, you trust and rely on the other people. We all get one another's stories."

Sky gave Maud and Steve a loving look. "Just like they saw us as a team. They trusted us long before we trusted them."

"And we did it with love," Maud said gently. She glanced at her husband. "And in time, all four of you began to trust us. We made a point of never allowing you to feel abandoned again."

"That must have been a lot of work," Gabe murmured.

"It was a 24/7/365 job," Steve said, "but we knew you were all shattered emotionally from being abandoned. Maud and I wanted to show you that adults could not only love and support you but not drop the ball and leave you without any protection."

"We wanted all of you to feel safe," Maud said. "And only time, consistency and being there for each of you was going to make the difference."

Luke studied the group. "I don't know about the other three of you, but I'm afraid to get too far into a relationship." He shrugged and added, "Maybe that's why I don't stay long with a woman in my life."

Gabe nodded, giving him an understanding nod. "I've often thought I chose undercover work because it was an excuse not to become entangled in a serious relationship. In my work, I'm gone weeks or months at a time. No relationship can stand that kind of strain."

Andy nodded. "I think, maybe, we all have to reach a point where we heal within ourselves. I know that the crash in Afghanistan made me see my life differently. Before that," and she glanced at Dev, "I dallied around with a guy, but if he started getting too serious, I ran. I was chicken. I didn't want to get corralled into a serious relationship."

"And deep down," Sky offered, "we're all afraid that anyone we might fall in love with will abandon us, too." She touched the area between her breasts. "I've never said this to anyone, but now is as good a time as ever because I trust all of you. When I analyzed why I run away from a potentially serious relationship, I found fear was the reason."

"Fear?" Andy asked, frowning.

"Yes, fear that I couldn't trust that person enough to take that next, serious step and make our relationship deeper and wider." She opened her hands. "Or maybe I haven't met the right guy yet. I don't know . . ."

"I think all of us go through a number of relationships," Maud told them. "And we've been hurt by them. So, we become gun-shy of the next person who comes along. None of the other relationships worked out, so I started thinking there was something wrong with me. There wasn't, but at the time I met your father, I had pretty much given up on ever finding a man who was compatible with my needs." She looked at her grown children with affection. "I would say that the right person hasn't come along yet, and to stay open to the possibility. There are good people out there we can trust over time."

"When I met you in that soup kitchen," Steve said, "near Princeton, I fell in love with you that morning. I didn't know it at first, but within three months, I was sure of it."

"I hope it happens to me like that," Sky said. "I'm pretty much given up on the whole idea."

Gabe and Luke agreed.

Dev glanced at Andy, who had clasped her hands in her lap, her gaze on them. She wasn't agreeing to it. He knew she was fully capable of speaking up for herself. Was she feeling the same way he was? That he wanted to get to know her better, have the time to fully explore her as a person? His gut said yes. That startled him. But it also fed him hope for a future that included Andy. Only time would tell him those things. It felt as if a silent step had been taken between them, a sensing and a knowing. Was Andy afraid to take the next step, trust him enough to go forward with whatever they had?

"I love the Wyoming night sky," Andy whispered as they walked to their cars. Dev was at her side, their hands sometimes lightly brushing each other.

"They're an amazing show every night," he agreed, looking up and slowing his pace after they went down the porch steps to the sidewalk.

She licked her lower lip. It was a moonless night, the stars shining like brilliant diamonds in the velvet darkness above them. The small posts on either side of the wooden gate lit the way for them. There was a breeze, and it was coolish but not cold. In the distance, she could hear cattle lowing in some of the grass lease pastures. "I'm sorry Luke asked you such a personal question. Did you feel embarrassed by it?"

Slowing, Dev opened the door to his truck and turned. Andy had leaned against the fender, her features muted and deeply shadowed. Her eyes were filled with concern for him. "It was unexpected. I didn't feel he did it to embarrass me."

"Oh, he's not mean-spirited like that at all," she said quickly. "And you're right, he's so quick mentally, being a Gemini and all, that he sometimes doesn't think before he speaks."

"I didn't take it personally, Andy. After all, everyone had been talking about relationships that were broken."

She wrapped her arms around herself, frowning. "You're right. But Luke has a lot of curiosity about the people he's interested in. And sometimes his social graces aren't as good as I'd like. He just blurts out something, not thinking ahead that whatever he's asking or saying might hurt that person."

"We all do it, now and then," and he smiled a little, leaning against the door of the truck, his hands stuffed in his pockets.

"He likes you. And Luke tends to get chummy quickly, far more personal than maybe he should be."

"Does that explain some of his many relationships?" Dev wondered. "Too fast for the woman? Crowding her, maybe?"

"For sure," she said with a little laugh.

"He's a Hotshot. He's used to going into situations that are dangerous," he teased, meeting her smile, seeing some of the trepidation dissolve in her eyes.

"Oh, he's used that excuse way too many times!"

"I learned with Sophie, my wife, to take things slow. To let things develop naturally, not try to push or crowd her. She was a great teacher for me."

"I think you're far more sensitive than Luke is at this

moment in his life. I think you read the tea leaves pretty well, Dev."

He felt her searching, reaching out to him. "Maybe tonight was for us to size up whatever it is that's growing between us." He saw surprise in her expression, but then, acceptance. "I feel what we have, whatever it is, or whatever you want to call it, is because of our five days on the run. I can't speak for you, Andy, but I felt as if we were melded together, because of our common goal, a common desire to survive, and it was a good feeling. I trusted you from the very beginning, no question. Did you feel that? Or am I the only one?" He saw her become pensive, look up at the stars twinkling above, and then her gaze meeting and holding his.

"We've never really sat down for a long, hard, in-depth talk about what that time did to us ourselves, much less what it did for us together. I did feel that melding, as you call it, happen. I've always been an intuitive person, but one of the many things that amazed me was that we were so intuitive, almost scarily telepathic. When we got separated in that cave on the second night? I was walking about fifty feet ahead of you and my flashlight batteries died? It went pitch black."

"Yes?"

"How God-awful dark it was? I couldn't even see my hand in front of my face. I lost my sense of direction and I was in total panic, thinking I was going to die and no one was ever going to find me. And then this peace came over me. Something told me you would find me. All I had to do was stay where I was. We couldn't call out to each other because the Taliban was nearby."

"I remember." He shook his head. "I'm glad we're discussing this. We were using only one flashlight to save our batteries. You had rounded a corner and I saw two tunnels ahead of you. When it went dark, I knew what had happened. I didn't know which tunnel you'd taken. Because I'd been in so many nighttime missions, I relied heavily on my gut feelings. That tunnel was ten feet across. I decided to be still, and something told me to listen to see if I couldn't pick up your breathing. I sensed you were scared to death. So was I. But something told me I could find you and we'd be okay."

"And sure enough, you found me ten minutes later."

"Yeah, I heard your breathing. I followed it and took the left tunnel and found you about twenty feet into it."

She managed a weak smile. "I gotta tell you, Dev, your arms going around me, hauling me against you? It was the most wonderful feeling in the world. I never forgot that moment."

"Me either," he admitted slowly, watching the changes in her eyes.

"Seeing you again here in Wyoming, I never felt so happy. We had trust, the best kind, already in place between us. It never lagged or broke while we were on the run. When I realized it was you, I felt that same thing, whatever you want to call it, bursting open and blossoming between us once more."

"I felt it, too."

"What does it mean, Dev? I've lain awake some nights trying to figure out how we're supposed to relate to each other. I know you're my boss and I'm your employee."

He managed a grunt and shook his head, holding her gaze. "We could have died so many times before and after our crashes. When people share an intense experience like that, I think it forms a connection few can understand. We had no one to rely on but ourselves. That has been branded into our souls as far as I'm concerned. I try to see you as an employee, but our past always outweighs that. Is it the same with you, or am I the only one fighting this?"

"I'm so glad you said something." She sighed. Unwinding her arms, she pushed off the fender, turned and walked up to him. Looking up, she whispered, "I don't know what we have, Dev. Personally? I'd like to see where it takes us. I have no idea what that means, but I've never been more interested in a man than I am in you. Tell me what you feel about us."

"It feels as if someone has taken a ton of weight off my shoulders that I've been carrying around since we met here in Wind River. I can't name what it is either, but I know it isn't anything bad. It's good."

She pushed some strands of hair away from her cheek. "I'd feel better if, when we're on the job, we keep our boss-and-employee position in alignment. I don't think either of us wants to upset the status quo there."

"You're right. I don't want that to happen either. What about our days off? When we have free time and no responsibilities like we have when we're on duty?"

"This is funny in an odd way, Dev. Today's whole discussion was about relationships. You and I didn't bring up the topic, but there it was."

"Sky said that because of being abandoned at birth, she couldn't trust a man in a serious relationship. Gabe and Luke both agreed, feeling the same way. But you didn't, Andy. I wanted to ask why you didn't agree with them. In my crazy-wishes world, I wanted to believe that whatever is growing between us is really good for you and for me. And that's why you didn't speak up and agree with your siblings. Am I right?"

She gave him a painful look. "Yes. We were thinking the

same thing and I didn't want to bring it up to the family today."

"Where does this leave us, then? Or where do you want to go in this thing we have but can't name?"

She smiled a little nervously. "I liked what you said about going slow, letting things take a natural course. I'm at a place where I really want this job. It's a new career for me. I desperately want to stay home, be near my folks and start to enjoy my life. I've risked my butt too many times, and now, I guess I'm at an age when I want peace. I don't want guns firing at me. I don't want to be crashing anymore." She touched her heart. "I have a sense that I can heal now. Before, I didn't. There's a hole in my heart, Dev. It's been there all my life. And I sense that here, in Wind River, I can settle down, be in calmer waters, do the inner work to get my wound cleaned out and finally dress it so I can get on with my life."

Pursing his lips, he said, "I completely agree with you. I'm not in a space to chase a woman or make demands on her like I did when I was much younger. Like you, I want a quiet backwater life, too. I like our deep talks. I'm hungry for them. They . . . you . . . feed my heart and soul. I always feel better after a conversation like we're having right now."

"Me too," she admitted.

"I'm glad we aired this. We can thank Luke for it."

She rolled her eyes. "He's always been the court jester in our family. Most of the time, he leaves us laughing."

"Court jesters sometimes speak the truth we all need to hear, and today he brought that home to us."

"And we had a wonderful meal. There's so much going on tomorrow . . . and I'm so proud of Mom and Dad spending a decade of hard work to make this dream of an airport come true for our valley."

"We have a lot to celebrate. I'll see you tomorrow," and he barely grazed her cheek with his fingertips, needing to touch this woman who was like an endless well of honesty and integrity. "I'm sure we'll see each other at the barn dance at your parents' barbeque."

"Mom and Dad will be hobnobbing with the senators and congresspeople, not to mention other county and state officials. I don't like that stuff, but she and Dad love it."

"And that's what it took to get our hub airport landed, pardon my pun," and he grinned. "Will you keep a dance open for me once we find each other tomorrow night?"

She smiled. "Absolutely. Good night, Dev. Thanks for being brave and telling me how you really feel."

"My wife taught me early on about communicating."

"She had to be an exceptional human being. I wish I could have known her."

"Maybe, over time, I'll fill you in about her. I'll always love her; she has a place in my heart and memory. But I learned about two years ago, after going through a long tunnel of grief over losing her, that I had to start living again."

"I'm sure both of us are going to value her in our lives. She was a teacher," Andy said gently. Lifting her hand, she squeezed his. "See you tomorrow . . ."

Chapter Twelve

July 4
Wednesday

Andy sat with her family in the front row looking up at the square, wooden dais decorated with Independence Day banners. She felt so proud to see her mother and father sitting up there, between the two Wyoming senators and congresspeople, as the governor of the state extolled the opening of the airport. There were at least a thousand people in attendance. American flags waved in the inconstant breeze, the eleven a.m. temperature pleasant, the sky a blinding blue with a few high, cirrus clouds wafting above the valley.

Next to her was Dev. It felt good to have him with her. They had all worked to make this opening something everyone in the valley could be proud of. They, along with the pilots and crew chiefs of their medevac service, plus the mechanics wore the dark-blue, one-piece flight uniform, adorned with patches, their names and the name of their company. After the speeches, the Wind River High School marching band provided stirring July 4 music between speakers, and then the official opening would be over.

There were four major airlines, along with regional airlines, that would be landing in an hour, officially opening the airport that was more than ready for their business.

Her siblings sat on one side of her, Dev, on the other. The mayor of Wind River, Trudy Hopkins, sat up on the dais, next to her parents. Everyone looked so proud. There was polite clapping when the governor finished. Andy had the list of speakers memorized. Next, the senators would praise the Nellie Tayloe Ross Regional Airport, then the congresspeople.

Finally, Maud would speak, and she knew her mother's goal for helping the people of this valley become economically stable was finally here. She glanced over at Dev, who slanted her a glance in return. He'd already admitted earlier, before they took their places, that he wasn't one to enjoy these kinds of things, and she wasn't either. What made it different for both of them was that it was her parents who had made this place, their dream for this valley, a reality. For this celebration, neither of them chaffed at having to sit for short speeches from all the officials.

As soon as the opening was finished, she and her cohorts, who sat directly behind them, would go to the medevac area. There, they would turn on their public relations for the people who would come to check out their office, view the Black Hawk sitting out in front, and they'd hand out brochures to those who wanted them.

The children would be allowed into the rear of the open sliding door of the helicopter, so they could see it up close and personal. Pete and Dev would be by the doors, explaining and answering questions about the medical side of the care this medevac was going to provide for the valley. She and the other pilots would be inside their facility, taking people around to see the various offices, the kitchen area and sleeping quarters for those on duty.

Keeping in mind these people who lived in Wind River contributed their taxes to the airport, Andy was happy to show them around. This was their hard-earned money at work for all of them. She could hardly wait until they could get on their feet, move around and interact with the people who were here. Everyone was dressed in their summer finery, a lot of red, white and blue worn throughout the assembled crowd. She smiled inwardly at her father, who was never without his black Stetson on his head. When he had left at eighteen for Princeton to chase his dream of becoming an architect, he'd not given up his daily uniform: cowboy boots, jeans, a wrangler's shirt and his black hat. Steve had teased his children, saying that when they buried him, it had to be in Western gear, plus his faithful black Stetson tucked inside his casket. It was a family joke, but his wishes, when that day came, would be lovingly carried out.

Her gaze moved to her mother, her short black-and-silver hair glistening from the sunlight. She was dressed in a simple, navy-blue linen suit, a classy white blouse and a red scarf around her neck. Her parents had flown in from New York City and now sat in the front row facing the dais. In the second row were the Whitcomb children, proud expressions on their faces. Her father's parents sat on the other side of Dev. She was glad both families were here, together, for this important event. Earlier, a photographer had taken the family picture. Photos would then be sent to everyone; a wonderful, lasting memento of this day.

She felt bad that Dev's parents could not come, his father having had appendicitis surgery a few days earlier. The operation was successful, but he couldn't travel. Maud had hired a videographer to film the whole ceremony. That video would be sent to them, and of course, there would be video of Dev, as well as where he worked, and, she hoped, some shots of him sitting in the Black Hawk helicopter's cockpit. He'd told Andy he'd spoken to his parents last night, finding out that his father was doing well. The good news was that this fall, in early September, his parents were going to fly here to visit Dev, staying for five days. She was looking forward to meeting his mother and father.

When it was Maud's turn to speak, Andy felt her chest expand with love and pride for her mother. The pleasure on her father's face as she spoke passionately of how the idea of an airport had become a reality for the people of the valley. Although her father had been just as instrumental in the design of the airport, supporting her mother for a decade to bring this dream to reality, he'd declined to speak. Steve had told everyone that this had been Maud's dream from the beginning, and she deserved the lion's share of praise for her hard, consistent work. And, of course, Maud had worked with her mother to contact key political people to make this airport happen. It took a village, for sure, to create something of this magnitude in such a deprived, economically hard-hit area.

Tonight, Dev would be coming back to her family's ranch for a celebratory dinner—a barbeque and then dancing.

After that, he'd suggested that a good way to end this incredible day would be to meet at the hot tub at their condo. He said they could celebrate by sitting in warm water and ease their painful feet after being on them for eight hours. Andy had laughed and agreed. She'd slipped and said, "That's a date, Mitchell." And then realized the word she'd used had triggered an expression in his eyes that gleamed with an emotion she couldn't name but felt. Yes, there was something good, something building between them, and she was going to surrender to it.

* * *

Andy slipped into the hot tub, the stars twinkling through the glass skylights above them in the clear night sky. It was nine p.m., and she sank gratefully into the warm, bubbling water, adjusting her one-piece black swimsuit straps before sitting down on the bench beneath the water. At this time of the evening, no one else was using the hot tub, so it was a favorite time of theirs to be alone, to talk in privacy. The lighting was a bluish color, just enough to see where one was going but keeping everything else in deep shadows. She liked that sense of being in a cocoon whenever they were able to meet here after a day's work.

Turning, she watched in admiring silence, drinking in Dev's tall, tightly muscled body. He wore a pair of dark green trunks that fell halfway down his thighs. It was a private pleasure to glance at him without being obvious, also admiring his broad set of shoulders, his chest sprinkled with dark hair, all lending him a decidedly sexy look. Andy had stopped trying to tell herself Dev was off-limits, her reasoning falling on the deaf ears of her own yearning heart.

Groaning, Dev said, "I've been waiting for this moment all day." He sank into the water near her. "Feel good to your feet?" he asked, meeting her shadowed eyes.

"My feet are barking. I don't know about yours, but this is heaven." Well, almost heaven. She couldn't stop herself from gazing one last time at his mouth, one of his many delicious features. Last night, despite how exhausted she was, she'd dreamed of kissing Dev. And it wasn't a peck on the cheek. It was hot, juicy and filled with many promises to come.

"We don't know how much we sit around until we're on our feet for unrelieved hours," he said, sluicing the water across his face.

Trying to ignore the water trickling down his strong

neck and onto his powerful chest, the way some droplets caught in the red hair, she felt her lower body clench. How many times had she thought about what it would feel like to slide her fingertips through that silky hair that only made him look more intensely masculine? Way too many. She pulled her thoughts back to his earlier comment. "We do sit a lot. I think if I was a waitress, on my feet eight hours a day, they'd hurt too. My mother hates sitting around for too long. She's usually up and out of her desk chair every twenty minutes or so. She's restless."

"I think Maud's speech, while short, was the best of all this morning," he said.

"All her life, whatever goals she sets, she's gone after them with passion," Andy agreed, her voice softening with pride. "She always told us kids never to leap into anything unless our heart's passion was connected to it. That we had to use that passion as fuel for our engine, ourselves, and lead a life that mattered for our planet and humanity."

"She seems to talk in symbols a lot," Dev murmured, running water through his opened fingers, watching it drop and momentarily glitter in the semidarkness.

"My mother sees life through a very different lens," Andy agreed. "My father sees everything through a historical and architectural lens."

"Brought up to see symbols and history isn't such a bad thing," he said, holding her gaze.

"No, I loved it. I think and see everything the way they see life. I guess that's what parents are supposed to do: give their children a grounding, a worldview, so they can successfully navigate life."

"Hmmm," he said, lifting his chin, looking up and out the window toward the swath of Milky Way stars, "that's true. My dad taught me to survive in the wilderness. We took a trip overnight to the woodlands when I was nine years old. He gave me a compass when I was six years old and taught me how to use it. He gave me a hard copy of a Google map. We had breakfast the next morning over a campfire and then he left. An hour later, I had to follow the map coordinates and locate where he was."

"Wow," Andy said, her eyes widening, "he was serious, wasn't he?"

Laughing a little, he said, "Yeah, but I ate it up. I loved being outdoors and being challenged by him. I usually found him. Or he found me because I screwed up on a coordinate and was lost."

She gave him a tender smile. "But he always found you, though, didn't he? You weren't abandoned." Even saying the word pinged a sharpened sadness that had never left the inside of her. There wasn't a day that went by that Andy didn't remember that she'd been abandoned. No matter how she tried to ignore that hole in her heart, it would never go away. Wanting to change the topic, she asked, "How did your mom see life? What was her lens?"

"Oh," he groaned, "she was a three-dimensional chess player."

"No!" Andy gasped and sat up. "I love chess! My dad is a chess master! Did you know that?"

He shook his head. "No, I didn't. Small world, huh? My mother is a chess master." He gave her a searching look. "What are the chances we'd both have parents who are that good at chess?"

She cupped water, sluicing it over her face. "I think the odds are pretty small. That's incredible, Dev."

"I feel strongly that after the crash in Afghanistan, the things my parents taught me as survival skills helped keep us alive. And yours did, too."

"That's amazing," she said wryly. "When we were out there running for our lives, I was thinking in chess terms.

Just knowing all the things my mom taught me about chess calmed me down and helped me stay focused. I looked at the mountains we were traveling through to get down on the other side of that range and find that Army outpost in the valley below. You knew where that firebase was located, had the coordinates, and you had your compass to guide us to it."

He chuckled. "Yeah, the same compass my dad gave me when I was six years old. I never flew without it, even though we had electronics that did all the math and coordinates for us."

"Yeah, but electronics stuff needs to be recharged and can die when you least expect it. That old-fashioned compass wouldn't die on us out in the middle of nowhere. I'm positive your compass got us back to the firebase."

"You bet it did. I couldn't retrieve my go bag from the Hawk after we crashed; the fire was too big and drove me back. I was lucky to have gotten out at all." He became pensive. "That was a terrible night, Andy. I'd lost two great friends an hour before I found you. I had a lot of grief inside me, but I knew I couldn't let it loose. The area we were in was a beehive of Taliban activity in every direction." Pursing his lips, he offered, "I didn't expect to survive that crash. I really didn't. And when I did, then realized where we crashed, I didn't think we'd get out of there alive."

"Honestly? I didn't either. But you and I ignored the fear and went for broke. I don't think it's in our DNA to give up, Dev. We'll die fighting until our last breath."

"You're right. We're not the type of people to sit down, cry and feel helpless, giving up without a fight."

"Every time your father took you out in the woods, he was developing your instincts in areas you weren't familiar with. I couldn't have made it out of there without you at my side."

"You brought your own skills to that dance," he told her, his voice deep with emotion. "I think that 'chess mind' that we both have helped us see the best places to climb, or to hide, or to sense where the Taliban might try to bushwhack us, and we avoided those areas. You saw details I didn't, and they were life-and-death important. Don't think you weren't contributing to our escape, because you were."

"That's good to know. Most of the time I was feeling like a third leg, not doing much at all except to try and keep up with the pace you set for us."

He reached out, trailing his fingers down her upper arm in a light caress. "You did. Neither of us would have survived without the other's contributions."

Her skin tingled where his fingers had briefly grazed her. His touch was unexpected. Wonderful. Welcomed by her, no question. Her brows drifted downward as she absorbed that light, intimate touch. Although his face was shadowed, she could see the interest burning in his eyes for her. Since their last talk, Dev hadn't tried to hide so much of how he felt toward her. He rarely touched her, but the expression in his eyes told her everything that lay quietly building between them.

"Two strangers thrown together in a hellish place where everything was against us," he said, giving her a sideway glance. "You know what was funny? Not funny ha-ha, but quirky?"

"What?"

"When we were making the last run for the firebase, I kept wanting to tell you that you were a great friend to me. I liked you because we worked seamlessly together, as if we were in telepathic contact with each other, like good friends sometimes are. We had five days together, very little speaking because voices carry. I wanted you to be single, not in a relationship. I wanted to ask if you had someone in your life or if you were married." His mouth twisted and he gave her a dry look. "Of course, I figured you did have a man in your life. Either that or you were married. I finally convinced myself to ask you once we got safely back to the firebase."

Shaking her head, she said, "You can tell we didn't share much telepathy between us, even though we truly did work well together on that run."

Giving her a quizzical look, Dev asked, "What are you talking about?"

"By the time we were let inside the base, I wanted to ask you the same things you wanted to ask me." She saw the surprise in his expression. "I was dying to know more about you, the man, not us in the middle of the crisis. And yes, I thought of you as a good friend, someone who was there for me, who had my back, like friends do."

"That is ironic," he muttered, awe in his tone. He sat up, sluicing his upper body with warm water.

"But then, at Bagram, they separated us and I never saw you again." She pressed her hand to her heart. "I wanted badly to reconnect with you."

Giving her a sad, searching look, he asked, "Did you feel I'd abandoned you? Knowing your mother gave you up puts a different light on what happened between us at Bagram. I'm trying to look through your eyes to see what your reaction might have been to us being split apart."

Her heart bloomed with warmth toward him. "You're the first guy I've met who has that kind of depth and self-awareness."

"I didn't know it then," he apologized, "but I do now. I'm trying to see life through your eyes, not mine. You know that old saying, walk a mile in my shoes?"

Reaching out, she grazed his wet, slick shoulder, his skin taut and muscles powerful beneath her fingertips.

Reluctantly, she lifted her hand away. "I was exhausted," she whispered unsteadily, "relieved to be alive, but I wanted you beside me. I wanted you near me, Dev." She blinked back tears that rushed forward, out of nowhere. "I . . . uh . . . yeah, the feeling of being abandoned once again hit me really hard. I tried to argue with myself that you had, after all, seen me through what I considered the worst time in my life, and we got safely back behind the wire." Ashamed, she quickly wiped her eyes, battling back the unbidden emotional boulder rising up within her. "I tried to find out where you were, later. No one would tell me. I finally got hold of the head nurse, and she told me you'd been ordered back to your squadron. She couldn't reveal any more than that. If I'd had a squadron number, I could have found you." Her voice lowered. "Your security clearance was way above mine. It meant they weren't going to tell me anything. I was so bummed out, Dev. I didn't even get to thank you. That's what hurt the most."

He murmured her name, enclosing her wet hand within his. "And I'm sure the abandonment felt like a knife going through you."

"Through my heart." Her fingers curled around his as she held his darkened gaze. "I knew we'd shared only five days, but I felt closer to you than to anyone else, except for my parents and siblings. I felt like we were one, working together, in unison, like a good team of plow horses," and she managed a trembling, slight smile that faintly curved one corner of her mouth.

The silence settled over them except for the soft, bubbling sounds of the water surrounding them.

"Are you glad we're back together again?" he asked her.

"At first, I was shocked it was you. And then? I'd never felt so happy."

He squeezed her fingers and released them. "I felt the

same way. I'd given up on finding you. I think the hardest thing I'd ever done was to let go of the idea that I'd find you someday."

Nodding, she whispered, "I'm not sorry we've met again, Dev. You make me feel good because you treat everyone fairly. I like that you're self-aware, and you try to put yourself in someone else's shoes. Those are important traits I've always wanted in a man but have never found."

"Until now," he rumbled, holding her glistening gaze.

"Until now," she agreed, clearing her throat.

"And with the craziness of everything going on with opening up the airport, getting this new medevac business on its feet, we're all running hard and there's barely any time to breathe, much less have downtime to just savor life."

Rolling her eyes, she said, "Oh, all of that."

"I think, from what your dad said to me one time, that everything slows down from Mach 3 with our hair on fire to January molasses from Vermont in the fall. Maybe then we'll have more time when we can do some things we enjoy doing together."

"September is when the snow starts flying," she warned him. "Yes, everything in this valley slows to a crawl from September through May. It's our eight months of winter."

"What would you like to do if we get a day off together?"

"That's easy. I love hiking. There are some fabulous areas in the Salt and Wilson Ranges."

"And you probably know them by heart?"

She grinned. "Yeah, I do. My parents took us kids out every weekend to the mountains. Sometimes, we trailered our horses and rode specific trails. Other times, it was hiking in and out on foot. We would leave on a Saturday morning, pitch our tents, sleep out overnight and hike back to the trailhead on Sunday morning. We loved those months and always looked forward to our weekends."

He studied her for a moment. "You mentioned earlier that at the crash you came to see me as your friend?"

"A close friend," she corrected. "Yes, the more time we spent together, the more I recognized that we worked well together. There was so little talking, but I saw again and again how you seemed to know what to do next, or get me to follow your hand signals, that it felt like I was with my best friend. I didn't know how you knew about me, Dev, but you did. I'm a very visual person, and you automatically seemed to know that. You'd draw a trail or where we were going in the dirt, showing me what you wanted us to do next."

"You were a combat pilot," he offered. "They're visual. They have to be."

Nodding, she said, "It was smart of you to realize that. But you were a Night Stalker pilot, so you're very visual, too."

"True," he said, "but my senses told me you needed to see, not have it told to you."

"Yeah, I'm really tired of mansplaining. A map drawn in the dirt was a very good way to communicate clearly and effectively with me."

"Anyone who ejects out of a jet has my admiration. I knew you were used to HUDS, heads-up displays, and other consoles with maps or targeting something, and I needed to reach you without words."

Propping her elbows on her drawn-up knees, she held his gaze. "Now I wonder about 'what if.' What if we hadn't been separated in the ER? What if we'd been able to reconnect sooner? What then?"

"I was going to find out if you were single and available. Like you, Andy, I felt like you were my combat buddy on a SERE: Survival, Evasion, Resistance, and Escape mission."

"Oh, SERE." She wrinkled her nose with utter distaste.

"We were assigned a buddy and then we had to escape together."

"I see what you're saying now. I hated SERE. I got hooked up with a guy who didn't have the nerve it took to get through capture and evasion. He always wanted to quit and surrender."

"Bad example, then," Dev agreed. "But you were the ideal SERE buddy, Andy. I wanted to tell you that. I try not to look at women as being the 'weaker sex' that all guys are brainwashed into believing. You were strong, smart and just as motivated as I was to get the hell out of there alive. And every day that passed, I had more and more respect for your intelligence, the details you saw that made a huge difference to us on the run."

"You didn't try to boss me around like a lot of other male pilots have in the past," she muttered, frowning, re-membering those intense days in flight training.

"From the get-go, you were right there."

"I saw myself as your wingman," she teased, smiling a little. "I took care of what was following and chasing us. You took care of the compass directions, what was in front of us, the route we needed to take to get up and over that mountain range."

"I began to lose the wingman symbol," he admitted, "the third day into our escape and evasion. You were like an old friend who knew me as few ever had. It blew me away, Andy. You had to have remarkable sensing about me in order to trust me."

"I did," and she looked around the moist, humid tiled room. "I've always had what I consider a paranormal sense about some situations and people. My senses are heightened, my hearing is beyond human range at those times, and so is my sense of smell."

"That's incredible."

"I attribute it to the adrenaline pouring into my blood-stream."

"Everything becomes more intense and beyond normal human ranges in emergencies," Dev said, nodding. "But your skills in those areas saved our bacon a number of times."

"Remember when I smelled tea on the night air?"

"Yes. And we halted, hid behind some large bushes and tried to locate what direction it was coming from."

"And I did. It was a group of Taliban getting ready to go to bed. They were having a final cup of tea before hitting the sack."

"Yes, and you sussed the area out, hand singling me which way to go so we didn't alert them to our presence. I was amazed that you could smell that tea on the air. I sure didn't."

"We all have our skills," Andy said. "You had your com-pass and I had my nose. My mom always told us kids that the secret to any good relationship started with a solid friendship. She said she was friends with Steve and it even-tually led to marriage."

Grinning, Dev laughed. "Good advice. But you also have a wolf nose, Andy. You sensed very accurately where the groups tracking us were located. That helped us figure out where to go next instead of running into them by mistake."

"It was a brutal time for us," she whispered, shaking her head. "Even now, I wonder how we got through it. I really do."

"I think part of it was our natural compatibility with each other," he suggested.

"And we respected what we each brought to the table," Andy said, nodding.

"And we were both well trained in SERE escape and evasion tactics."

"All of it conspired to get our asses out of that sling."

They chuckled together, giving each other knowing looks.

"Are you turning into a prune?" Dev teased, rising to his full height, water running off his body.

Holding up her hands, she muttered, "I *am* a prune, Mitchell."

"Grab my hand," he said, offering it to her, his foot on the step that led out of the hot tub.

Willingly, Andy did, allowing him to help her stand. She felt the strength of his fingers wrap around hers, though they didn't squeeze them too hard, as many men had in the past when they'd grabbed her hand. For a second, she drowned in his shadowed eyes, seeing the yearning in them, feeling the heat of his hand as the water sluiced off between them. Once out of the tub, he released her and gave her one of the fluffy bath towels. They were large enough to literally wrap up in. Both had brought terry-cloth robes, however, so they used them to pat off the water. Dev took her blue robe and held it open so she could shrug into it, and she thanked him. Then she turned around and did the same thing for him. They worked so well together on a nonverbal level that Andy wanted it to continue to be like this forever. She saw him head to the door and open it for her. Always the gentleman, a throwback gesture she appreciated.

"I have an idea," he told her as she passed by him and out into the carpeted hall.

"What?" She turned and halted, watching him close the door to the spa area.

Turning, Dev said in a low, quiet voice, "I like what we have, Andy. What do you think about learning to be good friends again? Like we were out there in the Sandbox?"

"Friendship is a great place to start," she agreed, falling into step with him as they ambled down the hall toward the elevator. "There are all kinds of good reasons to start there. You're okay with that?"

"Better than okay. I've spent a lot of nights thinking about us. And if we can have a friendship? Then anything is possible beyond that. My parents grew up next door to each other in Ireland. They were best friends throughout their school years. Later, they got married. And to this day, they're still the best of friends."

She slowed and pressed the elevator button, the brass doors soon sliding open. "I'm just amazed at the similarity between our two families," she confided, stepping aside so he could get in. She pressed the second-floor button, and the doors whooshed closed. "My parents met at a soup kitchen and food bank charity near Princeton, where my dad was going to school. They volunteered their time on weekends, and that's how they became fast friends. It was only later on, well into a year or so, before my dad had a talk with Mom about their friendship."

"They didn't get married for six years, though, as I understand it."

"That's right," Andy said, feeling the elevator halt, the doors opening to the second floor. "They both wanted their master's degrees and decided to do that first and then start their lives together."

"Did they live together, though?"

"Yes, after the first year, they agreed to work at their relationship. Mom's apartment was very close to the university and he moved in with her. My dad told me one time that it saved him a lot of money his folks didn't have to keep him at Princeton. He had scholarships, but none of them paid for his dorm room or food."

"So?" he said, ambling at her side, "they had a friendship that grew into a marriage. That's a sound plan."

"Exactly." She fished her card key from the pocket of her robe as she halted at her door. On the opposite side of the hall was Dev's condo. "It taught me that it was okay to wait." She pushed the door open.

Dev opened the door and placed his foot next to it, devoting his attention to her. "How about if we have any time of our own this summer, we start hiking together? Maybe even pitch a tent and stay overnight in the mountains? Continue to learn and earn each other's friendship and trust?"

"That," she said, smiling, "sounds wonderful. I really need to stay in shape, and hiking is far preferable to a gym. I like your idea."

"Good," Dev said, "now all we have to do is find those windows of opportunity and do it."

Her smile grew. "Oh, I have a feeling you'll be on the lookout for them."

Giving her a self-satisfied smile, he rumbled, "Got that right. Night, Andy. Sweet dreams."

"You too," she whispered, wanting to kiss him but afraid. She moved into her condo. Andy was sure her dreams would be torrid that night.

Chapter Thirteen

Dev counted this to be his lucky two days. It was his boss, Pete Turner, who made out the monthly flight schedule for himself, Andy, Alma, Tucker and Grace. The next two days he and Andy were assigned together. The pilots all rotated in pairs with one another and never with the same person on one forty-eight-hour period. He was the pilot-in-command today. Tomorrow, Andy would take the right-hand seat and be flying the Black Hawk. She sat in the copilot seat, dealing with navigation, radio and some throttle work. In the back was Larry Fowler, their crew chief and paramedic. They'd gotten a call into their unit at 0600 that a big rig had flipped over in the southern part of the valley on Highway 89, between Fairview and Smoot. It was about ten miles away from where they were taking off. The truck driver was pinned and he'd called it in on his cell phone.

As they lifted off from the airport, he could see two fire engines and an ambulance already speeding down the highway toward the crash, lights flashing and sirens screaming. That was sure to wake up folks who were sleeping in if they lived near Highway 89. The morning was cool, the sky clear with no breeze. It was perfect flight weather. Larry was getting everything set up on one of the two cots that were one above the other on the side of the helo. He was responsible for getting all the medical items ready in case the truck driver had suffered injury. Larry had placed an IV on a hook on the top cot, in case the trucker was losing blood. In an anchored ice chest, they had blood for transfusion, if necessary.

His mind was on the business of flying. There were electric lines on the right side of the highway as they passed the ambulance and firetrucks. The Hawk could go damned fast and they would arrive first at the scene. In the summer, hot-air balloons were up in the early dawn hours because the air was smooth and quiet.

"Balloon ten o'clock," Andy said into the mic near her lips, and lifted her Nomex gloved hand, pointing in that direction.

"Roger," Dev said, glancing to where she indicated. He spotted a green-and-yellow-striped one. It was coming up from Red Tail Ranch, the owners of whom offered hot-air balloon rides to tourists traveling through the valley toward the Salt River Range, part of their seventy-five-thousand-acre ranch. It was another way for locals struggling to stay in the valley. It was owned by the Dvorak family, a third-generation family living in the valley. Doug and Jenny were now in charge of continuing its legacy. Doug had been in the Army for four years, deployed to the Middle East, and was a renowned helicopter mechanic. He had gotten his civilian balloon pilot license when he returned from the military, taken over the reins of the ranch with Jenny, his parents ratcheting down their hard work, with the next generation taking over. Doug had developed his balloon flying skills; it was a way to make extra money, other than from cattle grass leases, during the summer. Every penny counted. Now, the owners had a small office inside the airport, touting their balloon rides. He'd talked to Doug yesterday at Kassie's Café and found out that since the airport had opened, their balloon ride trips had doubled.

"Wonder how many passengers Doug has with him?" Dev asked.

Andy leaned over, pulling the set of binoculars from the side pocket of her seat. She lifted them to her eyes, aimed at the balloon ascending from the ranch on her left. "Hmmm, looks like he's got six in the basket."

"Good," Larry chimed in from the rear of the helo, "that's money in the kitty for them."

"Hey, you two have no idea how much Doug and Jenny rely on what they make during the summer months. There were some years when it paid the property taxes on their land," Andy said.

"This airport is breathing new life into the valley," Dev agreed. He craned his neck. "Andy? I think I see the rig along the road. Get your eyes on it. Tell us what you see."

"Roger that," and she pulled the binoculars up. "Smoke coming from the engine. No fire. At least, not yet. The truck is on its left side, the driver's side. I don't see the driver. The driver's window is broken."

"That's why he's pinned," Larry said, coming and kneeling between the two seats, gloved hands on the tops of each of them.

"Yeah," Dev said.

"Two civilian cars had pulled off to help," she reported. "They're standing there, unsure what to do."

"Once we get there," Larry said, "Andy, will you come with me? I want you to get those people back to a safe distance. A battery can explode and start a fire."

"Or it can set the fuel on fire, and that truck has two forty-gallon tanks just behind the cab," Dev warned grimly.

"Roger, I'll go with you, Larry."

"Roger that. Thanks."

Dev began their descent, bringing the Hawk in on the same side as the truck, but far enough away from it so if it did explode, it wouldn't harm them or destroy the helo. They were all business now. Andy called into the medevac unit dispatcher, Lanny Jenkins, reporting their status and that they were landing.

The Hawk descended in the desolate area that reminded Andy of desert terrain, and she made sure there were no trees or possible power or electric lines nearby. Larry was looking out the starboard window and door, too, another set of experienced, valuable eyes on the landing zone coming up.

"All clear," he announced.

"All clear," Andy said.

"Roger," Dev said.

In moments, they were on the ground. Dev saw Larry pushing the throttles, located on the ceiling above and between them, into an idle position. They would never cut the engines, only to idle.

"Egress," he ordered them.

Larry unlocked and slid the door open. The four blades whooshed above them, slowing down to the point where dust was no longer being kicked up in billowing yellow clouds around them. As soon as he could see, he gestured to Andy to follow him. He hitched a large, heavy paramedic pack onto his back, settling the straps against his shoulders.

Andy bailed out, and they moved around the nose of the Black Hawk at a quick trot, heading toward the highway in the distance, where the eighteen-wheeler was overturned. She saw five more cars parked on the other side, opposite the truck, people getting out. None of them seemed to realize they were in a highly volatile and dangerous situation.

"Fire trucks and ambulance five minutes out," Dev informed them.

"Roger," Andy huffed.

"That's good," Larry said, lengthening his stride, leaping over the small, dry ditch, landing on the berm of the highway. "Do your best to get those people away from the site. When the fire engines arrive, the chief will have a couple of his men cordon off the area. And then, if I need help, I'll call you."

"Will do," Andy said between breaths. She wasn't as tall as Larry and was losing ground to him.

She peeled off, heading for the six people huddled near the cab of the truck. Larry went to the underside of the truck, on its side. Like a spider, he climbed upward, grabbing what he could to get him to the top of the cab so he could see what had to be done next.

Still wearing her helmet, Andy lifted her hands, making sharp gestures for the people to move quickly away from the truck. They instantly complied, seeing Larry up on top.

Dev sat in the helo, as was standard operating procedure. One never left a helicopter on idle without a pilot in the cockpit. He watched worriedly, knowing full well all the things that could go wrong. He had landed on the underside of the truck, so he couldn't see what the firefighters, who had just arrived, were doing. He knew they'd string out hose and get the nozzle ready to use. Another firefighter would begin to check out the two huge gasoline tanks on the truck to see if they were leaking fluid, another potential fire hazard.

Some relief went through him as he saw a firefighter

joining the gathering of curious automobile drivers and getting them far, far away from the dangerous situation.

"Hey, Andy," Larry called, "can you climb up here and help me? I need a second pair of hands."

"Roger that," she said, turning, then running across the highway.

Dev saw two sheriff's cruisers arrive. They stopped traffic about a quarter of a mile north and south of the wreck. He watched, seeing Andy trotting around the end of the rig and then rapidly climbing up the superstructure of the truck to the top of the cab.

His heart started beating harder as he saw her gingerly grab the frame of the truck's broken front window, scoot down and disappear from his view. Some of his trepidation left as he saw hoses being dragged from the two fire engines on the opposite side of the highway. That meant there might be leaking from one or both gas tank, and they were going to spray into the puddles gathering below to wash it away with the water, lessening the likelihood of an explosion occurring.

No auto accident was safe. Not one. The battery was always a major, deadly threat, and most people stopping to try to help a motorist who had crashed or needed help getting out of the vehicle never realized that. More batteries exploded in such situations, injuring all those who were nearby, never mind the acid that was thrown into the air and striking an unsuspecting civilian being a Good Samaritan. He worried about his crew. He tried to put his heart aside in this situation, not wanting Andy in such a circumstance but knowing she was a natural-born risk-taker and would, without a second thought, put herself in harm's way to save someone else. It was a part of her nature, and he understood that. But he didn't like it. Wishing he could see what was going on, frustrated, he waited for tense exchanges between Larry and Andy.

Andy hovered in a crouch near Larry. He was half into the cab, talking to the driver, who was conscious and still belted in, unable to get him free of it. Right now, he was cutting through it with a small saw he kept in his paramedic pack, which was laying open nearby, on the hood. She had her hand on the belt that had captured the driver's shoulder. His name was Eddy, they had learned, and he was in his late fifties, well over 250 pounds and balding. He looked scared as fumes continued to drift heavily into the cab.

It took sheer brute physical force to saw through the thick nylon harness. When it did, the man fell against the door, which was against the asphalt of the highway, outside the cab. His cry told Andy he was injured. Larry handed her the saw and she put it back in his pack, waiting for his next instruction.

"Andy, can you get down into the cab? You're small enough to get through the broken windshield area."

"Yeah," she said, taking off her helmet and setting it aside. Her hair was in a ponytail, so it would be out of the way. She would no longer have radio contact with anyone, only Larry's instructions above her.

"I need to get Eddy sitting up. We have to assess his condition before we try to get the passenger-side door open. There will be firefighters working on the door in a moment."

She heard metallic thumping sounds on the door. It sounded jammed shut. Sitting down after putting a small blanket across the jagged area where the glass remained here and there on the lower windshield frame, she eased down and into the cab. Eddy was trying to sit up.

"Hold on, Eddy," she told him. "Don't move yet. Let me get over to you. My name's Andy and I'm here to help you."

He was breathing hard, sweat running down his face. "Yeah, yeah, Andy . . . it's my shoulder. You're too small to help me. It hurts like hell. I can't use it. I'm sorry, but I can't get up."

Andy purposely kept her voice soft and soothing. "Eddy, it's okay that I'm small. I'll help you once I get the safety latch unbuckled so we can get the strap across your hips released." She saw him sag back, his hand on his left shoulder, grimacing, teeth clenched to stop from crying out.

Once in a position over him, her foot on the console, the other near Eddy's right shoulder, Larry handed her the small saw. She quickly and efficiently sawed through the nylon belt. "He's fully released now," she called, turning her head to Larry, who was stretched across the frame, watching her.

"Great," he praised, taking the saw from her and dropping it into his pack. "Eddy?"

"Yeah?"

"Andy's going to help you sit up now. She's stronger than you think. I can't grab your left arm because that shoulder is injured. I could do more damage."

Eddy was huffing and struggling, but it was no use. Between his weight and the gravity, he was stuck in that position. "I'm not gonna be much help," he apologized, giving them a mournful look. "I don't think you can move me, squirt. You're way too small to do it by yourself."

"Squirt? Is that my new nickname?" she teased, grinning down at him.

"Yeah, I think it is," he whispered, shutting his eyes against the pain.

"No worries," Andy reassured him. She planted her right boot on the dashboard, leaning down on her left knee next to his right hip. "I'm going to put one arm around your back and under your left armpit, Eddy. With my right hand, I'm going to come around the front of your chest and into your left armpit. I'm going to lock my hands, and then I'm going to slowly pull you up toward me. Use your legs and try to move your butt as I haul upward; try for a sitting position. Okay?"

He gave her a stare. "I'm twice your weight, squirt."

She gave him a feral grin. "Ask Larry. I'm small but mighty. Okay, let's do this, pardner . . ."

Andy knew how to use her legs, which were strong and immovable where they were placed, and pulled upward, using them like pistons. She slowly hauled Eddy up into a sitting position. It happened seamlessly, all of them working together.

"Excellent, Eddy!" Larry praised. "Now, just sit there. I know you're in pain."

Andy released him into an upright position. Eddy had done a lot of the work, too. He was leaning against the cab, his eyes closed, his face turning white, his right hand against his left shoulder. Finally, he barely opened his eyes, giving her a look of awe.

"You did it, squirt. Damn, you're a strong little thing."

Chuckling, she smoothed her gloved hand across his tense right shoulder. "It was easy-peasy, Eddy. Now, try taking some slow, deep breaths. It will help ease the pain."

The trucker did as she suggested, no longer questioning her in any way, shape or form.

Larry slid slowly through the driver's side window frame, resting his chest on the wheel. "Okay," he said to Eddy, gently removing his right hand from the injured area, "let me assess that shoulder. I'll try not to cause you more pain . . ."

Andy kept her hand on Eddy's right shoulder, stabilizing him, trying to give him some comfort under very stressful circumstances. She heard Larry talking to the fire chief, who stood outside the cab area, by radio, giving him medical information.

"Patient has a broken left collarbone. It's a closed fracture. Can we get that passenger-side door open?"

Andy heard the chief talking to the firefighters outside the door. Within a minute, she heard scraping and banging going on as they worked to open that door. There was no way to get Eddy through the windshield. He wouldn't fit. The only way up and out was to get that big, wide door open.

Larry quickly created a sling for Eddy's left arm, holding it against his body and thereby stabilizing the broken bone, which was attached through ligaments and tendons, to his left shoulder.

"Got it!" the fire chief crowed.

At the same moment, the door popped open. Someone used a gaff and pushed the door up and as wide as it would go. Soon, there were two ladders, and two firefighters, a man and a woman, appeared.

"Hey, Eddy," Andy said, giving him a grin, "the cavalry has just arrived! Ready to climb outta this beast? Get you out and into the ambulance, where they can give you a shot to help ease that shoulder of yours?"

Eddy looked up at the door above them. "Squirt, that blue sky and those two firefighters look damned good to me."

Laughing, Andy helped get him into a position where the firefighters had slid a short, stout ladder into the cab of the truck. It would help Eddy to exit. Andy could put her shoulder on his butt and keep him steady from below so he wouldn't get dizzy and fall backward.

For the next few minutes, Larry, from his position, gave the orders to everyone, slowly but surely guiding Eddy without any bumping around or falling back into the cab.

Within ten minutes, they had the truck driver out of the cab, on a wheeled gurney and sitting up in a comfortable position, a comfortable sitting angle that helped stabilize his back and injured shoulder so he was comfortable.

Andy was next to climb up and out of the cab. She waved from the top toward the idling Black Hawk helo, knowing Dev was watching. Without her helmet on, she had no way to communicate with him. Tossing him a brilliant smile and a happy wave, she turned around and, with the help of the firefighters, descended the second ladder to the ground.

Larry came down as he'd come up once he'd belted his knapsack paramedic bag across his broad back. He beat her to the ground.

"Hey, squirt!" he teased as Andy's boots met the berm, "hurry up! We can make breakfast back at the dining room!" He handed her the helmet.

Laughing, Andy said, "Fowler, you're always thinking about your stomach!" She pulled on her helmet and pushed the plug into the radio she wore on her uniform.

"Dev, we're ready to roll. Driver had a broken left collarbone, so all is okay to be transported to the hospital via ambulance. They aren't that far away from the hospital and he has no blood loss or any other major injuries. Riding in an ambulance will probably be more comfortable for him under the circumstances. We're heading in your direction."

"Roger, sounds good. I don't know about you, but I'm hungry as a wolf."

Shaking her head, she saw Larry's eyes light up with amusement. "You two guys must have holes in your legs! You're always bitching about not having enough to eat."

More laughter followed. Andy and Larry shook hands with the fire chief and the two firefighters who had helped them extricate Eddy. It was a job well done, with a lot of support. Part of the job of the firefighters was to remove the cables from the battery if they could get the hood open, and they'd been able to do that. The gasoline tank that had been leaking was patched, the gas on the highway and berm washed away. Fire was the most dangerous element in an auto accident.

She and Larry hotfooted it back to the helicopter. Andy saw the worry on Dev's face as she opened the door and climbed into the copilot's seat. Larry had gone around, hopped in the opened door and then turned around, closing and locking it.

Andy didn't have time for any personal comments to Dev. That would have been unprofessional. Later, she might get some one-on-one time with him after they chowed down in the dining room. From the look in his darkened eyes, she could tell he'd been worried. Belting into her harness, she threw him a thumbs-up that she was ready to start the Flight Check list with him. In the back, Larry had tucked away his paramedic pack into a special compartment and he, too, was ready.

Time to go home!

"Are you okay?" Dev asked Andy. The three of them had eaten a hearty breakfast in the small dining room upon their return to the airport. They were still on duty, but Pete had given them permission to go over to the hospital to check on the truck driver they'd rescued two hours earlier. It was only a five-minute drive and easy enough to get back if there was a call for another mission.

"I'm fine," she said as she walked alongside him in the late morning sunlight, wearing her blue baseball cap with the round embroidered insignia of their medevac unit on it. "Why do you ask?"

"I didn't realize how large that guy was until I saw him coming down that ladder and out of the cab. He was a big dude." He touched her shoulder briefly. "You're a mighty mite, but I worry about your back and knees. Eddy was a lot to heft out of the cab."

"I know how to use my body to lift, Dev. I know men rely on brute force and muscle, but women look for leverage instead. And a woman's legs are actually stronger than a man's. I used my legs to leverage his weight, let them do the work by pushing with his feet and not kill my shoulders and back."

"Larry said he was amazed."

Shrugging, she cut him a wry glance. "You guys . . . women are stronger than any man."

"My mother told me the same thing and I never argue with her on things like that." He chuckled, gesturing for her to go through the opening door to the ER.

Laughing, she aimed at the ER desk. "That's right."

His chest warmed with good feelings. Andy once more had shown she was a trooper when the chips were down. Instead of her relying on him, Larry was relying on her because she was small enough to slide through the main cab windshield to reach the trucker. She seemed almost high from the experience, and he'd known that feeling himself upon occasion. Having every right to feel good about the rescue, the mission had fed Andy on many levels and taken nothing away from her.

After they found out Eddy's room was on the second floor, they took the elevator.

"It probably isn't protocol to go visit someone you rescued," Andy said, "but I care about Eddy. He was in a world of hurt and was really strong through it all. Despite the pain, he followed our instructions. That takes grit, and he had it. I've seen others in the same situation who couldn't follow any directives. This dude is tough."

"I think Larry's and your attitude—soft, quiet voices, looking relaxed even if you weren't—helped Eddy react similarly," Dev said, walking at her shoulder down the white-and-green-tiled hall. At this time of day, the hospital didn't seem busy. He spotted the room number, pointing to it ahead. "There it is, on the right."

"You go in first," Andy urged. "You're the pilot in charge of the mission. He never got to meet you and he should."

Dev hesitated but nodded, slowing his pace. "Okay."

Eddy was sitting up in bed, his left arm in a sling. He was in a blue gown and had an IV in his right arm. Dev introduced himself, and Andy showed up a moment later. Instantly, Eddy's demeanor changed.

"Hey, squirt!" he called, lifting his right hand. "I didn't ever expect to see you again," and he broke out into a welcoming grin.

"Oh, no," Andy teased, going to the bed and gently squeezing his hand, "now my boss knows what you called me. I'll never live it down in our office, Eddy."

He released her hand and gave Dev a demanding look. "You should know what she did this morning, Mr. Mitchell."

"I do know," Dev said, coming to Andy's side. He gave Andy a smile. "Squirt, huh?"

Groaning, Andy rolled her eyes and looked at the trucker. "This is all your fault, Eddy!"

"Hey, it's a good nickname for you," he countered, smiling. "I'll never forget what you did. Ever. You folks saved my life."

Dev saw Andy's face turn to mush, the emotions clear in her expression.

"Hey, we were a team of a lot of people out there this

morning to help you survive that crash, Eddy," she said. "It was all of us, not just me."

"You know," Eddy said, "you remind me so much of my wife, Colleen. She's always been humble, never tooting her own horn."

"We," and Andy motioned to Dev, "joined medevac services for a reason. We love to help people."

"How are you feeling?" Dev asked.

Wrinkling his nose, which had a bulb at the end of it, he said, "I'd kill to get out of this bed, go down to the cafeteria and get the largest cup of thick, hot, black coffee around."

"Have you eaten?" Andy asked, alarmed. It was well past time.

"Oh, sure . . . but you know? They give you that dinky paper cup's worth of coffee that for a big-time java drinker like me, that's just two gulps."

"How about I go get you the Grande they have down there?" Dev asked. "They have a Starbucks."

Eyes widening with disbelief, Eddy said, "Hell yes, man!"

"We're paying for it," Andy said as he reached for his wallet, sitting nearby on a rolling tray table.

"Oh . . . well, thanks," Eddy said, suddenly emotional.

Dev touched her shoulder. "I'll be right back. Do you want anything?"

"Sure, I could use an Americano. Get one for yourself, too. We'll stay a bit; I want to see if Eddy's got a way to get home."

Nodding, Dev said, "Three it is. Back in sixty seconds or less."

Brightening, Eddy said, "Hey, that hombre isn't a bad fellow."

"What?" Andy teased him mercilessly, "you got a nick-name for him, too?"

Giving her a sly wink, Eddy said, "You're too young to know a cowboy TV show I used to watch as a kid. It was called *Have Gun—Will Travel*. The main character's name was Paladin. And it starred Richard Boone. Your pilot friend's nickname, at least to me, is Paladin. He looks a lot like him: real intense, his eyes focused and he has hair that's kinda Mediterranean-looking."

"Hmmm," she said, bringing the two chairs against the wall alongside the bed on Eddy's right side, "I'll have to check him out." She sat down. "Are you hungry, Eddy?"

"Probably will be in about an hour. I'm so upset by what happened that I kinda lost my appetite." And then he rallied. "Except for coffee. I want the biggest cup I can get. Good, strong coffee."

"Well, that wish is coming true for you. What happened out there this morning?"

With a grimace, he muttered, "A deer and her yearling crossed the highway right in front of me. I know I'm not supposed to try to stop, but hell, it was automatic. When I slammed on the brakes, it jackknifed the truck. I guess the only good thing out of this is that the mama and her baby got away safely."

"You're a softy at heart, Eddy." She reached out, gently squeezing the hand he had in a fist on his stomach. Releasing him, she said, "Does your family know about your wreck?"

"Yes. I live in Salt Lake City. It's not that far away. My wife is on her way by car to come and get me. The doc says he'll release me as soon as she shows up. I got my pain medicine prescription and he's given me the name of an orthopedic doc near where we live. They took care of me right and proper here."

"That's good," Andy murmured. "What about children?

Do you have any?" She assumed he did, but saw sadness come to his eyes.

Opening his large, meaty hand, he said, "It's a long story, squirt, but basically, our third son, Lawrence, was married and had two beautiful children, a boy and a girl. He got caught up in the opioid crisis three years ago. The state asked us to take in their children, and we did."

Making a mewing sound, Andy whispered, "I'm so sorry to hear that. It has to be hard on all of you."

"Yeah, in more ways than one. I was driving extra runs to make money to keep up with the kids' expenses at school. Children aren't cheap to raise anymore, like they were before."

"That's true."

"This accident is gonna cost me. I've already talked with my boss and the insurance adjuster."

"Are they going to hold you responsible?" Andy asked, fearing the answer.

"I'm not sure. I've never, in thirty years, had an accident. My boss is a good guy, and he likes that I'm trustworthy, responsible, come to work on time and do what's expected of me. He said he was going to fight for me."

"Does he know you have kids to feed and care for?"

"Yeah, Bob and I are pretty good friends. He's been my boss for the last twenty years at the trucking depot where I work out of Salt Lake."

"Well, let's keep our fingers crossed, then," Andy said, feeling deeply for him. "I hope someday those kids realize all the trials and tribulations you went through to keep them safe, loved and cared for."

"Oh, I think they will," he said, his voice warming. "They're good children. I've talked to both of them and they were crying on the phone, thinkin' I was hurt real bad."

Touched, Andy patted his hand. "I have a feeling it will turn out okay for you and the kids."

"Hope you're right, squirt, because at fifty, there aren't a whole lotta jobs out there. I'm worried sick about that."

Andy stood up and pulled out a business card from her back pocket. She sat down, pulled the rolling table to her and wrote something on the back of it. "Listen, my grand-mother owns a nationwide trucking company. If you're fired, the first thing you do is call me on the cell phone number I'm putting on this. Then, the next day, I want you to go over to their main terminal, which is located in Salt Lake City, and give this card to a Chuck Townsend. He's the boss over there. I'll call my grandmother, Martha Campbell, and ask her to call Chuck to tell him to give you a trucking job with high pay. Okay?" and she handed it to Eddy. He looked shocked.

"Are you serious about this, squirt?" and he held it up, squinting at the small print on the thick, white card.

"Totally," Andy promised him. "It's your lucky day after all, Eddy. Anyone who would take in two children like you and Colleen have deserves a break. I'm giving it to you. You've more than earned it in my eyes and heart."

Chapter Fourteen

July 10

Dev had arrived with coffee in hand just as Andy was explaining the business card she was giving Eddy. The trucker looked like he was going to cry. He wasn't that up on her family finances, so he waited to talk about it until after they'd said goodbye to Eddy and wished him well. Outside the hospital, walking toward the parking lot, he asked, "Does your grandmother own a trucking company in Salt Lake City?"

"Yes, she does. She owns lots of women-run businesses around the world. I always carry her business cards on me because Mom said we can use them to help others on a case-by-case basis. Sort of like paying it forward."

"Tell me more," he urged, taking the sidewalk to the parking lot, walking at her shoulder.

"Grandma Martha started working on Wall Street a long time ago. She's a feminist, and she saw how hard it was for women to be entrepreneurial, to start their own cottage businesses and to try to get bank loans. She became, in ten years, one of the most successful stockbrokers in the world. I don't normally talk about this, Dev, because there are too many people out there whose eyes glaze over when I tell them she's one of the richest women in the world. My grandmother is a dynamo on a mission to help women in any country. For example, Babs Trucking in Salt Lake City? She's one of the thousands of successful business stories my grandmother has underwritten. The company card I gave to Eddy? It's owned by Babs Fordham. It started as a local trucking company and Babs built it into a regional and, later, into a national one." She pointed toward the north. "There's a terminal at Jackson Hole as well. My mother is trying to get Babs to bring her trucking company down here, to the airport. We already have a trucking terminal built, as you know, and that's part of the larger vision Mom and Dad planned for this airport. It would be ideal, and Babs is considering it right now. My grandmother feels sure that she'll be in Wind River Valley sooner or later."

"I've seen Babs Trucking on the road," Dev said, impressed. "So, she'd move her Jackson Hole business down here to our airport instead?"

"Yes. I think it would be a good move, and so does everyone in my family. My grandmother has a whole team of men and women who run her international financial company, Hope Bank. Women are encouraged to go to that bank in their country to receive low-interest loans so they can start up businesses. Babs went to the Hope Bank in Salt Lake City twenty years ago, when she was nineteen years old, and got a loan."

"That's impressive," he murmured. "Now I know why you gave Eddy that business card."

"Yes. My mom has all of us kids carry cards on us wherever we go. She wants to help women around the world, and if we see someone, even a guy like Eddy, she encourages us to give a card to them. We're not anti-male, but because women aren't considered for bank loans as men are, we focus on them instead. If he gets fired from his job because of the crash, I know Babs will hire Eddy. One of the many things a woman getting a loan from my grandmother's bank has to promise is to give healthy paychecks. People have to make a living and be able to pay their bills. I know Babs will help Eddy, if he needs it."

"And here I thought you were just a Warthog pilot," he teased, giving her a grin.

Laughing, Andy said, "My family taught me to keep most of our financial history and background a secret. My grandparents have thousands of people sending them letters, emails and videos from around the world every year, begging for donations. She has a team who reads every letter, and often they'll recommend an action for that person. Sometimes, it's money. Sometimes, it's legal or business support. My mother, who grew up with this global charity in the household, didn't want that issue following the four of us kids. She taught all of us how to be discreet in the use of the business cards, and to use our judgment on whether to reach out to help someone or not. Our parents taught us a lot about evaluating a person and now, at my age, I'm grateful for that training."

"So," Dev said, slowing and opening the pickup door for her, "your parents taught you civics, social responsibility and being compassionate. Not a bad combo," and he stepped aside.

"Thanks," Andy murmured, climbing into the truck. "I love having those business cards. It's like giving a woman or a man, a get-out-of-jail-free kind of opportunity. And it always feels good when I can do it. It's human compassion and paying it forward. My mom taught us that from the time we could walk and talk."

Dev came around the truck and opened the door. "I won't say anything to anyone about this, Andy."

She strapped in. "Thanks, I appreciate it. That's why I made Eddy promise he wouldn't speak a word of what I'd done to help him. We kids and our family would visit my grandparents at their estate in the Hamptons, usually in the summertime. Growing up, we saw how overwhelmed they were sometimes, helping people who didn't have much."

"There are very few people who can help the world like your grandparents are doing," he said, putting the truck in gear and moving slowly out of the parking lot. "And I imagine there are stresses and pressures we can't even guess on them."

"Right," Andy said. "My parents never asked anything of them. With my mom's vision coupled with her MBA, they've taken the ranch from being barely in the black to being supersuccessful. They don't need my grandparents' money. They've made it on their own with pure hard work."

"And that's good," Dev said.

"What about your parents? Are they okay financially speaking?"

"Yes, they are. They're middle class, but coming from Ireland to the US when they did, at eighteen? They were poor as church mice. They were immigrants fleeing to America and then carving out a home and a business with decades of hard work. It put them at a level where they felt rich, very well off. I know they aren't wealthy by your grandmother's standards, but they're comfortable where they are, and that's what's most important."

"Money can't buy you happiness," Andy murmured. "But it sure can help folks who are economically deprived and stressed out because of having too little. My mom and dad took us on vacations every year to different countries around the world. My grandparents did the same for my mom. They took her to third-world countries and showed her the poverty, the horrible living conditions, the lack of so many things we take for granted here in America. It made a powerful impression on Mom. By the time we kids were in middle school, we knew just how lucky we were to be in this country. We never took money for granted again."

"Smart of Maud and Steve to give you all that travel opportunity. I know from my own globe-trotting how lucky we are to live in the US."

She snorted. "I'll tell you, deployed to Afghanistan? It's one of the worst-off countries in the world. My grandma really got involved. She connected with Delos Charities, who were in Central Asia already, delivering shoes, clothing, medicine and donated huge amounts of goods to try to make a difference in those people's poor, hard lives."

"I remember Delos jets flying into Bagram," he said. "Me and some of the other pilots, when we had a layover there, would volunteer our muscles to help offload and get the boxes to nearby warehouses."

She gave him a warm look. "That was so nice of you."

"Blame it on my parents' telling me their stories of near starvation and shoes being passed down to the next kid in their family, new soles being put on and worn until they fell apart."

"That's why you're the way you are."

Dev smiled a little, turning out into Highway 89, heading toward the airport. "I guess so. I don't like to see suffering. I don't have any friends who do either."

"Compassion," she said pensively, looking out the window, "can be learned, but basically, I think your heart either has it or it doesn't. I've seen plenty of hard-hearted men who don't."

"Not all men are that way," Dev countered.

"I realize that. But you see the brutality toward women and children in Afghanistan and it's horrifying. They consider women less valuable than a damned goat. And female children are seen as disposable if there is a boy in the household."

"Can't argue that," he admitted. "Glad we're out of there."

"Makes two of us."

There was silence for a moment, then Andy changed the subject.

"Any chance of us doing some hiking the day after we get off our forty-eight hours of duty?" she asked. "You might have other plans, but I'm free that day. I'd really like to break out in a sweat, do some serious trail work and get back to nature."

"I'm free on Thursday. Let's do it. Any place in particular you want to go?"

"Prater Canyon, up in the Salt River Range. It's one of my favorite places to hike."

"That was fast," and he grinned, meeting her sparkling gaze. "This will be good for both of us."

"Yes, I need a time-out, some relaxation from the push we've done since I got home."

"Agreed," Dev said.

"I wonder what adventures await us in Prater?" she mused, leaning back on the headrest, her eyes closed.

July 12
Thursday

The scent of pine was almost an aphrodisiac to Andy as she took the steeper trail out of Prater Canyon, a valley favorite. It was nine a.m., a weekday, but school was out, so there were a number of older teenagers who could drive flying their drones down below them. To her right was the river, which would eventually flow into the mighty

Snake River, farther away and to the west of the canyon. It was a perfect place to fly drones, plus hikers who wanted the quiet of nature around them could find it as they hiked out of the canyon and headed toward the waterfalls, a good mile farther up at seven thousand feet.

Andy smiled to herself as Dev came up as the trail widened to walk at her side. She could feel and see his appreciation for the mighty Douglas firs that covered the Salt Range like a green cloak.

"I've really missed this," she confessed, gesturing around her.

"What? The forest?"

"Yes, and giving myself permission to take time off. I've always been so driven. I think the smartest decision I made this year was to come home."

Nodding, Dev wiped the sweat from his brow and settled the red baseball cap Maud had given him before he left on their adventure back on his head. Maud was well known to wear the Wind River Ranch red baseball cap around the valley. In fact, Steve had joked once that Maud wanted it buried with her; it was that much a part of her identity, much as his black Stetson was his. Andy also wore one that had a lot of time and wrinkles to it, the bill well molded and narrowed. Dev wondered if she'd flown with it when she was in California.

"No place like home," he agreed.

"Tell me more about your upbringing?" she asked, keeping contact with his gaze for a moment. She saw his face soften with thought at her question.

"I grew up with sandy beaches, pine trees that flourish growing there and flying kites and, later, drones on the beach. My father loved surf fishing off the beach, catching some nice ones for our dinner. My mother always liked bringing a picnic basket to the beach while he fished, setting up a big umbrella to hide her fair Irish skin from the hot sun, knitting in her beach chair. They were born on the ocean, so the ocean is in their makeup."

"Is it in yours, too?"

"Yeah, in a sense," Dev murmured, sliding his hands under the shoulder straps of his knapsack. "I enjoy swimming. Most of all, I guess I was like my parents in that the sounds of the waves crashing into the beach, the cry of the gulls overhead, fed my Irish soul."

"I love when you wax poetic," she teased. His cheeks turned ruddy and his mouth flexed in a boyish grin. "It's nice to see a man able to reveal his emotional side to a woman. Refreshing, as a matter of fact."

"I don't imagine you had anyone in the military who waxed poetic," he said, trading a glance with Andy.

Snorting, she said, "Oh, no. It was all business, as it should have been. You can't be emotional in the cockpit, as you well know. It's all mental and logic."

"It's a place a pilot has to be at all times," he agreed. "But out here? It's nice to be able to let down, relax and just sort of let the day, the weather, the fragrances in the air feed us something so utterly necessary to every living thing. It nurses my soul, too."

"I've always heard the Irish are great storytellers and masters of word pictures," she said, smiling over at him. "You sure you aren't a poet? I've never seen you so relaxed, and you've unveiled your muse side here in the mountains."

Giving her an embarrassed chuckle, Dev said, "My mother speaks in wonderful word picture and I think I got a little of that ability through her. My father is a master storyteller. As a kid, I used to love sitting at his feet at night as he read the newspaper, weaving a story from some of the articles he'd read. I loved those times with him."

"Gosh, that sounds wonderful."

"I feel really lucky to have decent parents. So many of my friends were raised by single mothers, in broken families or dysfunctional ones. I didn't have any of that."

"And it's made you the man you are, Dev. Don't change. You're special, and there aren't many of your type around."

He moved his fingers up and down the straps, seeing a blue jay winging past them, crying out the alarm that there were two humans in its territorial vicinity. He held her smile with one of his own. "Don't go putting me up on a pedestal, Andy. I have feet of clay just like any other guy."

Laughing, she said, "Oh! No worries about that. I know that at my age and experience, both genders have feet of clay. Still, it's nice to see a guy allow his softer, vulnerable side to show and be shared. Women love that in a man."

He became sober. "That's funny . . . well, not ha-ha-ha funny, but ironic you said that."

"What did I say?"

"My wife, Sophie, said those very same words when we were planning our wedding. She was so mature for her age of eighteen . . . I never forgot those words. It made a lasting impact on me."

"I'm so sorry you lost her when you were both so young. That's tragic."

Shrugging, he managed, "Tragedy is in everyone's life."

Andy looked around, absorbing the silence broken by the blue jay and the soft wind singing through the pine far above them. Inhaling the camphorlike scent, believing it was truly feeding her soul, she whispered, "No question."

"There's a lot in life to deal with," Dev agreed quietly, avoiding a huge boulder in the middle of the well-used trail. Walking around it and meeting Andy on the other side, he said, "There are days when I think living on this planet of suffering is just that. I don't see much happiness in it, to tell you the truth. All I see is poverty, pain and suffering, and wish everyone could be lifted up to what I have. There are moments of happiness woven into it, of course, but by and large, we all, to a person, suffer, whether it's family- or career-related."

"Or a combination of both," she added gently. "My choices of men have been unmitigated disasters. I made a lot of mistakes."

"I think in our twenties we all make a ton of them," and he raised a brow, giving her a glance, seeing the unhappiness in her eyes.

"Well, I didn't do well in college either. Boys are idiots at that age, and so was I. And then, when I went into the Air Force, I met a slicker, more refined version of the idiots from college. I kept making bad choices. I called my mom more than once to ask what was wrong with me. I couldn't seem to find a guy who fit what I needed."

"And now, at this age?"

"Looking back on all the busted-up relationships, the pain it caused me, I feel more settled now, more secure. Mom told me once that men mature far more slowly than women do. A woman's brain is fully developed at age eighteen, whereas a man's brain isn't completely developed until he's around twenty-five or so." Her lips twisted. "She was right about a lack of maturity. I hit that wall many times with my choices. All I wanted was a man who didn't see me as a bed partner for his whims. I wanted a man who enjoyed all of me, and it wasn't always about sex. It was about one human getting to know another. Two people enjoying life in all its aspects, not just in bed."

It's about a relationship," he agreed. "Sophie and I were close from the first grade onward. We were buddies and, over the years, became fast friends. It was only when we were seventeen that we got serious in other ways."

"But your bedrock was your friendship. Right?"

"Right. And in my mind and heart, it's the best of all worlds when you want a long-term relationship. We worked out the kinks, the eccentricities, and found out who the other person was as friends."

"That takes time," she said, frowning. "I always thought I knew the guy and rushed in. I didn't give it a chance to mature, I guess."

He reached out, squeezing her left shoulder. "You're too hard on yourself, Andy. I don't know anyone who hasn't gone through a spotty past in their twenties. My mother once said that the twenties were our emotional-mistake years, learning what our parents didn't teach us or tell us about."

"Your mom is like the Delphi oracle," Andy teased with a grin. "She's got a lot of wisdom."

Chuckling, Dev said, "She told me when I hit my fifties, I'll be a little wiser, too."

"I can't even think in those numbers. I guess I just live the day as it unfolds before me."

"That's not a bad way to be," he said, looking up ahead, seeing a curve to the left between the thick woods.

"Hey," Andy said, halting. "Do you hear that? The waterfalls?" and she pointed toward the curve.

"Faintly," he said, halting and looking around. They were surrounded by trees, the ground covered with dead pine needles for a carpet, with black rocks covered with lichen, peeking up here and there. "How far are we from it?"

Looking at the Fitbit on her wrist, Andy said, "Half a mile. We've made good time."

"It's a great way to stay in shape," and he wiped sweat off his upper lip.

Andy frowned, tilting her head toward the curve in the trail ahead of them. "Did you hear that, Dev?"

"No. What did you hear?" He saw consternation in her

features as she turned slightly, lifting her head, one ear cocked toward the trail.

"There . . . there it is again. It's so faint. I'd swear I hear a woman calling for help." She scowled. "Do you hear anything?"

Dev listened intently. "No . . . sorry, I don't."

"It's my wolf-ear hearing," Andy muttered, walking around him. "Come on; I need to find out if I'm hearing things or there's someone in trouble."

Following quickly on her booted heels, the curve was long and then led steeply upward on a rocky patch of the trail. For a moment, Dev felt like the proverbial bighorn mountain sheep. Huffing, at the top, Andy halted, again tilting her head, listening intently, eyes closed. Breathing hard, he waited, hoping to hear what she heard.

". . . help . . . help me . . ."

Andy's eyes widened. She jerked a look up at Dev. "Did you hear that?"

"Yeah, I did." He pointed to the trail. "The sound is coming from that direction."

"Yes, it's a woman calling for help. Come on!" Andy dug the toes of her boots into the soft pine needles and soil, leaping forward, running full bore.

Dev ran easily behind her, the trail narrowing. They were on a somewhat level area, still a slope but not a steep one. The trail twisted again and again. They must have run nearly a quarter of a mile when he heard the woman's thin, reedy voice again. This time, much closer.

Andy slowed and shouted, "This way! There's a platform over the glacier river where tourists take photos. That's where it sounds like it's coming from. About three hundred yards. Let's hoof it!"

Nodding, Dev followed. He could smell the river now, more humidity in the air and the scent of water surrounding them. The trees were thick and he couldn't see beyond them, but he knew Andy had good knowledge of the terrain and area. She was running at a fast pace, her breath short and hard. This was a real climb. His mind moved forward. There was no question it was a woman. And in medical terms, he wondered how old she was. Was she out here alone? What had happened to her? Dev didn't know the terrain, but it was becoming rockier, even the path littered with rocks that could trip someone up, maybe break an ankle or leg.

They suddenly broke out of the tree line. In front of him, he saw the split-pea-soup-colored river. That color always signaled that its source was a glacier far above them, the water icy cold.

"Sandy!" Andy yelled, waving her hand frantically at a woman sitting near the wooden platform where photographers could shoot photos.

Dev saw a redheaded woman in her forties sitting down on the grassy bank, distressed. Her nose was bleeding and she was leaning over, her hands on her booted ankle.

"Andy!" she shrieked. "Oh my God! It's you!"

"Hold on," Andy yelled. "We're here to help!"

Dev quickly strode up to her shoulder.

"This is Sandy"

"Yeah," he huffed, "she's the radio dispatcher for the Lincoln County Sheriff's Department. We met her about a month ago when we were setting everything up."

"She's a good friend of my mother," Andy gasped, running hard now.

In less than a minute, they were there with Sandy, who was crying, her nose still bleeding, her lip split. Dev looked around. The bank area was spongy, wet with lots of long grass. What had happened to her? He saw a lot of grass smashed down around her.

"Hey," Andy said, kneeling down, her hand on her left shoulder, "what happened?"

Wiping her nose with a shaky hand, Sandy growled, "I was hiking this morning and two guys, druggies, attacked me." She pointed to the tree line. "I came out of the trees and they jumped me. I fought back." Her blue eyes slitted. "Those two are part of the Elson gang from the southern part of the valley."

Dev knelt down near her right shoulder. "How long ago did this happen, Sandy?"

"About an hour ago. I busted my ankle. It hurts like hell and it's swelling. Can you call dispatch at the sheriff's office? You're carrying a radio on you, aren't you?"

"Yes," he said quickly, shrugging out of his knapsack. Andy was digging into hers, bringing out a cloth, handing it to her so she could press it to her bleeding nose. Her khaki trouser leg had been pulled up to her knee, revealing the black, purple and blue colors, plus the swelling around the top of her boot, probably caused by her ankle. It didn't look good at all. "I'm going to call the sheriff's office, but we need to get the Black Hawk medevac up here to take you down. You can't walk on that thing."

She snorted, anger in her voice along with frustration. "Don't tell me about it. I tried to walk and I can't. The bones are grinding against one another." She looked beyond them at the meadow that stretched out to the north. "Can you land that thing up here?"

"Yeah," Andy said, straightening, looking warily at the tree line and then at the meadow. "There's plenty of space for it to land. Might be a little spongy and damp, but I don't think it will sink into the soil."

"Can you go check it out?" Dev asked her. He pulled out a holster that held a .45 pistol in it. "Strap this on, and take off the safety. There's a bullet in the chamber. We don't

know if these guys are still lurking around." He didn't want
to take chances with the two women.

"Thanks," Andy said, strapping on the weapon. She knew
how to handle a pistol and swiftly took the safety off it so
she could draw and shoot if necessary. "I'll stay in sight."

"We've had a few attacks up here," Sandy said, her
voice somewhat muffled, the cloth pressed to her nose.
"Maybe one a month or something like that, summer only."

Dev called in to the sheriff's office and told them what
was going on. The only helicopter in the valley was the
medevac. Two sheriff's deputies were going to ride up
with it to the meadow and stay behind to treat the area as a
crime scene. In the meantime, they'd get Sandy to the ER
at the Wind River Hospital. Dev was sure that if the
deputies found anything of import, they'd ask that they
fly up the forensic team when they came to pick them up
from the crime site.

He divided his attention between Sandy, who seemed
very self-sufficient and stable despite what she'd gone
through, and Andy, who was in the meadow now, testing
the impaction of the soil, determining where best to land
the Black Hawk to transport Sandy down the mountain.
Finally, she chose a spot, and taking long, orange plastic
strips out of her knapsack, which she always carried with
her, she laid out a ten-foot-long "X" where the Hawk
should land.

Andy returned as he signed off. He quickly told her
what was going on, and that the Hawk would be up there in
about twenty minutes.

"How are you feeling, Sandy?" she asked, kneeling
down, facing the tree line and watching for any unusual
movement.

"Much better." Her lips twisted. "My cell phone doesn't
work up here. My intuition told me to take a dispatch radio

with me, but I ignored it. If I'd had that on me, I could have radioed for help and not sat up here like a boob for an hour screaming for help." She pushed her fingers through her red hair, which was partially pulled out of her ponytail. "I'm so shaken by this, Andy. Prater Canyon is our most-used tourist place. Hikers from around the world use this trail. This is awful. Those two dudes were mean, and they meant business."

"But you fought them anyway," and Andy patted her shoulder gently.

"Hell yes! They jumped me from behind. You know I have a black belt in karate, right?"

"Yes, it's one of the first things Maud told me, proudly, about you. Kick ass, take names."

"Well," she grumped, glaring at the trail on which she'd been attacked, "I know for sure I broke one guy's arm. I heard it crack. That ended their attack on me. When I didn't melt and surrender, it surprised them."

"Were they carrying?" Dev asked. Standing up, he placed the radio on top of his knapsack. His gaze was sweeping the tree line.

"They looked like hikers," Sandy said, pulling the cloth away from her nose. "I didn't see any weapons on them." The bleeding had stopped. Andy took it and went to the bank of the river, kneeled down and washed out the blood and then returned to Sandy, who thanked her and placed the cold cloth against her swollen, lower split lip.

"Do you think you can identify them?" Andy asked, remaining close to her, looking at the continued swelling of her ankle above the boot. She had a bad break, there was no question, and she had to be in pain, but Sandy was so angry, the pain probably wasn't even registering on her right now.

"I've never seen either of them before. But once I get

this ankle taken care of, I want someone from the sheriff's department to send me photos of the Elson gang. Kaen's the one who says he owns these mountains, that this is their 'territory.'" She snorted, glaring at the trail behind her.

"So? It could be someone other than Elson?" Dev asked, above them, standing guard.

"Maybe," Sandy muttered. "But my gut tells me it was Elson's gang. He doesn't like Hispanics and blacks, and he only hires skinhead white supremacists and Nazi sympathizers." She looked up at him. "There were several Nazi tattoos on the backs of their necks."

"Damn," Andy said, shaking her head. "They attacked from the rear. What did they want?"

"My knapsack," and she jerked a thumb in the direction in which it was laying, one strap torn free from the red nylon body. "I think they were looking for money, credit cards, a cell phone to steal. All of those things can be sold. And junkies need to feed their habit. Why not jump a forty-year-old woman out in the middle of nowhere?"

"Bastards," Andy breathed, her anger rising.

"You said you broke one of their arms. Do you think they'll go to the hospital for help?"

"I don't know, but I'd be calling Wind River Hospital to talk to the head nurse, letting her know. Also, they need a deputy to get over there just in case. I didn't see any weapons on them, but they could be carrying them in their knapsacks."

"Good idea," Dev said, picking up the radio. He walked about ten feet away, closer to the wide, green river that was swiftly flowing and made the call to the nursing supervisor. He continued to sweep the area, not trusting that the two goons had left. What bothered him more was that he and Andy hadn't met them coming down from this area and the attack had occurred an hour ago. It was possible they'd trotted down the trail, made it to the parking lot below and were gone before they'd arrived. He wondered if any of the teens flying drones might have seen them. He'd be sure to let the deputies know about it for when they canvassed the area.

"I'm so pissed," Sandy growled, pointing at her bruised, swollen ankle. "I'll be in a cast for at least six weeks! This is the only time of the year, our short summer season, I get to hike. I love to hike. Damn them!"

Patting her shoulder, Andy said sympathetically, "At least we found you. This is a Thursday and not a lot of people are hiking, unless they're tourists."

"Yeah," she bit out, glaring at the surrounding area. "If no one came, the next problem I'd have is a grizzly getting my scent, attacking and killing me. I don't carry on the trail, but I'll tell, now I will. I have a license to carry a concealed weapon and it's way past time I start doing it." She patted her knapsack. "At least I carry a quart of bear spray on me."

Smoothing her hand gently across her grass-stained white tee, Andy said, "It's going to be all right, Sandy. Take a few deep breaths. We're here and we're going to get you taken care of."

Chapter Fifteen

The first snow had fallen five days earlier and Andy loved that small window of a week or so of Indian summer that would follow. She was hiking in the southern end of the valley in the Salt Range, showing Dev some of the little-known but beautiful hiking trails in the area. The morning air was near freezing and the higher in elevation they climbed, the colder it got. They were at five thousand feet, breathing hard with the change of altitude as they worked toward a small lake that sat at seven thousand feet above them. The river from that lake fed into the mighty Snake River, miles down on the other side of the mountain trail. The morning had a decided bite in the air and they were wearing goose down jackets, their knapsacks on their back. Dev walked ahead of her on the narrow, rarely used trail. The deciduous trees were in full autumn splendor, bright reds, yellows and orange leaves looking like errant splotches of tempera paint thrown between the dark green of the Douglas fir that surrounded them. She could smell the wonderful scent of decaying leaves across the brown pine needles that rolled out in front of them like an endless carpet.

Today was special. She sensed it. Since the incident with Sandy, who was well on her way to recovery, their relationship had changed, deepened, become central to her life. Living with Dev just across the hall from her, sharing a hot tub on most nights with him, was a pure pleasure she always looked forward to. She'd told her mother yesterday that she was falling in love with him, even though she'd never mentioned it to Dev. Yet. Today was the day. Andy could tell by the look in his large, intelligent eyes that he cared deeply for her. Since their talk about friendship, she'd felt him monitoring himself closely not to overstep his bounds with her. Sometimes, she saw he wanted to become more intimate, but he didn't go there. And she could swear there were a couple of times that he'd wanted to kiss her.

There were nothing but good things with Dev in her life. Maud had reminded her a week ago that she and Steve had been friends for a long time before stepping on to the next, serious step of an intimate, monogamous relationship. Andy had confided that she was ready to take that step, and Maud's eyes shone with happiness.

Tonight, they were pitching a tent, staying overnight and coming back next afternoon. One tent, two sleeping bags. Together. Yes, the time was right. And Dev knew it, too, even though he didn't say much about it. His actions always spoke louder than his words, and she smiled a secret smile as they crested a ridge. She ached for him, her heart never so full of happiness before now.

She saw Dev halt abruptly at the top, his hands going to his hips, his mouth moving into a thin line as he surveyed the meadow below him. Coming abreast of him, she asked, "What's wrong?"

"Look, bales of drugs are strung out all across that meadow," he muttered, scowling.

Her brows fell, too. "Crap. Drug smugglers dropping bales from a plane?" She saw that at least twenty bales, wrapped in thick black plastic, were scattered for nearly the entire half-mile-long oval meadow below them.

"Yes," he muttered, his hand going to the holster holding his pistol on his right thigh.

She studied the area. "There's an old US Forest road that comes into the north end of that meadow," she said, pointing in that direction, although the woods prevented them from seeing it from where they stood. "I was talking with Sarah, the sheriff, the other day. When I told her we were going up this trail, she said for us to be careful, that a lot of drug activity had started up in this area lately."

Dev turned, looking behind them. "I don't think we should go down there. We don't know when the druggies are going to pick these bales up. And they'll shoot us on sight, Andy." He gave her a concerned look, wanting her reaction.

Disappointed, she nodded. "I was thinking the same thing." They were in an isolated and mostly uninhabited area. Tourists never came down to this region. Most of the good hiking trails were around Prater Canyon, far to the north from where they were presently. Drug drops were done under cover of darkness, that much she knew. "I always thought these guys picked up their bales at night."

Shrugging, Dev continued to warily look around them. "Maybe their truck broke down? But yes, night drops and pickups are the norm. Not in broad daylight," and he gestured to the bales sitting out in the meadow for all to see.

"We're too deep into the mountains to call out on our radio or our cell phones. We're out of range. There's no way to contact Sarah at the sheriff's office to let her know what we stumbled on to either."

"We need to leave, Andy. This is too dangerous," he

muttered darkly, turning around, facing her. "Let's go back the way we came up. We're two miles from the trailhead where I parked my truck." He pulled out his iPhone and took photos of the drug drop below them. This would be proof for law enforcement, once they made it down the side of the mountain.

"Agreed. I wonder if our radio will work as we get to the lower altitude and closer to where the truck is parked."

"I don't know," Dev said. "Let me lead. You watch our six. If you need me, grab my arm, and no talking. We don't know if these drug soldiers are coming up the same trail we just took or not." He grimaced. "Feels like we're back in Afghanistan after the crash, dammit."

"Why would they be in our area? There's a dirt road at the end of that meadow they can drive up to those bales to get them."

"What if they have other drug soldiers around to ensure no one sees these bales coming up the trail as we just did?" he demanded, swiveling his gaze where they stood.

"Point well taken." Andy sighed. "Crap."

He reached out, grazing her cheek. "We had a lot of plans for this hike."

"I know." She caught his hand, placing a swift kiss on the back of it. The flare in his eyes told her it was well received. How badly she wanted to finally kiss this man and then love him. She knew without a doubt that Dev would be a considerate lover, putting her first, not last. Well, that was out the door, too, and she frowned. Releasing his hand, she said, "There are some feeder trails off this main one, if we spot someone or hear another party coming along."

"We have one pistol between us," he said in a quiet tone as he bent his head toward hers, wanting to keep noise to a minimum.

Her heart was starting a slow pound, and an ugly,

snaking sensation started deep in her stomach, tightening it. Compressing her lips, she rasped, "Dammit, you're right; this is just like Afghanistan."

He reached out, gripping her hand. "Yeah, drug soldiers instead of the Taliban. Both will kill us."

"I thought we were done with that."

His grin was sour as he regarded her. "I don't want a repeat either."

"There are no caves to hide in here either," she warned him.

"No, but there are lots of woods and they're thick, hard to see other people even if they're nearby, a camouflage of sorts."

"And we had shrubs and large bushes in places where the sun can get through the treetops," she said, pointing to a huge fourteen-foot bush that was at least six feet in length; no one could see through it to the other side.

He regarded the area. "You're right. Good to duck behind, so we could lay flat and not move if we heard or saw them coming."

Her nostrils quivered as she dragged in a huge breath of air. Her skin was covered with goose bumps. "Let's get going."

Nodding, Dev leaned down, pressing a kiss to her hair. "Stay close. We'll get out of this together."

Her scalp tingled. It was the first time he'd kissed her. The look in his dark-green eyes was filled with promise, tenderness, and then followed by a sense of protection coming around her. They might be equals, but she felt he wanted to make sure she wasn't a target, too. She felt similarly toward Dev and would rather have been in the lead instead of him. Knowing this area was her expertise.

They moved grimly down the narrow, rocky path. She

felt the hair on the back of her neck raise. Grabbing at Dev's arm, she gripped him hard.

Instantly, he stopped.

"There's someone nearby," she said in a low voice as he turned. She saw the hardness in his features now, just as before, in Afghanistan. His warrior side was operational, just as hers was.

"Where?"

"I don't know. The hair on the back of my neck is standing straight up. Whoever it is, they're close, Dev." She knew he understood her alarm. Her intuition wasn't logical, but it had saved them numerous times while running from the Taliban. He took her seriously, his head snapping up.

"Over there. Let's hide behind that bush." He wrapped his hand around her upper arm, leading her quickly over the two hundred foot downslope where they were.

His hand felt comforting, and Andy hurried to catch up to his long, ground-eating stride. In moments, they were flattened on their bellies, unmoving. Dev had drawn his pistol, his gaze pinned on the main hiking trail they'd just left. There was a curve in it and she couldn't see anyone coming.

Heart pounding in her throat, she suddenly saw a baldheaded man. Freezing, she hunkered down further, wanting to melt into the earth. In moments, eight men silently appeared, all in camo, carrying AR-15s or AK-47s, each with an extra loop of cartridges slung across one shoulder and their chests. They were all Caucasian, she noted, eyes squinted, peeking through some leaves. Dev was like a stone, unmoving. Fear arced through her. There was no question these were drug soldiers, their gazes pinned on the nearby ridge. *Oh God* . . . she began to pray not to be seen by them. They were two hundred feet away from the main trail. Sweat trickled down her temples as she suppressed the sound of her breathing by opening her mouth.

The drug soldiers didn't speak. Every one of them was hard-faced, focused, and she knew they'd kill them if they realized how close they were. It sent a savage chill down her spine, the same kind she'd experienced before in a far-off land. Only this time, it was her country, and that upset her deeply. Dev had slowly eased his iPhone into position, taking a number of photos of the men as they hustled by at a swift trot. He then moved it into his side pocket without rustling a leaf or making any sound. Andy knew these photos would be important to the FBI and other agencies who were working with the Lincoln County sheriff to rid them of these vermin.

A wall of relief flowed through Andy as the group disappeared over the top of the ridge, heading down below to the meadow. She saw Dev watching the trail intently, as if waiting to see more soldiers coming. The past melded into the present. She lay there, unmoving, not speaking, sensing he was using his acute radar, wanting to make sure they were safe to move. But move to where?

Dev slowly got to his knees, watching where he placed his legs so he didn't crack a branch or make some other sound. She mimicked him and leaned back on her heels, hands on her thighs, waiting to see what he was going to say. In Afghanistan, they would always speak in soft tones to see whether the other person disagreed with a plan.

"You know this area, Andy," he said close to her ear, his hand wrapping around her upper arm, their heads almost touching. "We need to get down in altitude, to a place where our radio will start working so we can call the sheriff's department."

"Agreed." She lifted her head away from his and turned, looking down the steeper slope below them. There was no trail and the floor was littered with dry pine. That carpet would be as slick as walking on ice. Swallowing, she shared her thoughts. "If we go down the trail, we might meet more drug soldiers," she warned.

"Yes," Dev said, giving a brusque nod. "So? Down this slope?" and he pointed toward it.

"Only choice. Want me to lead?"

"Yes, go ahead. I'll watch our six." He squeezed her arm. "We'll get out of this like we did before."

Meeting his narrowed eyes, she saw the grimness and determination in them, just as before. Reaching over, she gripped his hand at his side, giving it a strong squeeze. "Together. Like always."

He held her hand, his gaze becoming intense. "Andy . . . if anything happens? You need to know something . . . I'm falling in love with you. I have been for a long time, probably since the day I met you, but I wasn't aware of it at the time." His voice lowered, emotional and deep. "I love you. I need you to know that in case something happens . . ."

Her throat tightened, and she felt the warm strength of his hand around hers, protective and so necessary to her right now. "Same here," she choked out, her voice hoarse. "I've been falling in love with you, too, Dev." She saw relief come to his tightened features. "It feels good to finally tell you that. No matter what happens—"

"No. We're getting out of this alive, Andy. No question. We'll work together like we did in Afghanistan. It's nothing new to us. I need a future with you. We'll get out of this alive one way or another. All right?"

Andy wanted to protest because, above all, she was a realist, not an idealist. Seeing the raw determination in Dev's features, she swallowed what she was going to say. Instead, she leaned forward, placing her lips against his. "Kiss me," she whispered brokenly against his mouth. A forever kiss, in case they didn't get out of this dire situation alive. She saw his face grow tender, love for her fully unveiled in his eyes. Without a word, he released her hand and then framed her face.

She had kissed a number of men in her life, but as Dev slid his mouth lightly against her lips, as if slowly memorizing their shape, how they felt, finally sealing their secret longing and love for each other, made her lashes close, tears building behind them. This could be a goodbye kiss. Or it could become a kiss of possibility for them if they got out alive. As he leaned into her lips, gently parting them, tasting her, taking his time in exploring her, tears slid out of her eyes and down her cheeks. They trailed into the corners of their mouths.

Lifting his mouth away, he stared deeply into her glistening eyes as she lifted her lashes to meet that intense gaze of his. "Those had better be tears of joy, Andy, not tears of grief."

She managed a wobbly smile, her hands sliding over his shoulders and down his upper arms. "Tears of possibility," she rasped out brokenly. There was no way she was going to let Dev know that their lives weren't guaranteed. "You're the idealist. I'm the realist."

Releasing her hands he cupped her face and wiped away the tears with his thumbs. "Tears of possibility, then, sweetheart."

His touch was so light and caring, it broke her inwardly, but she shored up and didn't allow him to see how scared she was of losing him. So much could go wrong. Things they didn't know, enemies who were out there with military-grade weapons that could literally cut them in half if they hit one of them with a hollow-tipped bullet. Swallowing hard, her throat aching, she gave a jerky nod, unable to speak for fear of wailing out her terror.

"Good," he growled, releasing her. "Let's get going."

She slowly rose, sweeping her gaze from the ridge to the

trail below it before she attempted to move. Her heart was pounding. One wrong move, one foot put in the wrong place, could make a lot of sound. And if someone was nearby and heard it? Shaking her head, she stepped down the slope, watching where she placed her feet, keeping the wall of brush as a shield from prying eyes.

Her heart spun with joy, her lips tingling with the brush of a kiss he'd given her. Terror mounted and entwined with dread and hope. She could hear him behind her, walking so that sound was turned down in volume. There were so many pine needles on the ground, so many chances to walk on one, sending a crackling snap through the air. Loud enough to draw an enemy's attention. Her love for Dev was finally exposed. At the worst possible time. Would they be allowed a future together? Or their bodies found later? Seesawing between reality and hope, she forced herself to focus on where she was going to put her next step.

They had gone fifteen minutes down the slope, cautious and careful, watching where the woods were thicker, and therefore they were less likely to be spotted by the enemy. How many drug soldiers were around this area? Her mind spun with tactics, strategies, in case they were discovered. Her throat never stopped feeling tight, as if she couldn't draw in a full breath of air. Sometimes she would use a tree trunk, her hand pressed against it, to make a longer step to avoid a limb. The roughness of the bark brought her back to reality. Her knees were beginning to tighten up as the slope grew even steeper. There were rocks sticking up and out of the sea of brown pine needles here and there. Other rocks, much smaller, were hidden beneath the surface. She was always looking for any bump in the carpet beneath her feet that would signal a hidden rock. Those were easy to avoid. She wasn't concerned about those. Smaller rocks, all jagged, if stepped upon, could throw her off-balance. She could fall, and make noise if she did.

Everything about the five days of outrunning the Taliban came slamming back into Andy. Shocked at the intensity of her terror and worry, it cascaded around her. She wondered if Dev felt similarly. Oh, how she wanted a second chance with Dev. If only . . . if only . . .

Breathing hard, Dev reached out and touched Andy's shoulder, a nonverbal command. She halted immediately. They'd managed to come onto a plateau, and there she found an old, unused trail. Together, they'd jogged for at least a mile. It wasn't a downward trail, but it did lead them away from the area that could have more drug soldiers.

Halting, Andy turned and looked up at him. His dark-green T-shirt was wet with sweat beneath his arms, his face glistening from their push to get out of danger. His hands rested on her shoulders, caressing her as he leaned near her head.

"We've lost about a thousand feet. I'm going to try the radio now."

Nodding, she caressed the dampness on his cheek. Stepping away from him, she saw him unlock the pack on his back and swing it around, setting it on the ground between them. Her job was to be the lookout. Look for what was out of place. He'd taught her that during those five days, and she'd never forgotten it. Walking a good ten feet away from where he knelt on the trail, one knee down on the yellow soil, the radio to his mouth, she mentally crossed her fingers that they could make contact with someone at the sheriff's department.

Keeping an ear cocked on his quiet voice, which she honestly couldn't hear all that well, her gaze swept the area in a 360-degree sweep and saw nothing. Nor did she hear anything that was out of place. Above her, a squirrel chut-chut-chutted at her. The trail disappeared at the end of a low-hanging ledge. Below, it was the same as above.

Turning, she saw Dev talking, and her heart soared. He'd made contact! Still, she remained on guard. Hope rose in her chest and she wanted so badly to give in to it. She wanted to run to Dev, hug him with a fierceness she'd always hidden from him, let him know just how deeply she loved him.

After a ten-minute talk, Dev switched off the radio and put his pad and pencil in his pocket. He drew out his father's compass, the same one that had saved them before, setting the new direction for them. He smiled a little as he approached Andy, who remained on guard. She nodded, hope filling her as she watched him approach. Lifting his arm, he slid it around her shoulders, drawing her gently against him, his lips near her brow.

"I talked with Sarah. She's got everything we saw. She retrieved a map of where we are. I took down coordinates we can follow with my compass to get us down to the highway. She's alerting the ATF, the DEA, and the FBI. The Teton sheriff is sending their SWAT unit to meet up with them, plus their helicopter. The Air Force is going to have a high-altitude drone fly over that meadow to get real-time position info on this group and their cargo."

She wanted to collapse against him. Instead, she released a ragged sigh and pressed her brow against his chest. His heart pounded in her ear. "Is the drone up there now?"

"Yeah," he said wryly, "they were conducting high-altitude trainings for their pilots and just happened to be near this area. Sarah contacted them, and if we follow the compass direction she gave me, we'll avoid other parties who are in the area."

Frowning, she stepped away enough to look up at him. "More drug soldiers?"

"Yeah," he said unhappily. "There are two more groups. A second one about halfway up to where we were hiding near the ridge. The second group is where our truck is parked at the trailhead. They have four rental trucks in that lot right now with two men in each one, waiting for the bales to be carried down to them."

"So, they're going to haul these bales out by hand?" she asked, stunned. "Back on the ridge trail to the parking lot?"

"Yes, that's what they're doing. A large eighteen-wheeler broke down halfway to that meadow on the only dirt road leading in to it. Our guess is that they abandoned it and have initiated their plan B to get those bales out of there."

She stared in shock. "In broad daylight?"

"They have no choice," Dev said, looking up and around. "Their transport broke down, so it's Sarah's guess that the drug lord ordered the rental of the four trucks. She said there are twenty men coming up the slope from the meadow right now, each one carrying a bale. The second group halfway up the ridge trail will meet them and probably help carry the bales to the trucks to get them out of here as fast as they can."

"Whew," she muttered, absorbing his arm around her shoulders, wanting so much more from Dev. But now was not the time or place. "Sarah's given you coordinates to avoid all of them, right?"

"Yes. We have about three quarters of a mile before we'll be at the highway. She's sending a cruiser right now to pick us up. We should be able to make it to the highway in fifteen or so minutes." He held out his hand, showing her the old, brass compass. Giving her a look of irony, he said, "Once more, my dad's compass is saving us. Unbelievable."

"I'm ready to go," she said. "Are you?"

He grinned, pressed a kiss to her brow and released her. "Yeah, come on. We have a lot to talk about once we get out of this jam."

Grinning, she said, "A whole lot, Mitchell. Let's hoof it!"

September 5
2:00 p.m.

Andy began to feel disembodied as she walked out of the Lincoln County building. It came upon her suddenly, out of the blue. A sense of not being here-and-now overwhelmed her. There was a bench nearby and she slipped her hand into Dev's and said, "I need to sit down for a moment." She saw instant concern on his face. He, too, was exhausted by the intense meeting with another sheriff's deputy, getting all the information they could give him. The sheriff was delighted with the video Dev had taken with his iPhone. That information had already gone out to the task force that was now, he was sure, taking on the drug soldiers. He knew there would be a shoot-out. And so did Andy. He could see the worry in her expression. Sarah had nearly been killed by Brian Elson earlier. And now she was in the thick of it again, though this time the FBI was taking the lead, with twenty agents coming in from central Wyoming. It was going to be a war in that parking lot, no question. The only unanswered one was whether any of Sarah's deputies or anyone else on their side of law enforcement would be wounded.

Sitting, he placed his arm around her shoulders. The day had warmed up to the high seventies. "You all right? You look pale, Andy."

"I'm not sure," and she gave him a weary look and held out her hands. "All of a sudden, I feel shaky inside and out.

Look . . ." and she held out her hands in front of her, seeing the tremors, subtle but there.

Making a sound of sympathy, Dev removed his arm and turned, his knees pressed against hers while he gently gathered her hands with his. "It's adrenaline crash, Andy. Sit back, close your eyes and start taking nice, slow, deep breaths. That will help."

What helped was his unexpected, but oh so welcome attention. His hands were much larger than hers, rough but warm and caring. Gulping, she did as he requested, sinking against the back of the bench, feeling weakness stealing through every part of her. Tears jammed into her eyes and she gulped again. What the hell was going on? Confused, she opened them, staring at Dev. "I feel faint . . . want to cry. What's this all about, Dev?"

His mouth slashed and he squeezed her cold, damp fingers a little more surely between his own. "Did you have a letdown like this after we got to the ER at Bagram? After we were rescued?"

Frowning, she thought. "Yes . . . I did. It was so long ago, I'd forgotten about it."

"Do you think this morning triggered some of what was still hanging around in you? The trauma we experienced was five days long and we didn't know if we were going to survive it. That's big-time trauma."

Blinking, the tears running down her cheeks, she felt foolish. "I guess it is."

"We lived through a lot of trauma back then," Dev rasped, easing his fingers through the hair at her temple, smoothing it away from her eyes. "This one today was equally dangerous."

Her voice was raspy. "How are you feeling, then?"

Shrugging, he said, "It hasn't hit me like it has you. I feel exhausted. All I want to do is lay down and go to sleep."

Well, that was a half-truth. In reality, Dev wanted Andy in his arms, wanted to love her and then sleep with her. She wasn't ready for that, so he kept it to himself. Right now, she was having a flashback, married to the threat they'd just survived.

Wiping the tears from her cheeks, she muttered, "Maybe the difference between men and women, then?"

"Maybe. You've got a little color back in your cheeks. Are you feeling a bit better?" and he gazed at her intently.

There was such love in his gaze for her that Andy did feel better. "Yes . . . better."

"Love always does that, you know?" and he shared an affectionate look with her.

"At least," she whispered, "this forced us to fess up that we've fallen in love with each other . . ."

"One of several good things to come out of this. We're alive, too." He smoothed back her hair. "Do you feel like going home? My truck is still at that parking lot. One of the deputies said she'd drive us to our condo. We can use your truck for wheels after that."

"Yes, it's safe and sound in the condo parking lot. I hope they don't steal your truck or blow holes through it during the firefight."

Dev laughed a little and stood. "The good news is, we aren't in it if it happens. Right?"

She looked up at him, missing his bulk, his touch, wanting more, so much more. "Hadn't thought about that, but yes."

"I'll be right back. I'll let the deputy know we're ready to go home."

Home. The word had such promise. "That sounds so good to me, Dev."

Chapter Sixteen

As they approached their condo building, Andy gripped Dev's hand a little tighter. She halted.

He turned, a question in his eyes.

"I'm going to take a long bath in my apartment," she said. "And then I want to come over." Her voice grew soft with emotion. "I want to be in your bed with you. I want to be alone with you, Dev. And whatever happens, let it happen. How do you feel about my suggestion?" She studied his dark-green eyes that had turned molten with desire for her. It was raw. Her body responded to that one, intense look. She drowned in the hope that flooded her entire body as his gaze changed to one of tenderness.

Lifting his hand, he smoothed a tendril from her cheek. "I want the same thing."

Giving him another soft look, she whispered, "I saw it in your face."

"Yeah," he answered, a bit sheepishly. "Given how you're feeling, I wasn't sure if I should broach the topic. I know you're wiped out physically and emotionally."

"I guess we really do love each other. We both thought the same thing at the same time. My parents are like that."

He managed a twist of a smile. "So are mine."

"I'll see you in about an hour?"

He walked the few feet more with her. "Knock and I'll answer," he promised, leaning over, caressing her lips slowly, tasting her, their mouths fitting perfectly against each other. Dev didn't want to stop kissing her, but he forced himself to ease away and absorb her dreamy look as her lashes lifted and she stared up at him.

"I'll knock," she promised him throatily, stepping away, fishing out the card for her door. Andy didn't want to leave but did. She smelled of fear and sweat, and she wanted to get out of her dirty hiking gear and into the cleansing warmth of a tub. Never had she wanted a man like she did Dev. Relishing the glint in his gaze, that same desire burning in his eyes, she shut the door and went into the condo.

The phone rang and she picked it up.

"Andy, this is Sarah Carter."

Shocked, she said, "Sarah? Are you okay? What's going on?"

"I just wanted to let you know what happened out there at the parking lot. We've rounded up twenty drug soldiers, we've got twenty bales of drugs and no one got hurt." She then added, "Well, not quite true. Two drug soldiers were killed and the other twenty surrendered to us. The agents of the DEA, the ATF, and the FBI, plus Teton deputies, helped us. We're processing them all right now. I figured you'd want an update."

"Oh, yes," Andy whispered, her hand against her throat, her heart beating harder. "Dev and I were so worried for all of you."

She heard Sarah chuckle. "With your warning? We caught them completely off guard. Part of our force drove down the dirt road and directly into the meadow, surprising them. We also had the other team park a half a mile away, and we walked in and encircled the group. A few shots were fired. The two soldiers were killed, and the rest just dropped their weapons and surrendered."

"Wow," Andy said. "I'm so glad. I'll be seeing Dev in a little bit and I'll tell him the good news."

"We'll need you down here. Can you come at one o'clock tomorrow afternoon for another investigation session with one of my deputies? This is just a cleanup, after the fact."

"Sure, no problem. We'll be there. And thanks for calling. This lifts a lot of worry from us."

"I know; that's why I wanted to touch base with you. Get some rest. You've earned it."

Andy hung up, her hand over her heart, her eyes closed for a moment, relief washing powerfully through her. It was over. At least, this round was. She knew Sarah and other agencies were aggressively trying to drive the drug activity out of the southern valley once and for all.

Resting her fingertips on the phone, she wanted to call her mother and punched in the numbers. She was sure her father had already told her that they were safe, but she wanted that connection with her mother right now.

Maud answered the phone after the third ring. Andy sat down and told her what had happened and that she and Dev were safe, at home and okay. Her mother sounded relieved. Her hand tightened a little on the cell phone.

"Mom, I'm falling in love with Dev." She held her breath, waiting for her reaction.

"I think we knew it before you did," Maud teased her gently.

"Really?"

"Yes, at that first meal he shared with us. We both knew there was something good and special going on between the two of you."

"Well, since seeing him once again, I was trying to

justify so many things. My work, coming home, and that I didn't need a relationship. I wasn't looking for one at all."

Laughing a little, Maud said, "I wasn't looking for one when I met your father either."

"Did you fight it?"

"Yes, because I had many years of school ahead of me. I had other plans. It didn't work," and she laughed.

Leaning back on the chair, Andy asked hesitantly, "Are you and Dad okay with us getting together to see where it leads?"

"Of course we are," Maud said. "All four of you have what I call the delayed marriage syndrome."

Laughing, Andy said, "Oh, come on, Mom! We're all professionals with careers."

"I know, I know. But that doesn't stop us from wanting to see the four of our children happy like we are."

Swallowing, Andy whispered, "I've always wanted a marriage like yours, Mom. You guys are so happy together. It shows all the time. I guess since I was a kid, I dreamed of finding someone like Dad."

"Dev is a good man, and a good person," Maud said quietly. "He's sensitive, not the typical arrogant male."

"No, he wouldn't last two seconds around me if he was that way," she agreed. "He's gentle and sensitive underneath it all."

"So is your dad."

"I love that side of him. He's okay with being vulnerable when most men aren't."

"Dev is built the same way. You have our blessing."

Those words were sweet and welcome. "Thanks, Mom. I knew talking to you would help me see reality."

"If things keep going right, will you two start living together?"

"I'm sure we will. We haven't discussed it, but why not

cut our financial drain? Besides, I want to be with Dev. We have to maintain a certain professional demeanor when we're flying, but I'd love to be with him when we aren't. I'm sure he wants the same thing."

"I think it's a good idea," Maud said. "What sprung this loose in you two? That brush with the drug dealers today?"

"Yes." She chewed on her lower lip for a moment. "I had a pretty violent emotional reaction to it afterward. I agree with Dev that our five-day run to escape the Taliban traumatized me deeply. I'm still working it out. This run from the drug soldiers flattened me with the memories of the other. Dev realized first that I'm still working through that trauma. It surprised me, but he's been there for me."

"Doesn't surprise me, Andy. Most of our wranglers have PTSD and we've seen, even five or ten years later, they still have flashbacks or horrible nightmares. That kind of trauma stays with us for a long, long time."

"Dev admitted to me that it shook him inwardly, too. He was able to see it in me and himself."

"Then, it's good that you both recognized it and admitted your love for each other. Life's too short. So now you can move forward. Together."

Those healing words from her mother stayed with Andy after the call and taking a hot, soaking bath. She decided to wear a soft pink velour robe with a zipper down the front. She wore nothing beneath it. She didn't want to. Going across the hall, barefoot, she knocked lightly.

Dev answered it. "Come on in," he invited, stepping aside.

Andy liked that he had a towel around his neck, obviously having just come out of the shower. Her whole body responded to his naked upper body, the sheen of water across the tautness of his chest, the dark red hair sprinkled across it and tiny beads of water still there. He wore gray gym trousers, his large feet bare, making him look vulnerable, more like a little boy than a man. But there was no question his male sensuality affected her instantly and in the best of ways.

"Feel better?" he asked, closing the door after she walked into his condo.

She pushed her hair, the ends still damp, into some semblance of order with her fingers. "Much better. You?"

He took the towel and dried his shoulders, arms and chest, then looped it around his neck once more. "Just got out. I feel a hundred percent better."

"I want to lie down with you, Dev. Are you ready?" She saw his eyes gleam with amusement as he cupped her shoulders, drawing her against him. How lovely it felt to press her cheek against his powerful chest, to inhale his own, special male scent, the hair tickling her nose.

Dev brushed a kiss across her mussed hair. "More than ready."

"Lead on, Mitchell."

Chuckling, he pressed a second kiss to her hair. "This way . . ."

Andy liked that his bedroom wasn't dark or broody or had nothing but dark colors so she could barely see anything. Surprised that there were gossamer light-blue curtains, translucent almost, drawn across the huge picture window, allowing in soft light. The drapes were drawn back, a light blue to go with the cream on the walls. She saw a photo of him in his flight gear standing beside the open door of the Army Black Hawk, focused and obviously ready to get on with another black ops mission. Smiling to herself, she liked the look of the eagle about him. Her heart swelled with love for this man who never talked about his own heroism and courage in combat. She'd seen he was given a Bronze Star with a "V" for valor, to demonstrate his bravery under fire. That and a Purple Heart. He had two of those. But he was always humble about them, and unless she prodded him, he wouldn't have divulged that he'd earned those medals. He was a man who was comfortable in his own skin, not needing praise from the outside world.

Closing the door quietly behind him, they walked to the side of his king-size bed. Andy liked the old-fashioned, pale-lilac chenille bedspread. The headboard was made of light blond oak, plain and simple. It spoke a lot about Dev as she swept her gaze around the room. On the oak dresser were framed photos of his parents, both smiling. Two more that were probably of his teammates in the military. She wondered if those men were the ones who'd died in the crash he barely escaped from himself. At some point she would ask, but not now.

Hanging his towel over the back of a nearby chair, Dev drew her against him, holding her gaze. "It's been awhile since I loved a woman," he admitted.

She moved her hands slowly up and down his forearms, the sprinkle of hair increasing her keen yearning for him in every way. "It's been two years for me. I'm clean and no, I don't like condoms, and yes, I'm in my 'window' to love you and not get pregnant."

"Same here, except I can't get pregnant."

Laughing, Andy nodded. "You're good, Dev. Really good."

He became serious, searching her gaze. "We need to be communicating with each other. Tell me if I cause you any discomfort or pain. Or if you don't like something I'm doing."

"Always." She slid her hands up to his face. "Let's go slow this first time?"

"Yes," he agreed. "Now, come here. I've been dreaming

for months of doing just this," and he leaned over, sliding his arms beneath her legs and lifting her into his arms.

Andy smiled and wrapped her limbs around his neck as he carried her over to the bed. "You're sweeping me off my feet," she teased, caressing his cheek, then kissing it.

Laying her upon the bed, he joined her after pushing his gym shorts downward, falling around his feet and nudging them away. She stared at his erection and gave a nod, pleased. He pulled the zipper open where she sat, revealing her nakedness. Easing forward, he nipped her slender neck, hearing that happy sound vibrate in her exposed throat. The trust Andy gave him, the surrender of her body to him, made his eyes burn with unshed tears. He swore silently to her that he'd make this first time beautiful for her. His heart widened with such a rush of feeling that it caught him off-guard.

Guiding Andy onto her back, beautiful and naked, he straddled her, his knees beside her flared hips. He slid his mouth against hers, feeling her fuse with him, her moan deep and vibrating through him, hardening him.

Her hands ranged over his shoulders and back, memorizing him in a slow, delicious exploration. Strangling the desire with steely control, he took her willing mouth once more, gliding his lips against hers, feeling her smile beneath his kiss, feeling her enjoyment of everything he was doing with her. Leaving her wet, hungry lips, he lifted his leg, his knee opening her curved thighs. Brushing his fingers lightly against her core, his fingers instantly became soaked. She was so turned on. So ripe. So ready for him.

Andy was overwhelmed with the pleasure he'd been giving her. His continued caresses moving wickedly into her entrance, she absorbed his male scent and that taste that spun her into a dark, starving need of Dev. He placed himself against her entrance, slowly rubbing against her, teasing her. She instantly reacted, groaning out his name, her hands settling around his narrow hips, trying to pull him forward, trying to get him into her. He placed his elbows near her shoulders, his hands framing her flushed face, drowning in the glistening diamonds reflected in her half-closed eyes.

Somewhere in his cartwheeling mind, Dev realized she was such a sexual, sensual woman, so well hidden in their day-to-day work, but now, unveiling herself to him for the first time. Gritting his teeth, his hands closing more firmly around her face, he nudged his throbbing erection deeper into her, watching her eyes grow cloudy with urgency, her pleading whimpers tearing from her parted lips. Oh yes, she felt like a hot, tight, wet glove beginning to envelop him. Dev wasn't going to tease her; rather, he wanted to slowly open her, get her channel to widen and accept his girth and length. Her body relaxed as he eased another inch into her. Her cries of pleasure began, and she sobbed his name, the tightening of her channel constricting around him as he began to rock and give her pleasure. He felt her tearing apart as he lavished her with that ancient, rocking motion.

In moments, she cried out, her hands tight and almost painful against his shoulders as her lower body jerked, the orgasm overwhelming her. He kept stroking her slowly, increasing her gratification as it bloomed within her. Dev allowed her all the time she wanted to enjoy the depth and beauty of the intense orgasm as it flowed through her. He silently swore Andy would always come first, before him.

Another vibrating, low growl tore out of him as the release exploded through him. He stiffened, surging his hips against hers, fusing with her, unable to move, drowning in the scalding satisfaction throbbing between them. She kept her grip around his hips, thrusting into him, continuing to twist and rub against him. Dev fell against her, his head next to hers, breathing harshly, sweat running down his drawn features.

A smile drifted across Andy's mouth as she weakly enclosed him with her arms, needing this. Needing Dev. Nothing had ever felt so right as now, with him covering her, his weight like a heavy, warm blanket against her panting body. Their sweat mingled and small rivulets combined, tickling down across her skin here and there. He felt so wonderful, made her feel loved and protected by him. She leaned over, her mouth claiming his, tasting his lips against hers, sharing the intimacy with him as he moved his mouth urgently, making her moan. Threading his fingers through her hair, drawing her to him, his mouth claiming her swollen lips. She inhaled him, body, heart and soul.

Andy had no idea what time it was, only that it was dark. She was warm, cossetted against Dev's body, her butt and back against his front. Most of all, that strong, hairy arm across her waist, holding her close as he snored softly above her head, made everything feel so right. So incredibly wonderful. The sweet feeling of love flowed from her to him and she closed her eyes, never having felt like she belonged to someone as much as she did Dev. That hole in her heart began to close for the first time in her life. That sensation, that deep awareness told Andy that she had a partner for life in him. He wasn't a man who would ever walk out on her in a crisis. They'd already been tested twice now. The tenderness and care in how he loved her, wanting to be sure she was pleased first, touched her in ways she couldn't even give words.

Moving her fingers slowly down his forearm, she felt him stir. Dev moved, repositioning them so that he was able to slip one arm beneath her neck, settled her against the length of him as he eased her on her back. She lifted her lashes, drowning in the burning love she saw in his dark-green eyes as he silently absorbed her. Sliding his hand across her shoulder, down the length of her arm, he captured her hand, pressing a kiss to her fingers as she curved them around his large knuckles.

"I love you, Andy," he rumbled, holding her hand against his chest.

"I know you do, Dev." She reached up and caressed his cheek, feeling the stubble create tingles along her opened palm. "I love you so much . . ."

"I have something to tell you," he said, his voice still thick with sleep.

"What?"

"It was on the second night of our run for freedom after the crash. Do you remember we found a couple of caves about a quarter mile from the top of one of those mountain ridges? It was getting dark, we were freezing and our teeth were chattering."

Wrinkling her nose, she said distastefully, "Oh, I remember everything about it. It's never far away from me. Those caves were a godsend. We were so weary, our legs knotting and cramping constantly. It was one, long climb the whole day to stay ahead of the Taliban."

He kissed her fingertips, one at a time, holding her slumberous gaze. "And we settled on the second cave because it had a little pool of water."

"That was so wonderful. We had purification tablets for our water bottles, but we'd had no water for the whole day."

"We drank like drunken fools," he agreed. Releasing her hand, he said, "We each ate a protein bar and then we settled down to sleep."

"Well, I did. You stayed up on watch," she reminded him.

"We traded places every two hours and yes, I could see how exhausted you were, so I wanted to take that first watch." He leaned down, his lips against her wrinkled brow. "There was a full moon and the milky rays came down into our cave from the cracks above. I watched the moonlight move slowly across you as you slept. You looked so damned angelic to me, Andy. I never told you that before. I was going to tell you that if we ever got rescued. But that didn't go as planned either."

She searched his serious, deeply shadowed face. "That I looked like a bone-tired angel?" she teased, her lips drawing away from her teeth.

"It was more than that. I knew after those two days that you were a real combat warrior. I had never met a woman like you. Ever. I found myself thinking ahead, dreaming of what I'd say to you once we reached safety. That I wanted to know you better and under less dire circumstances." He lifted his chin, staring into the darkness before shifting his gaze to hers. "Don't ask me how I knew this, but I knew you were the woman I wanted as a lifelong partner. It was crazy. I thought I was going crazy and then that I was sure as hell sleep-deprived."

She frowned for a moment. "Seriously? You knew then, Dev?"

"Don't forget, we Irish can be pretty psychic on occasion."

"We'd hardly talked at all, using hand signals most of the time. I didn't know you from Adam. I didn't even know if you were married or not and figured you had to be. You were so handsome."

Giving her a pleased look, he said, "That's nice to know, too."

"But we got separated at Bagram ER. I never saw you again."

He touched an errant curl and slid it behind her ear. "There was one more thing that happened that night that you need to know. I was getting ready to wake you up when you suddenly started crying. It wasn't anything noisy, but I could see the silvery paths down your cheeks. You were having a reaction to everything that had happened to you, was my guess. I quietly got up and crawled over to where you were and gathered you in my arms. The minute I did that, you buried your head into my chest, your hand against your face, as if to protect yourself. I didn't want to wake you up and I kept you close to me, your sobs drowning in my flight suit. I rocked you, kissed your hair and your wet cheek, wanting to soothe you, wanting you to feel safe when we sure as hell weren't." He saw her eyes widen, and then tears filled them.

"I just held and gently rocked you in my arms, and gradually, you stopped weeping. You trusted me, and that's when I knew you were the only woman I ever wanted in my life."

Swallowing, she whispered brokenly, "Oh, Dev . . . you never got a chance to tell me that at Bagram . . ."

With a sorrowful look, he rasped, "It was the worst day of my life. I knew in my heart, in my soul, you were the woman I wanted to spend my life with, as crazy as that sounds. And the way I felt wasn't because of all the stress and pressure we were under either. My mother has that; she knows what she knows without ever knowing why she knows it. And she's never wrong when she has one of those feelings." He slanted her a wry look. "I had that feeling about you."

"It must have been devastating to you when we couldn't find each other," she managed.

Dev wiped the tears away from her cheeks with his roughened fingertips. "I wasn't a happy camper, believe me."

"No wonder you turned white, like you'd seen a ghost when you first saw me."

"Yeah," he said, shaking his head. "I thought I was seeing things. But I wasn't."

"And you still felt the same way about me? Even four years later?"

"If anything? Finding you again just increased the love, the need for you I'd had during our escape and those four years we were separated."

Slowly sitting up, she caressed his mussed hair, seeing the pain, the disbelief and joy in his gaze. "Thank you for telling me that, Dev. That must have been tough on you. I'm sure you didn't know I was drawn powerfully to you. Did you?"

"At first, I didn't see anything in your expression, your vocal tone or eyes that you might be attracted to me."

"I was, but I hid it behind my game face."

"You could have told me," he said, smiling a little, smoothing the last of the tears from her cheeks.

"I was afraid, Dev. I'd had so many crash-and-burn relationships with pilots. You're a pilot. I was projecting on you that you'd be the same as the others."

"Yeah, I can understand that reaction based on your prior experience," he growled, mouth quirking.

"Still, over time you wore me down," Andy admitted, her fingertips tracing the strength of his mouth. "I had to get over my own past, put my career in another slot, of being less important than getting to know you."

"Until that hike when we ran into the drug soldiers. That ripped off our dance with each other. Up until that point, we hadn't admitted we loved each other."

"That did it," Andy said softly agreeing, leaning over,

kissing him gently, her hand coming to rest against the side of his face. His mouth was strong and cherishing and she soaked up his strength, but also his tenderness. As she eased away, she said, "I have a confession to make, too, Dev."

"What is it?" and he smoothed her hair along the top of her head.

"Because of being abandoned at birth, I always had this hole in my heart," and she brushed her fingers between her breasts. "After we'd loved each other, I fell asleep. I woke up just now and you had curved me beside you, and I felt so protected. I felt safe, and I'd never felt that way before." Her voice lowered. "I felt the hole in my heart beginning to close, that sense that no one loved me, that I'd been thrown away. And then I felt a hope I'd never felt before, that you loved me, you wanted me in your life. I was important to you. I'd never felt those things before in any relationship I'd had in the past."

He kissed her cheek, whispering, "I need you like I need air to breathe, sweetheart." Pulling away, Dev rasped, "I can't conceive of a life without you in it every day, Andy. For the rest of my life and yours. What we share? It began four years ago, and it didn't go away. It just grew and grew, and I think like you, I was looking for you in every person because I couldn't find you. And I never settled for someone less."

She snorted softly. "Same here. I had some relationships, but they never were as good as when I was with you in Afghanistan. Even under that life-and-death situation? I trusted you. I had fallen in love with you but just didn't know it."

He sat up, back against the headboard, and gathered her into his arms, positioning her such that they faced each other. "Do you feel the same? That this is a forever kind of relationship?"

"I do," she said, giving him a trembly look. "You've always made me feel safe in an unsafe world."

Nodding, he gave her a pleased look. "I'm going to spend the rest of my life showing you and telling you how you fill my heart. I lost Sophie, and she will always be a wonderful part of my life. With you, I want to look forward to old age, with us both growing silver-haired together."

Laughing a bit, she touched her hair. "Well, we're not quite there yet, Mitchell."

He laughed with her. Holding her, kissing her here and there, her shoulder, her temple, he said, "Your parents need to know."

"They already do," she said wryly. "Months ago."

Eyes widening, Dev sat there digesting her words and saw her give him a devilish grin. "Which condo do you want to live in, then, with me?"

"I like mine better," she said.

"Done. I need to call my parents, and I would like you to talk with them."

"I'll do it."

"We need to maybe drop over and talk to your parents sometime today?"

"How about tomorrow?" She would tell Dev about her earlier phone call with her mother later.

"Sounds good."

"Knowing Mom?" Andy said, irony in her tone, "She probably already knows."

They laughed together, holding each other, going silent for a long time, absorbing the warmth and care they shared. Dev brought up the chenille bedspread and pulled it over them because it was getting chilly in the early morning hours.

"We should live together for a while," he suggested.

"Yes. But knowing my parents, Mom is going to be nagging me about a date to get married before too long."

"Well, we can't have that. Why not live together, and by next June, we'll know, and it's the nicest month in the valley from what your dad has told me."

"A June wedding would be wonderful. Would your parents be able to make it up here?"

"I'm sure they will. That's plenty of time for them to prepare to fly up here."

She moved her finger down the center of his powerful chest. "Maybe my parents, you and I could fly down there this Christmas and share it with them? Do you think they'd like that?"

"My mom and dad would be over the moon," Dev said.

"Well," she said, snuggling into his welcoming arms and body, "let's talk more about that tomorrow morning when we wake up."

"And after at least two or three cups of coffee," Dev warned her good-naturedly.

Andy closed her eyes, utterly relaxed against his tall, firm body. She kissed his chest and nestled into his warm flesh, the hair across it like a soft pillow. "Tomorrow," she murmured drowsily. "A new and wonderful day."

He slid them down onto the bed, tucking her in with the sheet and blankets, and then bringing her along his length. "The first day of forever with you," he said thickly, kissing her slowly, appreciating her for who she was.

"Forever," Andy agreed. "Just like our parents, who have loved one another forever. I like that idea . . ."

Don't miss Lindsay McKenna's next book
in the Wind River Valley series:

WIND RIVER UNDERCOVER!

Coming to readers in April 2020

In the meantime,
if you've missed the previous book in the series,

HOME TO WIND RIVER,

turn the page and enjoy a quick peek!

The book is available
at your favorite retailer
and e-retailer.

June 1

How was Jake Murdoch, her foreman, going to react to the news?

Maud Whitcomb, owner of the Wind River Ranch, pushed her fingers through her dark hair that was threaded with silver. Sitting in her large office, she waited with anticipation. Jake was an ex-recon Marine with severe PTSD he dealt with day in and day out. As the foreman for their hundred-thousand-acre ranch for the last three years, he'd proved himself invaluable despite his war wounds. She was pretty sure he wouldn't be happy.

Jake's symptoms made him a loner, boarded up like Fort Knox, and he liked living alone in the huge cedar log cabin a mile from the main ranch area. Dragging in steadying breath, Maud heard heavy footsteps echoing outside her open office door. It was early June and, for once, there was bright sunshine and a blue sky in western Wyoming.

She saw Jake's shadow first and then him. He was six-foot, two-inches tall, a solid two hundred pounds of hard muscle. His shoulders were almost as broad as the doorway he stood within. At thirty years old, any woman worth her salt would turn her head to appreciate his raw good looks and powerful physique. His temperament, however, was open to question. He was known as "Bear" around the ranch. Bear as in grizzly bear. He was terse, not PC, completely honest and didn't brook idiots for more than two seconds.

Swiftly glancing up at him as he entered, Maud watched him take off his dark brown Stetson and saw his expression was set; any emotion he felt was hiding behind what he called his game face.

"Jake. Come on in," she said, waving a hand toward a wooden chair in front of her desk. "How's your mom doing?"

Grunting, Jake hung up his Stetson on a nearby hat tree and turned, boots thunking across the highly polished oak floor.

Maud girded herself. He wasn't happy. At all. "Coffee?" It was nine a.m., and usually by this time he was out on the range, managing their wranglers. He probably wanted to be out with his hardworking crew rather than in here with her. But they had to talk.

"Yeah, coffee's good," he said, making a beeline for the service on the other side of the room. He poured two cups, black, and turned. Setting one in front of her, he sat down and took a quick sip of the steaming brew. "You know my mother broke her thigh bone a couple of days ago. I just finished talking to her surgeon before coming here, and they said she pulled through the operation with flying colors. She's resting in her room right now."

"That's great to hear," Maud said, relief in her tone as she sipped the coffee. "I know they call it breaking a hip, but in reality, people break their femur or thigh bone."

Shaking his head, Jake muttered, "Yeah. Bad anatomy, if you ask me."

"So? What's her prognosis?"

She saw him grimace and set the coffee down in front of him. "The surgeon says she's going to need eight to ten weeks of care. She lives alone in Casper. And she's fighting having a caregiver in her home twenty-four hours a day."

Managing a sour smile, Maud said, "Like mother, like son. Right?" She saw worry in Jake's forest-green eyes. He had been close to both his parents; his father had died at the age of fifty-five of a sudden and unexpected heart attack. For the last ten years, his mother had been on her own. Now, at sixty-five, she had a broken bone and needed help. Jake's expression turned dark, and she saw him wrestling with the whole situation.

"I'm afraid you're right, Maud."

"So? What do you want to do about it?" She leaned back in her squeaky leather chair, holding his narrowing gaze. "How can we gather the wagons and help you out?" Maud made a point of being there for the people who worked for them. Jake had not asked for anything. He never did. Her experience with her wrangler vets, however, had taught her early on that those with PTSD, man or woman, never asked for help, never asked for support, and she knew it came from the shame that they had been broken by combat. "Well?" she prodded, arching a brow.

Jake squirmed. "Mom asked if I could come home and help her for those two months." Mouth quirking, he mumbled, "I told her I couldn't, that we had fifty grass leases with fifty different ranchers coming here, bringing in their herds by truck, in the next two weeks. I told her the Wyoming grass was thick, rich and nutritious, that the cattle would fatten up far more quickly on these lands than being put into a livestock pen. That I couldn't leave because our work triples from June through September."

"How did Jenna take the news?" Maud heard the pain

in Jake's low, deep tone. He was a man who hated showing any emotions, but they were plainly written all over him now. Some of it Maud attributed to their strong relationship. Jake could let his guard down around her, one of the few people in his life he did trust.

"She was disappointed but understood." His black brows fell and he looked away. "She needs help. I don't know what to do. That's why I'm here." He gave her a hopeful look. "You're the go-to gal for ideas, Maud. I'm hopin' you can come up with a fix."

"I think I have one, Jake, but I don't know how you will react to it. Here's my plan. I talked to Steve last night and he's in agreement with me. I hope you will be, too." She straightened, resting her elbows on the desk, her hands clasped, her full attention on her foreman. "We both feel Jenna could be brought by ambulance to the ranch. The foreman's house is two stories, has three bedrooms, three baths, and is large enough for you to take care of your mom as well as an in-house caregiver." She saw his brows raise momentarily. "I know you'd rather live alone, but honestly, your cabin is the second largest on the ranch, next to where we live. It has plenty of room for you, your mom and a hired caregiver."

She took a breath, watching his face go from hard and unreadable to something akin to discomfort, coupled with relief. Jake had a set of good parents, that she knew. And he'd been very close to both of them. As well, Jake had protective instincts toward women. His mother was no exception to that rule. Maud knew he wanted desperately to support and care for her, but he hadn't thought outside the box on how to do it. That was her job.

"Now," she said firmly, "before you say no, I talked to Dr. Taylor Douglas, our PA, physician's assistant, in town. She said I needed to find someone with a medical background, preferably a registered nurse, who could take care of Jenna: help her walk, be there to assist her with the mandatory exercises, as well as cook and clean for you. Taylor put the word out in Wind River for such a person. I haven't gotten any bites on this yet, but I'll keep at it. Your mom and the caregiver could have the two bedrooms on the first floor. You have the master bedroom upstairs. If I find a caretaker for Jenna, would this work for you? It would be for a minimum of two months."

Jake rolled his shoulders, scowling in thought. "Maybe. But I can't afford to hire a caregiver for Jenna."

"No worries," Maud answered briskly. "Your mother is on Medicare and our umbrella insurance on the ranch will cover a full-time caregiver until she doesn't need one anymore. I'll pay for the caregiver because you're so important to the daily work that goes on around here, Jake. I'd do it for any of our wranglers. We meant it when we said they were family, and that's what you do for your family." Opening her hands, she added, "We're grateful to have made money and we aren't taking it with us. Your mom will have the best of care and we'll cover any additional expenses. How does that sound?"

"You've always been more than fair with us vets," he said, his voice low with emotion. "And I appreciate it, Maud."

"So? Is that a yes? Can we move ahead with this idea? Are you okay with it?"

Rubbing his stubbled jaw, Jake studied the fifty-five-year-old woman. "I don't like takin' handouts, Maud."

"This isn't a handout. Our insurance covers it. You've earned this, Jake."

He made a low, growling sound and stared hard at her. "I've never been in a position like this before. I like living alone, but I want to help my mom, too. I guess my uneasiness with havin' two women underfoot for two months or so isn't gonna kill me."

Giving him a half grin, Maud said, "No, it won't. And you can always hide up on the second floor if you're feeling overwhelmed with estrogen in your household." She heard him chuckle and saw his shoulders drop, indicating he was relaxed at last. Jake wasn't the kind of person she could trap and put in a corner. He had to come to this decision entirely on his own. And he was an honorable man, if nothing else. Jake would never knowingly hurt someone. At least, as a civilian. What he did as a recon Marine was different, and although he never talked about it, she knew enough to realize he'd been in harm's way all the time. It wouldn't surprise her that he'd killed the enemy either. She knew the burden of killing another human being through some of her other wranglers. It stayed with them the rest of their lives.

"I'll probably make the second floor my home."

"If I can find a caregiver, she'll do the cooking for the three of you. That won't be so bad, will it?"

"No, that sounds kinda good, to tell you the truth. And she'll housekeep, instead of me doing it. I like that part of it, too."

"I thought you might." She allowed the humor to come through in her voice and Jake gave her a slight grin. "It's only two months."

"But they're the busiest months of our year, Maud. I won't be around that much."

"And that's why a caregiver is essential. You won't have time to drive Jenna to her rehab exercises in Wind River, or to see an ortho doctor if necessary."

"Well," he said, straightening, "if you can find a caregiver, then we're set?"

"Yes." Maud looked at the bright red landline phone on

her desk. "I'm calling Kassie and her husband, Travis. They're plugged in with everyone in town. Maybe one of them can give me some leads."

Rising, he said, "If there's such a person around Wind River, Kassie will know. She's gossip central at her café," and he grinned a little.

"I'll let you know," Maud promised. "Once we hire someone, we can get Jenna out of the Casper hospital and over here to heal up."

Walking to the hat rack, he gripped the edge of his Stetson. "That sounds like a good plan, Maud." Settling it on his head, he turned, giving her a grateful smile. "I don't think outside the box like you do."

"Oh," she laughed, standing and walking around the desk and heading toward where he stood, "yes, you do! Every day around here, I see you thinking of ways to do something that needs to be fixed." She slid her hand on his shoulder, patting him in a motherly fashion. "All humans are good at something. Your skill set happens to be in ranching, Jake. Mine is about seeing patterns and putting dots together," and she chuckled with him. Jake rarely smiled. When he did? She saw the kindness and sensitivity he held protectively away from the world. Allowing her hand to fall to her side, she walked him to the door. "I'll be in touch by cell phone once I get something."

He nodded. "Thanks, Maud. I honestly don't know how I landed at your ranch, but I have to be the luckiest bastard in the world to have you as my boss."

"Get outta here, Murdoch. You got a shitload of eighteen-wheelers on your plate with these leases trucking in the beef right now."

He gave her a sour grin, opened the door and thunked down the wooden stairs.

Maud watched him climb into the white, dusty-looking

Ford pickup with the name of their ranch in big red letters
on each door. Turning, she felt lighter. Jake had never been
in this kind of situation before, and she hadn't been sure
how he was going to react to it. His care and love for his
mother was heartwarming. He was such a gruff person,
hardly letting anyone near him or his vulnerability. Maud
sensed Jake's life was going to take a turn for the better.
She didn't know how, as she walked to her desk, sat down
and dialed up Kassie's Café, but she knew it was going to
happen.

Lily Thompson was working in the no-kill animal shelter run by Maud and Steve Whitcomb, when Suzy, her
boss, who manned the front desk, stuck her head around
the door.

"Lily! Maud Whitcomb is on the line for you!"

"What?" She knew Maud was the owner of this large
shelter, but in the two weeks since she was hired, she
hadn't met the woman personally. She closed the cage on a
black Lab with a gray muzzle, after giving him a bowl of
fresh water. "Hold on . . ." and she hurried across the spot-
lessly clean concrete floor, wrapping the hose she'd used
and hanging it on the wall. Rubbing her hands down her
jeans, she asked breathlessly, "What does she want?"

Suzy, who was in her early twenties, shrugged dramatically. "I don't know."

Squeezing out the door, they walked down the hall
toward the reception area. "Does she always call her employees?" Lily wondered.

"No . . . not usually," Suzy responded, giving her a concerned look.

"Oh, dear," she muttered. "I wonder if I've done something wrong."

"I doubt that! All the animals love you. Some of them love you to death!"

Wincing inwardly at the word, Lily nodded and picked up the phone. "Hello? This is Lily Thompson." Her heart was pounding in her chest and she curled her fingers into her damp palm. Was she going to get fired? God, she hoped not.

"Lily, this is Maud. I just got done speaking to Kassie, and she mentioned you were an RN. Is that true?"

"Yes, ma'am, it is." She gulped, unsure of where this was going.

"Suzy told me you have a part-time job there, fifteen hours a week?"

"Yes, ma'am, I do. I love it." Inwardly, she was praying the owner wasn't going to tell her to leave. It would devastate her in ways most people wouldn't understand. This was the first real job she'd been able to find since receiving an honorable medical discharge from the Army due to her extreme PTSD symptoms.

"Are you looking for full-time work?"

"Well . . . uh . . . that would depend. I really love animals." *Because they give me peace. They accept me for who I am now. Not who I used to be*, but she didn't divulge that.

"Can you drive out to our ranch? I'd love to talk to you face-to-face about a job possibility. I assume you're looking for full-time work?"

Was she ever! Licking her lower lip, Lily said, "Yes, ma'am, I am. But I can't work in a hospital or anything like that." Lily had to be honest about her skills and how much she'd been harmed by her time in Afghanistan.

"This is a job in a home, as a caregiver for a sixty-five-year-old woman who has broken her femur. You would cook three meals a day and do some light housework besides helping the woman with exercise and walking to strengthen herself once more. It should last around two months, full-time. Are you still interested?"

"Maybe," she answered tentatively. "Could you tell me more?"

"Come out to the Wind River Ranch. We'll talk. Can you make it at one p.m.?"

"Yes, ma'am. I'm done today at noon. I know where your ranch is located and can drive out there. I'll be on time, I promise."

"Great. Just come to the office. That's where I'll be."

Lily hung up, her heart pounding even harder. *A job. A real job.* A caregiver. Well, she could do that.

Suzy glowed as Lily told her about the call. "You said you wanted another job, that this one wouldn't pay your monthly bills."

Lily smoothed out her jeans, some damp spots of water on them from watering all the cats and dogs in the shelter that morning. "I did."

"Kassie's a good go-to person to find a job. You must have told her you were looking for another one."

"Yes, I'd love to find something full-time. I don't want to leave the shelter," she said, looking around the small but homey office. "I love the animals."

"It's only a two-month job, Lily."

"It's better than nothing. And it sounds like something I can manage. I always enjoy helping animals and people."

Suzy sat down. "Hey, good luck on it. Maud's a really nice person. You'll instantly feel at ease with her. She has a heart of gold, so don't sweat the interview. Okay?"

Easier said than done. Nodding, Lily picked up her jacket and pulled it on. It might be June 2, but it was only forty-five degrees outside despite the blue sky and sunshine. "I'll see you tomorrow morning at six a.m.," she promised Suzy, lifting her hand in farewell as she pushed the outer door open.

Outdoors, she halted and looked around. It was something she did without thinking about it. There were a lot of things she thought about since being in the Army, since that village was attacked . . . Resolutely, Lily compressed her lips and walked doggedly toward her dark blue pickup. Her parents had bought it for her when she returned home, wanting, in some way, to help her adjust to civilian life. It was used but in good condition, and as she climbed in, her heart warmed at their helping her after the Army released her.

To her right was the Wilson Range, rising out of the flat plain west of the one-hundred-mile, oblong-shaped Wind River Valley. It was covered with snow on its blue granite flanks, then surrounded with thick evergreens from ten thousand feet downward and flowing onto the flat of the valley. The shelter had been built on the southern end of the town. The parking lot was gravel, with a wooden corral around it except for the entrance and exit points. The tires made crunching sounds as she backed out and headed toward the ribbon of two-lane asphalt that went through the valley.

Since discovering this small town nestled between the Salt River Range to the east and the Wilson Range on the west, she'd found some level of peace. Her money was running out, although she knew her parents would give her more if she asked. They'd done so much already, trying to help her with her devastating PTSD symptoms.

Driving slowly through town, she parked at Kassie's Café. Kassie had given her a back room in the large restaurant, free, until she could find a job. She, like Maud Whitcomb, was partial to military vets and had married one, Travis Grant.

Lily left the pickup and walked around to a side door. The little apartment had a bathroom with a tub, which she loved to soak in. Water always calmed her. The bedroom had a queen-size bed and a purple comforter that was cozy and warm for the freezing nights that occurred even in June around here. There was also a small kitchenette. She discovered either Kassie or one of her women vet waitresses had thoughtfully put a bowl of fresh fruit on the table for her. When she opened the fridge, she found three complete meals wrapped in Saran wrap.

Lily didn't know how she'd managed to luck out, but Kassie and Travis had been saviors to her. She'd come here two weeks ago, low on money, low on morale and questioning whether she'd done the right thing by leaving her home in Blackfoot, Idaho. She was looking for a job that had low stress, something that would pay her a salary she could live on.

As a vet with PTSD, her career as an RN was pretty much over. She didn't have the ability to stand the stress of working in a busy hospital. Or even a doctor's office. Sometimes, crowds of people, noise and the combination of the two, made her mind blank out and she was paralyzed for moments, unable to think or react.

During her therapy, after breaking emotionally over what she'd witnessed in an Afghan village, her therapist gently told her she would never be the same person again. Lily found those words disheartening, but Major Ann Dawson had shown her the strength that was still within her, helped her to understand how she could call upon it to heal. That, too, was a part of her.

The first three months after her breakdown out in the field had been the hardest. They'd put her on medications that made her feel out of her body. Her mind didn't work, and she was in some kind of cottony cocoon she couldn't wrestle out of.

Only after the medication was slowly withdrawn and she started with therapy sessions with Major Dawson had she started to come alive once more. And as she recounted the horrific attack by the Taliban at dawn, the murdering of innocent men, women and children, she broke down and wept until she had no more tears to shed. But the pain, the anguish of watching people systematically beheaded with swords, stabbed with knives, shot in the head, still peppered her dreams nightly. Dawson had urged her to remember, not push away what she'd experienced. It had been so hard. It was still hard, but her emotional reaction to it had diminished in intensity. Her therapist said that with time, it would lose its grip on her, and Lily believed her. She just wished it would hurry up and happen. Unfortunately, the therapist told her it would be many years before it slowly took place.

Lily went to the kitchen counter and made a pot of coffee. If she took certain antianxiety meds, she'd calm down. But they interfered so much with her ability to feel connected to life that she finally refused to take them anymore. Lily would rather suffer and feel alive than be anesthetized and slog through the day feeling robotically removed from everything. Truly, the meds had turned her into a zombie.

Because Kassie had given her this space to live until she could get back on her feet, Lily wanted to help where she could. The dishwasher room, where dirty plates and flatware were cleaned, was too loud and jarring to her sensitive nervous system. Noise could bring on a flashback of that dawn morning in the village. And getting a flashback made her curl into a knot, her head buried against her drawn-up knees, arms tightly wrapped around them, unable to do anything but remember to breathe in and out until it passed. It could take an hour, but then the rest of the day or a sleepless night followed.

She felt helpless. Alone. Broken. Too fragile to live in this rough-and-tumble world civilians easily dealt with day in and day out. At one time, she could do it, too. But no longer. Major Dawson had told her to find a low-stress job, doing something that made her look forward to working daily. The shelter in Wind River was perfect for her. Dogs barking didn't bring on a nasty reaction within her. The dogs and cats loved her, and she wallowed in their unselfish adoration, lapping it up like the starving emotional being she'd become. These last two weeks had been heaven for her because she was the only human with all the animals. Things always went better when there wasn't a crowd of people around her.

She sat down at the table that had two chairs around it and ate a tuna sandwich she'd made last night. Luckily, she'd slept well, a rare thing but so welcome. Major Dawson had told her that over time, years, the anxiety, the hyper-vigilance, the nightmares and those dreaded flashbacks would begin to ease. Lily took it as a good-luck sign that Wind River was a place of healing for her. In the last two weeks, she'd had seven nights of solid, unbroken sleep. A new record! Attributing it to her beloved dogs and cats, she remembered her caring therapist telling her she would find an inner strength that would support her healing. It would be a journey that would consume her life to come, but a worthy one.

Well, she'd found it. Kassie and Travis Grant were her guardian angels. Just as Maud Whitcomb had been, by hiring her part-time at the animal shelter. Yes, this place, the kindness of so many people who lived here, was the medication she needed to get her feet solidly under her.

Tonight, she'd call her mom and dad in Idaho and let them know what had transpired. Idaho Falls was about six hours north of where she lived now, but sometimes it seemed like half a continent away. Other times, a six-hour trip by pickup home to see them would be easy for her to accomplish.

Sitting and munching on her sandwich, she went over her short talk with Maud. She'd never been a personal caregiver but liked the idea of helping a sixty-five-year-old woman rehabilitate. After all, she'd worked in orthopedics while going through her last two years before receiving her RN degree. Maybe that would help her get the job. But it was only for two months. Then she'd be back to square one. Still, it felt hopeful, and she had to try.

Fear was something she had rarely felt until after joining the Army. Then it had been a daily companion after her breakdown. She felt the emotions rising in her, felt her stomach shrinking, as if a hand had grabbed it and was squeezing it until it was painful. Fear of rejection. Yes, that was it. Shame and humiliation were the two biggest feelings in her life. Ashamed that she couldn't *take it*. Some of the male vets in her hospital ward due to their own PTSD had called her weak. Fragile. Even though they themselves were in as bad shape emotionally as she was. How many times at night, in her bed, had she cried, face pressed deep into the pillow to stop the sounds? Lily had lost count. Crying helped relieve the pressure within her. Better out than in. Crying was healthy, and she saw the difference in her state of mind since giving herself permission to do just that.

Humiliation haunted her daily, reminding her that she couldn't take real life, the natural stress everyone around her could deal with without blinking an eye. She couldn't handle a crowd on a sidewalk, or be squeezed into a theater, or be comfortable in a department store. Instead, walks around the hospital grounds, green grass, trees, colorful flower beds, birds singing, all combined to ramp down the anxiety that savaged her. Lily understood what fragile meant because that was how far she'd sunk into her own wounded being. There was so much she could no longer handle.

Frowning, she wondered what Maud would think of her. Because she wouldn't lie about what had happened to her, and how it affected her daily. If she lost the job, so be it. Lily wasn't about to put herself into a position where there was high stress, loud noises or too much hustle and bustle. In an hour, she'd find out a lot more. The fear grew in her, making her feel hyper with anxiety.

Books by Bestselling Author
Fern Michaels

___The Jury	0-8217-7878-1	$6.99US/$9.99CAN
___Sweet Revenge	0-8217-7879-X	$6.99US/$9.99CAN
___Lethal Justice	0-8217-7880-3	$6.99US/$9.99CAN
___Free Fall	0-8217-7881-1	$6.99US/$9.99CAN
___Fool Me Once	0-8217-8071-9	$7.99US/$10.99CAN
___Vegas Rich	0-8217-8112-X	$7.99US/$10.99CAN
___Hide and Seek	1-4201-0184-6	$6.99US/$9.99CAN
___Hokus Pokus	1-4201-0185-4	$6.99US/$9.99CAN
___Fast Track	1-4201-0186-2	$6.99US/$9.99CAN
___Collateral Damage	1-4201-0187-0	$6.99US/$9.99CAN
___Final Justice	1-4201-0188-9	$6.99US/$9.99CAN
___Up Close and Personal	0-8217-7956-7	$7.99US/$9.99CAN
___Under the Radar	1-4201-0683-X	$6.99US/$9.99CAN
___Razor Sharp	1-4201-0684-8	$7.99US/$10.99CAN
___Yesterday	1-4201-1494-8	$5.99US/$6.99CAN
___Vanishing Act	1-4201-0685-6	$7.99US/$10.99CAN
___Sara's Song	1-4201-1493-X	$5.99US/$6.99CAN
___Deadly Deals	1-4201-0686-4	$7.99US/$10.99CAN
___Game Over	1-4201-0687-2	$7.99US/$10.99CAN
___Sins of Omission	1-4201-1153-1	$7.99US/$10.99CAN
___Sins of the Flesh	1-4201-1154-X	$7.99US/$10.99CAN
___Cross Roads	1-4201-1192-2	$7.99US/$10.99CAN

Available Wherever Books Are Sold!
Check out our website at www.kensingtonbooks.com